BILLIONAIRE'S PROMISE

A BROTHER'S BEST FRIEND BILLIONAIRE ROMANCE

SUMMER COOPER

SUSU CHIN

Lovy Books Ltd
20-22 Wenlock Road
London N1 7GU

Created with Vellum
Cover by SC Creative

ALSO BY

Also by Susu Chin
This is Susu's first novel. Be on the lookout for more passionate tales and unforgettable characters coming soon!

Also by Summer Cooper

DARK DESIRES
A billionaire dark romance series
Dark Desire (FREE now!)
Dark Rules
Dark Secret
Dark Time
Dark Truth

BARRE TO BAR
A billionaire second chance series
Dancing With Lies (FREE!)
Dancing With Temptation
Dancing With Doubt
Dancing With Guilt

Dancing With Redemption

TWISTED INTENTION
A billionaire revenge romance series
Twisted Beauty (FREE now!)
Twisted Love
Twisted Fate

Mafia's Obsession
A hot mafia romance series
Mafia's Dirty Secret (FREE now!)
Mafia's Fake Bride
Mafia's Final Play

Screaming Demons
An MC romance series full of suspense
Rough Start (FREE now!)
Rough Ride
Rough Choice
Rough Return
Rough Patch
Rough Road
Rough Trip
Rough Night
Rough Love

Check out Summer's entire collection at
www.summercooper.com/books

📚 FREE BOOK ALERT! 🎁

From Summer Cooper
Download your FREE digital copy of ***Protecting Her***, a Billionaire
Romance (usually $4.99) by signing up for our mailing list. 💜
Join now ➡️ https://www.summercooper.com/sign-up

Thank you for being a part of this literary journey! 🙏
Happy reading!

PROLOGUE

13 Years Ago
June

"I love you. In case I die."

Something we heard someone say while we were at school. We thought it was silly. No one was going to die, not for a very, very long time at least.

But we were wrong.

I was wrong.

Now I regret not saying those 'silly' words to my best friend.

"Happy 18TH Birthday!" Liam and Lincoln burst into my bedroom at midnight and repeated the same words again and again and again. Even though the night light in my room was dim, I could tell that my two brothers had some kind of party hats on.

"Get up! Get up! Get up!" Lincoln had a thing about repeating things three times since he started college. Perhaps his thick skull thought that no one could understand him. He shook my bed like a silly child, trying to get me up.

But I remained unmotivated.

I had never spent a birthday without Chloe in my life. Okay, that wasn't entirely true, perhaps once or twice in my life, but that must have been before I could remember things. As we didn't officially meet until we were three.

Oh, in case it wasn't clear, Chloe Abshire was my best friend. She wasn't just any ordinary best friend, though. She was the best kind.

The kind who would fight for you, literally, even though an injury could cost her the ballet career she dreamed of. The kind who would burst out into swear words and stand up for you even though she would get in trouble with the principal and her parents. The kind who never forgot about your birthday. The kind who was your favorite everything.

But all that meant nothing now.

It'd been six months since Chloe's death.

Lincoln insisted that she was just missing. But the idiot was just saying that to make me feel better. It wasn't what the locals said about her. Or the coroner. I even went to her funeral. Hers and her parents.

Tears fell down my cheeks again.

Mom had demanded that I stop this *nonsense* soon.

She said it like I actually enjoyed having tears flood my face. I couldn't help it.

On the night of her *death*, she'd been here. In this very bedroom, sitting on this very bed, watching the latest episode of Pretty Little Liars. I haven't watched any episodes that came out after that. It hurt too much knowing that Chloe would never find out what happened to the girls, to her favorite character Emily Fields, played by her favorite actress Shay Mitchell.

"Yiyi, I drove all the way back for you." Lincoln sank next to me and planted a kiss on my forehead. *Yiyi*, my family only called me by my nickname – a shortened form of Horyi – when they wanted to remind me that I was the youngest in the family. An immature little child.

Liam had now turned the main light on, and the brightness hurt my already swollen eyes.

"I'm not in the mood for a stupid birthday," I snapped.

When will my brothers ever take me seriously? Why would they go behind my back and organize something that I had said multiple times I didn't want? Brothers, huh? They never listen.

I tucked my head further inside the blanket, wishing the boys would leave me alone.

"I know you miss her." Lincoln's soft whisper triggered something deep inside me. Though tears had been hard to hold back, I hadn't done this since her funeral – cried out loud.

Ugly. Cry. Out. Loud.

"Shhh, shhh, shhh..."

Liam stood at the end of my bed staring like an idiot. I had no idea why my best friend had a crush on my geeky and emotionless brother. That was something I would never get. I could never think of my own brothers as gorgeous or hot or *sexy*. Eww. Okay, I know they aren't ugly Why else would my classmates all pine over them like they were members of One Direction? Giggling, taking pictures of them, like they were the prettiest cake in the most Instagrammable cafe in town. They were always begging for opportunities to be introduced to them.

"I got you a present," Liam announced as if that would make me stop crying instantly. To be fair, it would have worked when I was eight, or even ten. Or fourteen. I could still be excited at receiving presents at fourteen. Only the good ones though.

But right now, all I wanted was to be able to celebrate my birthday with Chloe again.

I never thought that this would be something I'd ever have to wish for. I felt a strong wrench in my stomach just at that thought.

I'm not naive. I knew that this year would probably be the last time we'd celebrate our birthdays together before we parted ways for college. Eventually, we'd get to celebrate together again, but this year would be our last chance. But we didn't even get that last chance.

Our *friendship* ended so unexpectedly. I knew I was being silly. There was no such thing as till death do us part for besties. Still, it would have been nice if I was at least given a chance to say my goodbyes, even if I wasn't ready to.

"Is, uh–" An unfamiliar voice came from behind my half-open door, "everything okay?"

My brothers brought someone home?

How could they?

Not only did they not respect the fact that I didn't want a celebration, they brought a stranger home. I was not in the mood to deal with any strangers.

But I would have to deal with my brothers now. I climbed out of my bed ready to give them an earful – not caring what the stranger would think of me, I was beyond caring.

Then I saw him.

The most beautiful man I've ever seen in real life.

Like he'd just walked out of one of those Korean dramas that Mom was so obsessed with. I watched them with her sometimes, but I never cared about the story line, I was just in awe of how beautiful everyone was.

And this guy, he's even prettier than Lee Min-ho. What kind of screwed up mess was this?

"Who is that?" I asked as I retreated back into bed. Using the duvet cover, I quickly wiped the tears off my puffy eyes caused by six months of grief.

"It's just me, little sis, Kai. Happy birthday." Spoken in a strong London accent with a hint of nasal twang. Cute.

"Liam!" I cried out. But Lincoln stood up instead. I guess out of my two brothers, Lincoln had always been the one who could truly translate all my different cries. Though he was also the one who never let me get my way. Right at this very moment, my tone said I didn't want to be seen like this, and he understood perfectly.

My big brother walked straight over to Kai and whispered something in his ear that made him nod repeatedly before leaving the room.

Once again, I hid under the covers – trying to hide my embarrassment. Why didn't my big brothers tell me that they were going to bring someone? Why would they do that to me?

Normally, this wasn't something I cared about.

My emotions were all out of whack. They had been for months now.

A girl should be allowed to throw a tantrum in her own space whenever she wants though. *Women were born with complex hormones, and they shouldn't be ashamed to be emotional.* Chloe's little voice rang in my head, but for the first time, it didn't make me cry.

Thanks bestie.

"He's gone," Liam said, his voice heavy. "I'm sorry, sweetie."

That was all he could mutter. Obviously, he didn't know what else to say to his little sister. Although he was better looking than Lincoln, he was never going to be as popular with that dullness of his. Poor thing. He never knew the right thing to say to me, or to anyone, let alone in a situation like this.

I knew that losing Chloe wasn't just hard for me, it was devastating for him too. I suspected that he had a crush on Chloe, but Liam had a very strict plan for his life. He wanted to become a world class surgeon – and that would take a lot of hard work. At this stage in his life, Liam just wanted to stay focused on getting into the best medical school.

Still, Chloe's affection towards him didn't go unnoticed. A smile spread across my face. He wasn't as emotionless as I thought. When Chloe told me that she thought they almost kissed, I laughed in her face. There wasn't a remotely romantic bone in Liam's body, and he wouldn't do anything like that.

I had to reconsider my stance on the day of her funeral. Despite being in deep sorrow, I hadn't failed to notice that my brother shed a tear or two at her funeral. Was that just sorrow over a young life lost, or had there been more and I'd been too blind to notice? Perhaps that kiss wasn't imaginary after all. There was a possibility that Liam was grieving for a friend, but they'd barely spoken to each other.

I wondered what would have happened if Lincoln didn't ruin their moment and they had kissed. And I could totally see Lincoln interrupting them, rudely. On purpose. That was just the kind of thing my big brother did for sport – ruin everything that was remotely good for me, *and Chloe.*

My girl hated Lincoln's stupid pranks.

"We should go," Lincoln said to Liam.

I popped my head out of the duvet like a turtle, the tears on my cheeks now dried. "Where are you going?"

"Sleep," Liam said. Lincoln opened his mouth but decided to let Liam finish his sentence. "I know you said you didn't want to celebrate your birthday this year. But you're turning 18 and that's a big deal."

Lincoln nodded.

"We threw you a small party downstairs." His voice was unexpectedly soft and gentle, without a trace of his usual bossy tone.

"But you brought friends." That was a comeback to the word

small. For us, small also meant intimate. Just the three of us without our parents, *plus Chloe, or minus.*

"Just one," Lincoln said. "You've met Kai before. Why does him being here upset you?"

Lincoln was right. When he first met Kai, I'd said that I wanted to meet him since he was actually from China. Though I was quarter Chinese ethnically, I had never actually known one personally who wasn't related to me. Until Kai. So why did his being here upset me now? He was as much a part of Lincoln's life as Trevon was.

"I guess because I told you I didn't want to make a big deal about today?"

"Well, it is kind of my birthday present for you. I know you can't take your eyes off him."

"Cheapskate."

"You know, I'm a poor college student and all."

"Whatever. I'll be right down. I hope that seeing your friend again isn't my *only* present." I hopped out of my bed and ushered my brothers out of my room. "Five seconds."

One sec was way too unrealistic, Chloe would say, so we had decided that we would say anything but one sec.

I'd thought that I would prefer to spend my birthday alone this year. I even went out of my way to send Mom and Dad away on a trip. I'd had an idea of what I wanted to do on this special day. Cry my eyes out for my bestie. Light a fire and burn some of her favorite things for her to receive in the afterlife. Being able to send the dead things by burning materialistic items made with origami used to sound silly to me. But right now, it felt rather comforting that my ancestors had such a strong belief in life after death. There was so much I wanted to send to her.

I wondered if people would cry for me if I died.

I think I would be really upset if no one cried for me. Am I not worth the tears? Not that I could control such things. I loved Chloe so much and my tears were proof.

Grief was a tricky thing. I never knew grief until now. Now, whenever I think of her, it *burns.* My tears shed uncontrollably again as my thoughts turned to her sweet face being burned alive.

Downstairs had been transformed. All the available wall space had been filled with string lights. Our home was modern and very tidy due to Mom's obsession with cleaning – not necessarily done by herself, but by the cleaning staff. But today, the house looked totally different, like a dream.

I felt like I had stepped into a fairy land.

Like a *princess.* I had never felt that way before.

Suddenly, Kai appeared from nowhere, holding his hand out as I stepped off the stairs. I couldn't help but feel like a *real* princess. With her prince by her side.

I never knew my brothers would care this much about me. Before this, I thought the only thing they were capable of was annoying the hell out of me. There was no way my brothers did all this by themselves.

I stared at the beautiful man in front of me and knew that this fantasy prince was too good to be true. He probably wasn't interested in girls. In my whole life up to that point, the only people good at decorating that I knew of – either from real life or on TV – were gay men. "You guys did all this?"

"We had help," Lincoln said. *I knew it.* I was a little disappointed, but my face couldn't help turning scorching hot as Kai winked at me.

It was such a shame. The first person I've ever been really attracted to was gay. Congratulations to me, I'll probably die alone. He was simply *too* pretty to be straight.

Kai led me to the dining room where they all started singing Happy Birthday and I tried very hard not to cry. The short song felt extremely long and slow. At the end of the song, I closed my eyes and made a wish that I knew would never come true.

I wanted another chance to celebrate my birthday with Chloe again.

I knew it was silly. I should have wished to make it into the medical school of my choice *easily* without studying past midnight like Liam. But that was the only thing I wanted right now. Nodding, agreeing that I would have this wish no matter what, I opened my eyes and carefully blew out the candles. It was hard not to spit any of my snot onto the cake. My face was a mess again and my eyes were out of focus. My brothers bent down to give me hugs and kisses then they went to get me my presents from their rooms.

Kai stood next to me and stooped down, his hand lightly cupping the side of my head as he planted a kiss on my forehead. "Happy birthday, princess."

Did he think that the kisses were a custom or cultural thing? He really didn't have to. But I was glad that he did. And for some messed up reason, my eyes were back in focus and suddenly my tears had dried.

I can't be in love with this guy, can I? What kind of nonsense was true love anyway? Clearly that was a lie made up by adults. Just a fairy tale. It clearly did not exist.

Was that how Chloe felt about Liam? No matter how stupid his face looked, Chloe had said that it always made her happy when she saw him. Lincoln, on the other hand, always made Chloe angry for no reason, even when he was just doing nothing quietly at the far end of the room.

"This is for you." Kai handed me a pale blue paper bag. I couldn't believe that this guy I barely knew had bought me a present from Tiffany & Co.

Really?" My heart was racing and the boy just grinned like it was nothing for him. I reached inside the bag and found a thick envelope. "What is this?"

"Open it," Liam said, as curious as everyone else in the room apart from Kai himself.

Perhaps it was just a birthday card with a small book. I reminded myself that we really didn't know each other well, and he really didn't need to get me anything.

"What the f–" *Fuck!*

"Ahem…" Lincoln cleared his throat. I rolled my eyes at my big brother for trying to control what came out of my mouth. "*You're a lady*," Lincoln mouthed. I never understood why it was cute when Chloe swore, but not me. Such a double standard.

I took out a big fat stash of cash, all in one-hundred-dollar bills.

"What the fuck!" Both my brothers cried in disbelief.

"Ahem…" I mimicked Lincoln. He could have a taste of his own medicine.

"I'm sorry. I didn't know that it was your birthday until this afternoon, and it was too late to get you something nice."

They looked at each other for a few seconds, then I burst out in laughter, and the others followed. I had no idea why it was funny. Maybe my laughter had been suppressed for so long, it just needed to be let out. Tears were falling from my eyes now for a different reason for the first time in months.

"I can't take this, but can I count it please? I've never seen so much cash in my life."

"Oh? I'm sorry. Should I write you a check instead?" I busted out laughing again. Louder than the last time. This was a joke, right? I couldn't tell anymore.

I counted ninety-nine.

I counted again.

Ninety-nine.

Did he mean to give me ten grand but miscounted? I wasn't

greedy but the perfectionist side of me needed things to be neat, and ninety-nine wasn't neat.

"Ninety-nine," Kai confirmed.

"Right. And it was *intentional.*" *But why?* The question was eating me up inside, though I felt too awkward to ask the beautiful man.

"Ninety-nine means longevity in Chinese. I thought you guys knew." Kai looked confused.

I smiled in agreement. "Oh, I have heard that before."

"She's lying," Lincoln chimed in. "Our parents never taught us anything related to our Chinese heritage."

"Yeah, sorry." I shrugged and another smile escaped my mouth.

After having the birthday cake and some food, Liam kissed me good night and went to bed. He had an exam the next morning and he needed his rest. Lincoln volunteered to clean up the dishes and any mess that they had made while Kai and I argued about whether or not ninety-nine hundred dollars was an appropriate to gift to accept from a stranger.

Kai was still convinced that it was a good gift. It would have been an acceptable gift in China – a little too generous, but acceptable.

In the end, I said I would happily accept his ninety-nine hundred dollars as a birthday present in ten years' time, if we still knew each other.

"*Friends*," he said.

That would be very nice indeed. If I could be his friend, and maybe more.

"Do you like KTV?" Kai changed the subject.

I had no idea what he meant. I had heard of MTV, but I had a feeling he was talking about something else. "I'm not too sure."

"Come. I'll show you." Kai held out a hand and led me out to the living room. Being up-close to him made me realize how tall he was. A little over six foot, perhaps. And it made me feel a bit fuzzy, in a good way.

Kai turned on the television, along with two boxes that I had never seen before. As the TV came alive, the screen showed an original music video of a song by the Spice Girls without the singing voices. "Karaoke." I recognized it right away.

"Yes, some people call it karaoke." Kai gave me a microphone and a remote control. "You can find any song you want."

"Any song?"

"Yes, any song. As long as you have the internet, you can connect to the server I subscribe to in China and download any song in the world."

"Where did you get this?" Kai had these deep eyes that were like black holes that could suck out your soul. I shook my head to apologize for my behavior. If only Kai knew what I was thinking as I stared at him.

Someone as beautiful as Kai must get stared at a lot. On that note, I suddenly felt not as guilty.

"From China of course," he explained.

Beautiful people are meant to be shared, no I mean stared at. Or shared. No, shut up.

"You brought this thing all the way from China?" Why would someone go through the trouble of shipping something like this over? "We have karaoke here you know?"

He turned his face and looked directly at me. "I know you have everything here, princess, but yours suck so bad."

I was shocked but I didn't know whether I was more shocked that he dared to suggest that our precious American products could possibly suck, or that he just called me princess again.

"Why do you keep calling me princess? Do you call every girl princess?"

He shrugged. "Not every girl. You know, when I was young,

and reading those silly illustrated books about fairy tales...well, you're exactly what I imagined a princess would look like."

"I see."

I shook off the thought of him being my prince and me being his princess and changed the topic.

Although I was genuinely curious about how the subscription worked, how artists get paid, whether it was legal at all... right now, I just wanted to enjoy the rest of my evening with this man. This man who had the ability to distract me from my pain, my grief, even just for a little bit.

My big brother joined us for a while before passing out on the couch.

I didn't want the night to end. Chloe's sudden departure had made me cling onto the present so much tighter than I used to.

The next morning, I woke up in my bed. The boys had gone back to their life, doing whatever they were supposed to be doing.

The last thing I remembered was leaning on Kai's shoulder, singing to Jeff Buckley, wondering if it was less painful to die drowning compared to being burnt alive. And that his cologne smells ridiculously amazing, calming and *addictive*. I closed my eyes again, hoping that making a second, more realistic wish now, long after blowing out the candles would still count. *I want to sniff him again.*

Weird.

1

June

id I have social anxiety or was I just an introvert? I don't know. But my work required me to face the public sometimes, and to conquer that fear, I had to fight and convince the trillions of tiny reluctant cells within my body.

Sunglasses. Hat. Facemask. Check. Check. Check.

I knew that I looked like someone who was about to commit a serious crime. Then a part of me also knew that in this day and age, wearing a face cover was just part of daily life for many, especially for someone like me who worked in a medical setting.

My blood pressure monitor didn't work last night, despite swapping the batteries out from one of my favorite toys. After following a strict two-week regime of intermittent fasting, along with a low carb diet, I was dying to find out if this peculiar experiment recommended by a colleague of mine would fix my blood pressure reading.

For the millionth time, I went over the reasons, or worse the diseases, that could be causing my abnormally high blood pressure. I ate well. Went to the gym three times a week religiously. Quit drinking. Didn't smoke. My blood results were normal – I had it tested multiple times just to be sure. Since the laboratory had my name on it, I could run personal tests for free as many times as I wanted. Though, I had to be careful not to draw any unwanted attention. I didn't want word to get around that I was sick, or worse, dying.

Anyway, it just didn't make sense.

Well, sleep was the only thing in my life that wasn't in order. Stress might be playing a part too.

But that was just an occupational hazard.

I'm not sure I could call myself a doctor if I rested and slept well and didn't suffer from any stress. Liam and Dad reminded me repeatedly that a doctor's life wasn't an easy one, physically or mentally, though it was definitely a satisfying one.

I had come to accept that – one day, if I'm lucky – I would sleep well, and *enough. It's just too bad that it would be* on the day I retired or dropped dead.

At 10 a.m. in the morning, the Bennet Pharmacy shouldn't be busy at all, and I knew that very well myself. For the past year, I had made it my life's mission to learn the ins and outs of my family's business – the pharmacies, various medical centers, and hospitals – including small details like the opening and closing times, and the busy hours of those facilities. Especially those that were close to my home. Before 11am was usually a quiet time to go shopping on the weekends but quite the opposite during weekdays.

My other option would be to go to the hospital to use the equipment. I had an old-fashioned blood pressure monitor that required no batteries there. But I preferred my Saturday mornings to be strictly mine. Going into the hospital meant work, regardless of why I was there, people would find work for me. It might be a quick chat about a patient, or taking a glance at some charts, or double checking on some decorations, or even something like whether we should source a different toilet paper to save money. And before I knew it, I would have spent hours going through things that weren't in my job description.

My trouble was, I didn't really know how to say no, especially when it came to small favors. And it seemed everyone had got the memo about this, because people kept asking for favors that I simply couldn't refuse.

Sometimes I wondered if I should be a mean bitch. I could set up some kind of consultation fee with HR, and every time someone came and asked me for shit, I'd just have HR deduct their pay. After all, I was sure none of their job descriptions included making their superior work harder. It should very much be the other way round.

Mean bitches are happy. And have better lives.

That was one thing I noticed from my mother. She cared about nothing but herself.

I marched quickly towards the electrical section and grabbed a Broun monitor that looked very similar to my old one. I would have no problem using any brand, but I felt like I owed some loyalty to Broun. Their CEO, Brian Broun, had been generously sponsoring many health campaigns and charity events organized by our hospitals. Over the years, our charity managed to raise significant money to help the less fortunate in the world. The very least I could do was support them by buying their products. Technically, I wasn't supposed to have any bias when it came to recommending any home medical equipment for my patients, but a lot of them seemed to prefer using the same one that their doctors were using.

There was talk of Brian's ulterior motives for his recent support whenever I tried to raise money for charity. That he was interested in purchasing a pharmaceutical company to raise his company's portfolio. And having a good relationship with hospitals would definitely help them distribute those drugs to the public. It was only a rumor, at the moment.

Whatever the real reasons were, anyone was welcome to help. And personally, I wouldn't reject money for charity.

The real reason I stayed loyal to Broun though, was that it was the first blood pressure monitor I had ever known. My family had been using the same one for years and it rarely broke. And I'm extremely reluctant when it comes to trying out new things.

Reluctant to change or supremely royal? I guessed they were kind of the same.

I walked into the pharmacy, wondering if a new blood pressure monitor would be better. I'd just picked up the latest model and turned to go and pay for it when I found a body in my way. A very tall body that towered over me.

"Dr. Bennet, fancy seeing you here today."

Damn it.

I really thought that no one would bother me today. I haven't had any proper me time for three years now. If my blood pressure reading was good, I was going to reward myself with a spa day. If not, that was more reason to unwind. So, either way, I was going to have a spa day today.

That's why I hated it when I went anywhere owned by my family. Everyone recognized me. Well, almost. Of course, not every single person who worked at Bennet Medical Group knew who I was. That would be insane. Because there were just too many faces in the company. I put on a well-practiced smile because it didn't cost anything to be polite, and people could still tell that you were smiling when you wore a face covering. "You–", the upward curve on my mouth dropped as soon as I saw his face. I felt like my eyes were about to pop out of their sockets. He wasn't wearing a face mask so there was no chance that he could be someone else. *Mack What's-his-face.*

"It's me. Mack Johnson." Of course, I knew who he was. I dreaded running into someone like him. Or anyone connected to him.

I pulled off the little piece of cloth covering half my face. There was no point hiding who I was anymore. Mack must have done his research to find me here. He'd probably been watching me or following me before reaching out.

A few months ago, I let my brother Liam talk me into a major ad campaign. My face was now on the pharmacy's promotional posters. These posters got plastered across the walls of every corner where they could possibly attract customers, and not only in New York. The campaign was so successful that the medical group had decided to use it across the whole country, and in parts of Europe and Asia too. Not only that, but the digital version was also haunting everyone that might need medical help on social media. That meant pretty much every single person in the United States of America. So now, everyone knows me as the face of Bennet Medical Group, and some people even called me the face of women's health.

"Hi," I said coldly and cursed my British blood for the need to be polite. I wanted no interaction with Mack. "Sorry, I'm in a rush. I'll catch you another time."

I marched straight to the self-pay machine, my eyes too afraid to look around.

"Come on. Surely you have time for a coffee?"

I was kicking myself inside for not going somewhere else for the monitor. The thing was if I bought one from somewhere else, I'd feel like I was betraying my own business. On the other hand, at Bennet pharmacies, the staff would automatically apply my VIP discount, and the business wouldn't be making much profit anyway. Then it was almost like I was ripping my own business off.

Welcome to the over-thinking mind of Dr. June Bennet.

"No." Short sentences with a stern voice, that's the key to delivering a concise, straight to the point message–a tip I learned from my best friend Chloe.

"For old time's sake."

Clearly short and concise didn't work on Mack as he forcibly pulled me towards him for a sideways hug.

It had been more than 10 years since I last saw Mack. I may have even had different colored hair back then. And I didn't answer to June back then, but my middle name. Despite my efforts to avoid certain people from my past life, one of them had found their way to me.

Mack smelled like he had been smoking weed and probably hadn't had a wash for days. With all the energy I could muster, I struggled to get myself out from his grip and shoved him.

"Don't!" *Do that*, I finished the sentence in my head. This time louder and in a higher pitch. Everyone–though not many– started to stare, and I didn't care, I needed some witnesses if this guy was about to try anything.

My palms started to sweat. It wasn't in my nature to cause a scene. I dreaded attention. I had always hated it.

Perhaps the real reason I agreed to do the marketing campaign was just to shut my brothers up. I was so sick of them constantly comparing me to my sister-in-law, Chloe. My supposedly dead best friend. The one who had a crush on Liam thirteen years ago but ended up marrying Lincoln. She turned out to be alive all these years, hiding from the gang who killed her parents. She'd been working at a strip joint all this time. They kept saying that Chloe was much more worldly than me. So stunning, and fearless on stage. And that I should really step out of my comfort zone and be a little bit like her.

It was true that I admired Chloe deeply and wanted to be more like her.

Bolder. More confident. More everything…

But I feared *him* more.

I dropped the monitor in the baggage section and headed for the door. At this moment, my blood pressure was no longer an issue. Well, it wasn't my highest priority right now anyway.

My face was warm, my heart was beating fast, and my blood boiling – I didn't need a monitor to know that my pressure was high.

Quickly, I walked to my red Tesla and jumped in.

"Hold on." Mack grabbed the door with his gorilla sized hand.

"Let go." I was ready to slam my door, and Mack would lose his fingers – the red of my car was perfect for covering his blood.

"I'll be quick. I just need some cash."

Cash? So, Mack was just here for some money.

I was a little taken aback by his audacity though. So straight to the point, he'd wasted no time at all. Secretly, I let out a small sigh of relief. Mom had led me to believe that if a problem could easily go away with money, then it was not a problem at all. Side note: you had to have the money in the first place.

I knew full well that I was really fortunate to be in that position, and that without my parents, I might never have been.

"Cash machine isn't far from here. That shop over there has one." I pointed at a convenience shop on the next block. I immediately regretted my smart reply, I shouldn't have teased him like that because I wanted this conversation to be over as soon as possible.

"Bitch!" Mack's free hand punched the roof of my precious Tesla. My body shrunk and my eyes started to water. A minute ago, I was ready for this to get bloody and now...what was going on? I couldn't just back down. His gorilla hand would pay for that bang.

I had no idea what I was feeling at that moment.

Fear–yes.

Anger—most definitely.

"Stop being smart with me, June Horyi Melisa Bennet."

Did he just call me by my full name?

"How much?" I hated myself for surrendering so quickly. No one even knew my full name. I hated it being so long, so I never used it, not even at school. And I sure never told Mack about it. The way Mack said it, indicated that he knew more about me than just my full name.

"Ten grand."

That wasn't a lot of money. Not for Mack. Not for me.

"Fine." I knew that there was a possibility that Mack was toying with me. Testing me. Now I'd just given him the upper hand.

"I'll be in touch." Mack said as he tried to slip me something, a card or a piece of paper from his pocket. I took the opportunity to shut my car door and drove away as quickly as possible. No blood.

Mack shouted behind me. I had no intention of finding out what the bad man was saying. What could he possibly have said really? I'd rather not know what he wanted to do to me if I didn't give him his money.

My escape plan had been rather smooth. At least I didn't have to clean off any blood or pick up any severed fingers. But when my car approached my building, I drove straight past it. I couldn't bring myself to go home.

I needed time to think.

I needed someone to talk to, but who?

Chloe. The best friend who had left me grieving for 10 years would be my first choice. She had dealt with many lowlifes and scumbags as a stripper in her past life. She would know what to do – or even know a few people who could help in this kind of situation. It turned out that her cousin Marie – whom she never knew she had – was the head of the Mafia or something like that.

The only problem was I didn't want my brother Lincoln to find out about this. The sweet couple had been through enough over the years. Not just ordinary tough times that normal human beings went through, but black mailing, kidnapping, and robbery just to name a few.

In some ways, they were the perfect people to go to for advice. But I really didn't want my brother to think that I couldn't deal with my own problems. My problem was nothing compared to what they'd faced, so if they could do it, I could as well. I just needed to figure out how. Besides, they were all the way in Myrtle Beach, and I wasn't eager to drive or fly there right this very second. And I was definitely not calling.

Dad? Nope, he just remarried not too long ago and should enjoy his honeymoon with his new bride.

Mother? I could just picture her wrinkling her nose, squinting her eyes at me – wondering how on earth I brought this on myself. Her solution could be powerful though, but a bit unconventional and not quite legal. I wouldn't mind illegal conduct to be honest, if it was done properly and untraceably. Could I trust my mother on this one though? Probably not.

Liam, my other brother, would not be a good option. He was very *nice*, clean cut and...geeky. Sure, my geeky brother made a great surgeon, but he would be useless in this situation.

"Call the police," I could hear Liam saying already.

There was one other person...

The car behind me had been the same silver SUV for a while now. The same car with a bird dropping at the top right corner of the windscreen–that really annoying spot that was just out of the wiper's reach. I remembered thinking how much it would be bothering me if I couldn't get the bird shit out of my sight. But that thought was almost ten blocks away.

Could it be Mack?

When he said he wanted ten grand, I thought I heard him wrong. For someone like Mack, who did nothing other than eat, drink and party, ten thousand dollars wouldn't last him long – especially when he had such expensive tastes.

"Call Chloe Bennet," I gave a command to my car. My fear had overridden my reluctance to call her.

No answer.

"Wendy Gupta," I shouted at my car. The Indian Goddess who had helped to hide Chloe and helped her avoid many other troubles along the way. She might have an idea or two. I was convinced that she was connected to some powerful people.

"Wendy!" I called out as soon as she picked up.

"Hey, greetings to you too." Wendy's sarcastic tone had no effect on me. I was just overjoyed there was someone to talk to right now.

"It's so good to hear your voice." Realizing that it was an odd thing to say to someone I had only met a handful of times, I continued, "I'm sorry I haven't been in touch. I don't really have an ex–"

"Are you in trouble?" I almost screamed and I knew that I had called the right person. Not only was I useless at thinking when I was nervous, I also sucked at getting my words out.

"Yes."

"Are you safe?"

"Yes." Then weakly, I said, "Maybe not."

"Put me on video," she demanded.

"If you can…" Wendy added cautiously.

"Hi," I felt better as soon as I saw Wendy's round face. I realized that my face had turned rather purple from holding my breath in.

"You're in a car?" My head bobbled, yes. "I can't see anyone else in the car with you. Please don't tell me you killed someone and you're looking for a place in New York to hide the body."

"No." I really should've just spat out the words, or Wendy would think of another scenario to have me nod to, and really, it was just wasting time. "I think someone is following me."

I breathed heavily, as if I was about to give birth. If I didn't get any air into me, my brain was going to explode.

"Car chase?" Wendy's eyes widened. "In New York?"

"No chasing, no. Following. The same car, for many blocks now." I tried to say words that made sense. That was one of the reasons I practiced meditation, it wasn't just a trendy fad that I followed, I really needed it to ease my anxiety.

"Deep breaths, girl."

I took a few more deep breaths, following Wendy's instruction through the screen. It was just a simple breathing exercise that I had used and even taught and guided many of my patients through during their fertility procedures. Somehow, it went right out the window just when I needed it.

"Good girl." I felt like I was being talked to like a puppy. I wasn't sure if it was the words, or Wendy's voice, but my anxiety had started to ease. "Listen carefully, you will need to do a sharp turn at the next junction. And no brake, no signal. I repeat. No brake, no signal."

"Okay. Left or right turn?" I asked.

"Doesn't matter. Make sure you don't run over anyone."

I took another deep breath before turning my steering wheel as hard as I could and felt as though the car almost lifted at one corner. Almost.

"Is the car still there?" Wendy's voice was loud and clear through the speaker.

I thought for a second that it was all okay now – that I'd made a silly mistake, no one was actually following me. There was no sign of the silver SUV with the poop stain.

Two seconds later, the shit car reappeared.

"It's back," I announced. "And driving faster towards me."

"Okay, listen." If Wendy was going to suggest another crazy move, I was going to cry. I wasn't known for my reckless driving. "I'm going to send you a location and you're going to drive there like nothing has happened, you clear? Just drive normally, okay? No more sharp turns."

In the middle of New York on a Saturday morning, I had no idea where I was. I couldn't tell my whereabouts or recognize any streets or buildings. My mind was blank.

"Don't leave me," I begged. "I can't think."

Wendy's brow furrowed. "I'm sorry I can't be a better help. I'll stay until you get here."

It suddenly occurred to me that Wendy was actually in New York right now. And she was bringing me to her.

My phone pinged with a notification–the shared location that Wendy had sent. I clicked on it right away and obediently followed the navigation. She said nothing else for the rest of the journey – having her on my screen was enough though.

Along the way, the silver SUV had disappeared a few times– being overtaken by other vehicles–but came back right away each time.

Ten long minutes later, I arrived at an abandoned warehouse. Was this a joke? Despite my sixth sense telling me to run for the hills, I put my foot down on the brake.

So did the silver SUV.

2

———

Kai

No one knew I was back in New York.

Apart from my security team. Dave, my personal bodyguard, had let them know when I would be landing, and they were told to be on-call and ready.

My flight landed about two hours ago and the first thing I wanted was to get some sleep. Flying made me nervous, and I could never get a proper rest. Despite what the science told me, I still prayed that the plane wouldn't come crashing down every time I took one.

Even though my family owned a private plane, and a prestige membership with a private plane company, I still choose to fly commercial. There were many reasons – if the captain was responsible for many lives on board, then there was less reason for the pilot to fail. Right? And there would be more than one good looking flight attendant to serve me. This trip alone, three gorgeous members of the flight crew had approached me, giving me some hints about getting to know me. Interacting with beautiful ladies definitely helped ease my anxiety.

Having said that, my biggest nightmare about flying commercial was the possibility of snakes on the plane. God, that movie was so stupid…but great. Not likely to happen in real life, I know. Still, if anyone could explain and reason away irrational fear, all the psychologists would be out of jobs.

I'd missed America. New York in particular. Even though the air constantly smelled like garbage or farts.

But the freedom I got here was priceless. I could walk the streets without anyone recognizing me. There was no need to report back to mommy dearest about my whereabouts. I didn't need approval for everything I did. No media or IG account would criticize what I wore, or what I did, or even what I ate.

I could do anything I wanted. Or go anywhere. Well, with the protection of my bodyguards that is.

So, if freedom smells like farts, then so be it.

I would never dream of going anywhere without my CD – Clare and Dave. They were both hand-selected from the best candidates, all to make sure that I could live a life as safe and free as anyone else.

Dave – or Da Wei – graduated top of his class in military school. If it wasn't for his wife's death, he wouldn't have left the marines. Now in his early fifties, he was still as tough as he looked. Two years ago, when Dave turned fifty, my mother had wanted to replace him with someone younger and fitter, but I refused.

I decided that, instead of fighting my mother, I'd compromise. That was when Clare joined me, as my second bodyguard. My mother disapproved of my choice – a young and gorgeous blonde; she nearly had her sign some kind of contract to say she would not date me. Not that I would date my staff. To me that was just unprofessional. But Clare really wasn't my type either – too bossy for my liking.

I know my mother had a lot of say in my life, especially

whenever I was back in Shanghai. But I let her walk all over me because I loved her. The poor woman had lost her husband to another woman, a secretary I might add. And I had promised that I would always be on her side no matter what happened.

Rushing straight to my penthouse in Central Park Tower, my mood was getting crankier the longer I was away from my bed. I stood outside the door impatiently, waiting for Dave and Clare to clear the building.

"Sir, we have a problem," Clare reported as soon as she reappeared.

I couldn't believe my luck. But judging from her facial expression, there was no danger.

"What now?" The last thing I wanted to hear about was some kind of rat problem or something. Well, it's New York, so totally possible.

"Someone is here." Her left hand on her earpiece, receiving further information from Dave. "Your cousin–" She didn't sound convinced at all. Clare had to memorize all the information about my family, close relatives and friends. But her memory just wasn't as good as Dave's. Dave on the other hand, had met everyone. After all, he had been with me from the beginning, the first day I was assigned security.

"Jenny." Clare spat out the word without any emotion.

"Jenny?" Did I hear her right?

"Yes, Cousin Jenny."

It made no sense. What was Cousin Jenny doing in New York? She had two school age children in Shanghai and the kids needed their mother. The thing is, Dave had basically watched both Jenny and me growing up together so there was no way he would make a mistake identifying her.

Dashing straight past Clare, I wanted to find out what on earth was going on in my house.

"Where is she?" I yelled.

"Rose Gold guest room."

I sprinted up the stairs, since taking the elevator would take too long.

"Jenny," I screamed, as I approached the bedroom.

There she was. On the floor in front of the coffee table, sitting in a pile of trash.

"Qing-qing!"

Now I knew why it took a while for Dave to identify her.

Her face was covered in old makeup – maybe last week's, or even last month's. Streaks of dried, blurred eye shadow or eyeliner or whatever paint that she used covered her face. Matted hair was covering her previously beautiful dark purple straight hair.

"You look like hell," I said, disgusted with the state of the room. I wasn't joking when I said she was in a pile of trash. The small living room section of the room was covered with paper, tissues, some unidentifiable items and food wrappers. Lots of them – but potato chips mainly. Jenny never touched that kind of food. They had too many carbs or calories, she used to say.

Jenny didn't make a sound, her eyes fixed on the 60-inch television in front of her, with America's Top Model playing in the background.

I knew that I wasn't going to get a response out of her. I'd vaguely heard my staff whispering about Jenny lately and had no idea what was going on. The woman had been through some serious mental health problems in the last few years which started with postpartum depression when her second child was born. It got worse as Jenny's demanding mother-in-law blamed her for getting a diagnosis for her child, which confirmed his autism. The old woman believed that ignorance is bliss, and if Jenny had never taken the child to the clinic, they would have never *confirmed* the child's condition. Then they could have pretended that the problem didn't exist in the first place.

Ever since my dad nearly died from Covid, my family had become really cautious with our social events. I thought it was kind of silly because Dad didn't actually live with us. Sure, he would come home three times a week religiously to have dinner with Mom and the kids – but that was as much time as he was willing to give us. The rest of it was reserved for Mary – the other woman.

I didn't know how much Mom still cared about him until he got sick. She was calling in every favor she could to get him the best treatments available and get him on top of the priority care list.

Mom had made the Li family cancel pretty much all of their face-to-face appointments. Mary had objections to begin with but she had this fear of Mom so she would eventually do whatever she said. Well, within reason.

Anyway, Dad's sickness was one of the reasons I hadn't been able to come back to the States, or even leave my province.

Now that my dad had fully recovered, and was able to play golf again, my mother was a little more relaxed about me traveling. Though she had no idea that I had left the country. I basically told her that I was just *popping out* for a bit. I knew that my mother would find out sooner or later, but I still hoped that Cousin Jenny wouldn't rat me out too soon.

"Anyone know you're here?"

Jenny shook her head. That was an improvement from her blanking me, giving me her signature dead fish impression – the bottom half of the white of her eyes showing. She actually came up with that name herself when we were kids, as she struggled to properly roll her eyes for years. She would often check with me whether she had managed to roll them or was just doing her *dead fish* impression. Except today, it wasn't just her eyes doing a *dead* impression.

"Have you seen a doctor?" I wondered if she had been taking

her pills. As far as I knew, she had never stopped her medication.

She nodded.

I wasn't sure if I believed her. Anyhow, if she needed any meds it shouldn't be any trouble here in America. Don't get me wrong, I thought it was nice that people were so open about their anxiety and what not. But I did wonder if the rate the medication was prescribed in this country was a little unnecessary. Then again, no one asked me, and my opinion didn't matter here.

All I cared about, at the moment, was that I could get Jenny her medication if need be.

"Do you want me to go away?"

She threw me a sideways glance that meant yes. I knew her well enough to know that.

I turned around and walked towards the bedroom door. "But promise me you'll at least clean up here. Otherwise, I'm kicking you out."

Another sideways glance.

I was bluffing and she knew it. She was my favorite cousin, and she was always welcome in my home.

I walked out of the guest room, and past a few more rooms down the hallway until I was sure that Jenny couldn't hear me. I instructed Clare to send a team to look after her. Clare made a note to contact the cleaning staff, medical team, a stylist, and hire a driver and personal assistant for her. Of course, it wasn't a secret that I wanted her taken care of, but she might want to stay the way she was for a little longer, in her wallowing mood. But until then, the team could stand by for when she was ready to come out of her shell.

While I was talking to Jenny, Dave had divided my current security team into two and had one of them watching my cousin.

I didn't really know how long she had been away from home, but I knew people would be frantically searching for her. If she wanted to stay hidden, I was going to make sure her wishes were respected.

Dave was in-charge of dropping a hint to Jenny's family security team, letting them know that she was safe without revealing any other information. They weren't even going to know that Dave was the one dropping the hint – he was great at this kind of 007 stuff.

"Sir, I'm glad you are taking care of her." Dave turned around from the driver seat as I settled in the back of a black Porsche Panamera. Clare sat next to him silently and I appreciated her not making any comments about my cousin. She was good at her job, and I liked that she spoke her mind, but sometimes people didn't need to hear everything she had to say.

I let out a sigh and a light nod.

The whole Law family must have been looking for her, as well as the Chens, her husband's family. The last time she ran away, it was one of Jenny's friends who found her in a hospital in Taipei, disoriented and without any memory of who she was. Then as soon as she arrived back in Shanghai, a medical team sent by her husband was waiting for her at the airport and she was taken into a facility for God knows how long.

No one I spoke to really knew what they did to her in that facility. Jenny's husband wasn't going to tell me no matter how many times I'd asked. She refused to talk about it. But every time I asked her, tears would stream down her face so quickly that I wished that I hadn't bothered to ask. Part of me knew that we should revisit that topic again, if and when Jenny was ready to open up.

At least part of the problem was that Jenny was a really vain person and she only ever wanted to show her perfect beautiful

side to the world. It was an eye opener to see the opposite side of
her, where she no longer cared about her appearance.

My instinct told me to help her. But how?

Right this second, what I could do was give her what she
needed – some space.

"Where to, sir?" Dave asked.

"The warehouse."

I rang my friend Trevon Smith on the way to his place, the
warehouse, but Trevon didn't pick up. He was probably busy. In
fact, Trevon was always busy, non-stop working on his latest
project, and it would have been a real shocker if he ever picked
up his phone.

So, I sent Trevon a message letting him know that I would be
staying at the warehouse for a couple of days. Or until further
notice.

I hated hotels and I would avoid them if possible. I hadn't
always been like this though. When I was a child, I used to love
staying in hotels. When staying in hotels meant holidays, it
meant my parents finally had time to take me away on a vacation. Later on, staying in hotels meant that my dad had done
something bad and was trying to make up for it by taking Mom
and I on a vacation. But these make-up vacations always ended
in my parents fighting. Then after that, it just became a place
where I stayed when I was on a business trip. So, like I said, not
many great memories in hotels.

Trevon and I were roommates when we went to the same
boarding school in the United Kingdom. It had been the first
time both of us were away from home – me from China, and
Trevon from the United States. Weekends were always tough for
me. A lot of us would be sent "home", either to our parents, or to
family friends who would host us. I was supposed to go to Uncle
Roger's house, who was my dad's business associate. He always

made me really uncomfortable. He was constantly trying to sell me his business ideas, hoping that I would pass it to my parents.

When Trevon found out about this, he invited me to stay with his aunt every single weekend. And since then, I never went back to Uncle Roger's house. To me, Trevon was like family.

So, staying at Trevon's place during times like this was a no brainer, and he wouldn't mind, I was sure of that.

A few years ago, Trevon bought an abandoned building and intended to transform it into a working storage unit for his online retail store. His plan was to fix up the place and then hire people who had fallen on hard times to work there, while providing training, fair wages, food and shelter for them.

The building consisted of three floors and Trevon had turned the top floor into an office with a living space for himself. More than a living space really. It was so nicely decorated the standard of the interior could compete with an uptown penthouse. I hadn't actually been to the building before, but I had seen enough pictures from Trevon in our private group chat. He was so damn proud of this place.

On the outside though, it still looked like an abandoned building. Trevon had to stop the work on the warehouse because of the pandemic, which was a shame because this place had so much potential. And it would bring so much good to the local community.

"Lao ban." That means boss in Mandarin. And I hated when people addressed me so formally.

"Don't call me *lao ban*," I growled at Clare.

"Shao yeh." *Little master*. This one was even worse.

"Who the fuck taught you that?" I sometimes wondered if my mother was right, that I had been too relaxed with my staff. And now they have started calling me *names*. Sure, I was certain that most employees made fun of their bosses. *Behind their back.* Not in front of them like Clare just did.

"Goo–."

"Perfect." I snapped.

"Sir," Dave cut in. "I think we have a situation."

Again? Just my luck, huh?

I straightened up, and immediately spotted a red car parked outside of the warehouse and another one approaching slowly. Normally, this wouldn't be suspicious at all in New York, but this was an abandoned-looking building owned by my friend. Not some random drug den. Why would two cars choose to stop in front of it?

"Slow down," I demanded.

The whole car was in alert mode. Clare had even pulled out her gun, ready to shoot at anyone coming near us.

"Maybe someone is dealing near here?" Clare spoke up without thinking again but she may be right. But I didn't think Trevon would allow that. If someone was doing any illegal dealings anywhere near him, it would have been sorted out within hours. No one was allowed to piss on Trevon's territory.

"I don't think so," Dave announced as a man came out of the silver SUV and started trying to force the driver's door of the red Tesla open. "It looks like someone might be in trouble though."

"What is going on? Who is that?"

I felt stupid for asking. They knew as much as me at this point about the situation ahead.

"Mrs. Li said we should stay away from trouble." *No one asked her.*

Sometimes, I wondered if Clare worked for me or my mother. But if my mother was here, she would definitely advise us against getting involved in matters that could cause us harm. Then she would remind me that I was the only son in the Li family – the only legit son at least. The only heir to the Li

Empire, I could hear my mother saying. Although lately, I suspected that might not have been true.

"Sir," Dave hesitated, "you, um, you–"

"I what?" I blurted out.

"You know the driver in the Tesla."

My mind raced to a million places. My rib cage felt a sharp invisible pain – which triggered whenever I felt nervous or scared. The pain was a scar, a reminder left by my kidnappers years ago. Fragmented memories flashed through my mind – two guys kicking me in my stomach, refusing to stop no matter how much I begged. They wanted me to call Mom and Dad.

My arms reached for my chest, folded tightly. That usually helped sooth the panic attack that was creeping up on me. I had thought about seeing a therapist for a while, but I just couldn't seem to bring myself to do it. There was no way I would let my family even know about the mere thought of attending therapy sessions – they would see it as weakness – not a desired quality for the heir of their Li Empire. That's why I envied Jenny's courage for seeking help.

"Gun!" Clare shouted. "The asshole's got a gun."

Damn it. My newer bodyguard's tendency to loudly narrate everything wasn't good for my anxiety. I had lost my ability to think.

I tried not to look but my curiosity took over and I couldn't help it. Looking out the window, I saw a guy standing next to the driver side of the car, pointing his gun at the window, and the next second the car door opened slowly.

Should I help? I was in a great position to help. Clare and Dave should be able to handle any average guy. Again, my mother's words were ringing louder now in my head, reminding me that I shouldn't put myself and my team in danger. And this right here, definitely smelled and tasted like danger.

"Hurry. Drive faster," Clare instructed Dave, her voice was so loud that I wondered if the asshole outside could hear her.

My anxiety was sky high now. I could feel it as my lungs struggled to secure me oxygen. Another flashback – someone pointed their gun at my driver and me. He unlocked the door, and they helped themselves to the terrified boy sitting at the back of the car. Then before I knew it, chloroform was on my face, and I woke up with a black bag over my head in a smelly place where no one could hear me for days no matter how loud I screamed. I knew my assailants were there watching but they just decided to ignore me.

My mind was split in two.

Help or walk away.

"We should let Trevon know." My lips trembled, but that was all I could do. I felt like a coward.

Should we call the police and let them handle it? Or would it be too late?

Back then, I was taken in broad daylight outside of school. If someone had tried to help me, maybe I wouldn't have been taken, and I wouldn't have the scars on my body as a souvenir.

Our car drove past without any issues. Whoever it was, didn't really care that he was spotted pointing a gun at someone in the middle of the day. Much like my kidnappers. I sat up straight, adjusting my collapsing posture which did nothing for my confidence. Then I saw it, *her*, in the rearview mirror.

"Turn around!" I shouted.

"Sir," Clare complained. I didn't know how I knew, but I could just tell that Clare wouldn't like what we were about to do.

Well, last time I checked, I was the boss. "Get ready. Now."

"Sir." Clare again, louder this time.

"Shut the fuck up or get the fuck out." She wasn't expecting me to snap. She had never seen this side of me before. She had gotten used to bossing everyone around, including me. But guess what? Mr. Nice Guy had left the building.

I suddenly realized what Dave meant a few moments earlier.

I did know the driver. Very well indeed.

June Bennet.

The driver in the red Tesla.

The trouble that I was told to stay away from.

3

June

I didn't expect Mack to point a gun at me. The Mack I knew had always been fun and cool. How much of that had to do with the drugs though? Perhaps his coolness wasn't a projection of his real personality; I clearly didn't know him that well.

He wasn't a nice guy. That much I knew.

Mack ran a lot of "errands" for my ex, Dannie Wu. Dannie never told me what exactly Mack did for him, but those errands definitely weren't legal. One time, he rushed into Dannie's apartment panicking and covered in blood that wasn't his. Dannie wasn't a nice guy either, but I didn't know that until much later.

"Calm down." I lowered my voice, hoping that it would somehow help soothe Mack's nerves. My pulse was racing but I tried my best not to show it.

"I'm here," I whispered to my phone and wondered when the help would arrive. Wendy seemed to have gone completely quiet on the other end.

Bang. Mack kicked my brand-new Tesla. "Who are you talking to? Get the fuck out of the car now."

"Okay, okay." I sounded reluctant and he could probably hear it in my voice. I couldn't help it though. I got out of the car and held both my hands up.

"Who are you talking to?" *Shit.* He heard that – I wasn't as subtle as I thought I was.

"No one. Just a friend…" I stared at the dated abandoned building and was really skeptical about the help Wendy spoke of now.

"I thought we were friends." My voice came out a little shaky, but I wanted to know what he had in mind. The only way I knew how was to keep him talking – much like when I treated my patients. You don't want them keeping everything to themselves, because there was no way you could help patients like that.

"Friends don't run away from each other like that," he snapped.

"It's nothing personal, Mack. I have a problem being with people. You know, staying at home for too long will do that to you." I kind of lied. I knew that this was something that many people suffered from after the pandemic, including my mother.

"Is that so?"

"Of course." I could feel my teeth knocking together. "Lots of doctors died, you know? It could easily have been me."

I had to keep the conversation going in hope of keeping Mack relaxed.

"I guess you're right. I did think of you during the lockdown you know." I let out a small sigh as Mack showed signs of relaxing as he lowered his gun.

"Who else is here? Is it just you? We should go grab a coffee. I know a place not too far–"

Suddenly, a black car that drove past earlier turned around and sped towards us.

"What the fuck?" Mack's anger was back. "Get on your knees, now."

"Please, Mack."

"Get down or I'll shoot you."

I did as I was told.

Two people got out of the car and neither of them were Wendy. I didn't know the woman, but I recognized the large Asian man. A bodyguard. Did he work for Wendy now? What was he even doing in the country?

"Put down your gun." I heard Wendy's voice, from somewhere up high. Glancing up, I saw Wendy standing on the top floor balcony holding a megaphone.

What the actual fuck!

I felt confused. I was scared about being held at gunpoint, but at the same time I was excited about Wendy. She looked like a superhero about to save my ass – overlooking me and my whole situation from above.

How was it possible to be feeling such despair and hope at the same time?

A few seconds ago, I was convinced that I nearly had Mack. Not in a way where I could swing around and disarm him of his gun. But I was certain that he was about to let me go. We could have easily resolved this issue without any violence. Besides, Mack was almost certainly under the influence of something and not thinking clearly. My money was on some kind of drug.

If Mack acted alone, then all I needed to do was give him whatever he wanted. Probably some money. I shook off the thought of Dannie coming for me.

"You're surrounded, asshole. Surrender now or else..."

Surrender now or else what?

I really wanted to know. Or else what? That line was only ever said on TV. Actually, the whole situation kind of tickled me a little. I had a gun pointed at my head and I felt like laughing –

the stress of it all must have gotten to me. I had officially gone mad.

"Mack, listen to me. We can still go get that coffee if you want." I tried, but he wasn't listening.

"Surrounded by who exactly?" Two people pointing their guns at him didn't seem like a big enough threat to Mack.

Those *errands* that Mack used to run, I knew for sure that it involved physically harming human beings – not animals like Dannie had claimed. Not that it was okay to harm any animal. But Dannie told me back then that Mack was attacked by a stray dog and had to kill it to save his life.

I was sure that those clean-cut bodyguards in their suits just seemed like some jokers to him.

"Five. Four. Three. Two. One," Wendy counted, then three police cars rushed in. "Well, do you need a formal introduction?" she added.

"Tell them we're friends," Mack instructed me, knocking his gun on my skull which sent an electric buzz down my spine.

"Friends don't do that," a familiar voice answered but it wasn't Wendy on her megaphone.

Kai stepped out of the car, looking like a knight coming to my rescue. I didn't know how to react at the sight of him.

"Who the fuck are you?"

Exactly. I wanted to know that myself. Who the fuck gave him the right to rescue me? I wasn't some kind of princess in distress.

"Her friend." The corner of this mouth lifted, and I recognized that sarcastic smile on his. "If you drop the gun, we could be friends, too. I'll do whatever I can to help you."

Friend huh. Maybe that was what Kai thought of me as well. *Just friends.*

"If I don't?" Mack's hand jerked and the gun knocked on my skull one more time. Gah, I hated that. I could feel another piece of my soul being knocked out of my body every time he did that.

"Dead people can't be friends," Kai said, with another sarcastic smile.

"What about them?" Mack's face turned towards the police.

Kai laughed.

"They can be bought." Then he stopped his laughter. "Oh, I'm sorry officers, that's not what I mean, you know, bloody foreigner."

Fuck Kai. He thought he was being clever. I was freaking out right now. My forehead and my palms were covered in cold sweat, and I was in no mood to laugh at his stupid jokes. Was it so hard to understand that the only thing I wanted right now was to *not* have a gun pressed into the back of my skull.

The next thing I knew, Mack was tackled by a large man, and he almost took me with them.

A crowd of police dashed in, surrounding me, the man, and Mack. Two police officers helped me up, and two others held Mack on the ground as they cuffed him. That was when I realized that it was Dave who jumped Mack.

"Are you okay?" Kai asked.

I nodded even though I didn't really know how I felt.

"Please don't tell my brothers," I muttered, "or Chloe."

Kai said okay, and I made a mental note to repeat the same thing to Wendy. My brothers could be overly protective, and I didn't want them on my case right now. Kai held me close, rubbing my back with his large hands. It felt nice and may or may not have had the effect of soothing my nerves. But I enjoyed it.

Tears started pouring out of my eyes, which surprised the hell out of me. Hiding my emotions had been my practice for the last few years, and I had managed really well until now.

Perhaps Kai's touch did that to me.

But I was still kind of angry at him. Why? I didn't actually remember anymore. Whatever he did that pissed me off was a long time ago. He might not even have been aware of it. But never mind that. I wanted to be mad at him and I should be allowed.

"Wait, I need to talk to Mack." I struggled out of Kai's arms and called out as one of the police cars started to drive Mack away.

"You should stay away from him," Wendy said.

"Where are they taking him?" I demanded an answer, but my voice could never do stern very well.

"It's obvious, isn't it?" Wendy ushered me towards the entrance of the warehouse. "Come, I'll make you a cup of tea."

I followed Wendy inside the building and up some flights of stairs. There were rows of tall industrial shelves on the bottom floor with a few forklifts lying around. The second floor was in the process of some renovations and was mostly covered in dust sheets. The top floor was guarded with a heavy-duty metal door, and Wendy scanned her thumb print on the code reader to unlock the door. Inside it was an apartment.

"What's going to happen to him?" I couldn't care less about the gorgeous apartment in front of me. The light that came through the floor to ceiling windows was so bright it hurt my eyes a little. It bothered me that Wendy hadn't told me what I wanted to know.

"Hell. Of course." Wendy let out a laugh that made me think of the wicked witch of the west.

I sat down in the living room while Wendy made tea and coffee. Looking around the rather empty apartment, I noticed the furniture was clean and simple but expensive. Oh, *empty* might have been the wrong word – it was spacious, very much so. There was so much empty space and not enough furniture or personal belongings to fill it. It was entirely possible that the interior designer was going for a minimalist concept, I suppose.

I had redecorated my apartment not long ago and had spent far too much time looking through pricey furniture catalogs – so I could tell the furnishings here were far from cheap. My interior designer tried to convince me that price was often correlated with the time it would last. How could I know for sure? I guess only time will tell.

The high ceiling and large windows let in lots of natural light, although those windows could really do with a clean. I somehow didn't think that this space belonged to Wendy at all. It was simply too macho for her. Knowing her fashion choices – rather radiant, feminine and creative – I didn't think she would go for something so masculine and austere.

Even for an abandoned warehouse like this, it would have been really expensive to buy such a large building in New York. And to have bought it and not be fully utilizing it – it was almost a crime.

Kai came back to the lounge area after finishing up whatever he was doing with his team.

"Are you feeling better?" I had a feeling Kai didn't know what else to say to me.

"Long time no see." My sarcastic tone sounded more bitter than I had imagined, which wasn't a bad thing. Bitter was good too.

I couldn't bring myself to look at him. His eyes had the power to melt me, make my knees weak, and reduce all my logic to nothing.

"Yes, I just landed." Kai volunteered that information. "I'm sorry I haven't been in touch. Things have been crazy back home."

Needless to say. Because the truth was, things had been crazy for everyone for the last few years.

Every. Single. Person. On. This. Earth.

On that note, I really had no reason to be mad at him for disappearing. I didn't know why I was being so harsh when it came to him.

Fine. If I really had to spit out a reason, it was because three years ago he was kind of leading me on. And I thought we were going somewhere. Seriously. I even bought some sexy lingerie that's still sitting in my wardrobe, tags and the original wrapping still on. I wanted to take them back to the shop, but I wasn't going to let the shopkeeper think that I couldn't keep a man. That might be true. But nope. I wasn't going to let people talk.

"How are you?" I still sounded bitter.

"I'm fine. I've missed you." He smiled and my heart skipped a beat. Damn him. "I've missed Link, and I've missed New York."

Fuck. Of course. He didn't really miss me. That was just something he said to everyone.

Stop being so pathetic. I really should work on that when it comes to him.

This man in front of me was my first ever crush. His smile alone could cure cancer, my cancer anyway. I didn't think he would still have that power over me today, not any more after all these years, but how wrong I was.

I didn't know if this was true for everyone. But sometimes you come across someone in your life who has the power to make you crazy, to make you an unreasonable bitch. Simply because they would never see you the way you see them, love you back the way you love them. Life could be so unfair.

Oh well, I tried to knock some sense into myself and reminded myself that I was no longer a silly teen crushing hard for my brother's bestie.

Wendy broke my train of thought as she walked into the living room with a tray of refreshments – a variety of cut up fruit and some cookies. *Yum cookies.* "Where are your bodyguards?"

"Downstairs," Kai replied without thinking. I could have bodyguards too if I wanted, and Wendy could have been talking to me.

"Right." Wendy adjusted her robe awkwardly – seemingly having just gotten out of bed not too long ago. "I'm helping Trev with his warehouse project and staying here from time to time."

Trev as in Trevon Smith? Lincoln's other best friend?

I thought that it was strange that Wendy tried to hide her whereabouts during our call earlier. What was that girl hiding? "So, you planned for Kai to come here?"

"Oh no, that wasn't planned. He came uninvited." Kai cleared his throat, and I wasn't sure what he did that for. Part of me was glad that they weren't meeting here privately, using their friend's place as some kind of love nest.

"I called the police of course. I just needed you to lure him somewhere quiet so the police could get to work." I nodded. Sure. It made sense. But she still wasn't telling me the whole truth, though it didn't really bother me. She would tell me when the time was right, or not, completely up to her. It was never my right to nose in other people's business.

Kai stood up and started wandering the hallway.

"Which bedroom should I take? I need somewhere to stay." Wendy followed him around but didn't say anything.

I couldn't watch the two of them any longer, as much as I wanted to see Kai embarrass himself. "Mr. Li, a word please. In the kitchen."

Explaining to Kai that Wendy and Trevon probably needed their space was tricky. Kai would never understand why his bachelor best friend would be interested in a relationship after all these years. Trevon was a gorgeous man, but he was interested in money, in making his business a success, more than women, and that was why he hadn't been in a relationship for so long.

"I think Wendy and Trevon might want a little privacy."

"What for?" Kai asked innocently.

"Hello..." I jerked my eyebrows up and down hoping Kai would finally get the hint.

"How sure are you that they're seeing each other?" Kai wouldn't budge on the idea of staying at the warehouse.

"Not a hundred percent. But would you want to mess it up for Trevon, even if there was only a one percent chance that they could be interested in each other?"

I felt a presence behind me and turned around to find Wendy lurking. The woman's smile was strange, but if I had to guess, she was trying to say thank you. But then, that was just a wild guess.

"Just thirsty for some water." Wendy tiptoed around us.

"Is there any reason why you aren't staying at your own place?" Her voice a little timid.

Wendy was right. I knew that Kai and my brother had the habit of staying at each other's properties, but that was only when they didn't have a place of their own. A few years ago, Kai practically lived in one of Link's apartments in Myrtle Beach for a year.

"Funny story," Kai started to explain. He frowned a deep frown that was somehow...appealing.

"Not that funny actually. I showed up at my own place today and found my um–" he paused for a long second, "someone was living there. So, I need some place else to stay instead."

Simultaneously, Wendy looked my way, and I gave her a glance back. I wanted to know who was staying with Kai so I could get jealous. Wendy though, probably just wanted the gossip.

"Who is it?" Wendy was much more eager than me.

I leaned in, in hopes that it would pressure him into talking.

Because if he was seeing someone, I would want to know. Always.

"Did you do something? Is she mad at you?" Wendy pressed on.

"Maybe." He swallowed so hard it practically echoed through the room. "I just need to leave her alone."

Pride filled Wendy's face. "Sure, leave *her* alone."

Okay, right then I realized that Wendy just made Kai confirm that it was a woman. And he was probably trying to hide her, and *she* was possibly mad at him. "I think you should stay with June."

Now that took me by surprise.

I couldn't believe what Wendy just said and I wished that she'd choke on her water. "Thanks Wendy. I don't need–"

"That's a great idea actually." Kai grinned at Wendy, then me.

"I think someone like you can afford a hotel." Part of me wanted Kai to stay with me. Since I had been dreaming about seeing him, waking up to the sight of him since I was eighteen. But I really couldn't risk having my world turned upside down anymore. Not at this age. If I were to see someone now, it would be my *forever*, not Mr. Playboy Kai.

"Sure. I could ask your sister-in-law. I'm sure the James' or the Thompsons would make one of their best suites available for me. But I really hate hotels." He was right about that. He was one phone call away from the best hotel suite in New York.

"Why?"

"Why what?"

"Why do you hate hotels?" I had met up with him in hotels before, but I had no idea that he hated them. And no, we weren't meeting up for a screw.

"I can't say."

I rolled my eyes at him. "If you don't tell, you can't stay with me. You know I could make those phone calls myself, I'm sure the Thompsons would help me out as they would you."

That much was true. I had met Chloe's friends, Emily and her family. Their family had hotels in every corner of the world. There wasn't a major city on Earth that they hadn't built their hotels in. Okay, a slight exaggeration on my part, Pyongyang and a few others might be an exception.

I knew I shouldn't tease him but still, it was fun. After what I had suffered through this morning, I would much prefer to see someone else in agony, and Kai was an obvious choice. "Because all hotel rooms are haunted, and I'm scared of ghosts."

Wendy almost spit out her water and Kai smiled.

"Fine." I tried not to laugh. I wasn't sure I believed him, but I knew that a lot of Asians believed in ghosts, my mother included. "On second thought, you have bodyguards, right? What do you hire them for?"

I tried to keep a straight face. I tried really hard.

"Oh yes, they will need to stay with us," he said shamelessly as if I had already promised to let him stay.

"What?"

"I think you need another tea." Wendy excused herself from the now slightly heated conversation.

"You won't even know they're there. I promise."

My idea of having Kai to myself had been shattered. I didn't factor in his precious bodyguards who never left his side. How naive was I?

And suddenly, I remembered what Chloe told me years ago when Link's life was in danger. Kai and his family always had security in plain sight, protecting him wherever he went, and ready to pounce on anyone who might cause him harm.

"Like ninjas." I recalled saying the same words to Chloe.

"Exactly."

4

———————

Kai

June's apartment was nice, but it didn't seem to suit her. Most of the walls were painted white, with a select few that were covered in this dark blue wallpaper with a floral pattern in gold foil. The furniture was all either black, white or beige. Everything was neutral, and unremarkable. It did give it a modern feel, like most five-star hotels have, but at the end of the day, none of them were remarkable enough that you would ever want to go back.

"Who's your interior designer?" I took the opportunity to ask as June joined me in the living room after showing Clare and Dave their room.

June frowned slightly. "Um, something Apex I think."

That's exactly what I thought.

Unremarkable.

So unremarkable that even the owner of the apartment couldn't remember. This tiny apartment had two bedrooms and a small room she used for exercise. A bit tight for me and my guys. I wondered what the second bedroom was for. Was someone else living here with her? I couldn't wait to snoop around for some men's items.

"It just doesn't feel like you." I thought about not mentioning anything, but I had done enough of that at home. And here, with June, I felt like I could just say anything I had on my mind.

"Emily recommended them. Do you remember her? The Thompson's girl who's friends with Chloe." I nodded.

"The Emily you were going to call to get me a suite." Of course, I knew who Emily was. I had attended many charity events organized by Emily before June even heard about her. The Thompson family was known for their hotel business and had been trying to branch out to other sectors. Though they had some success in America in the food industry, lately they had been thinking about expanding abroad. Emily's brother Trent Thompson, and husband Dylan James, had both reached out to me separately, in hopes to secure a collaboration in China. Those two, they never saw eye-to-eye when it came to business.

"Yes, I know Emily Thompson."

"James," June corrected me as she sank into one of the cream-colored sofas.

She wasn't wrong but I didn't feel the need to tell her that Emily still uses her Thompson surname for work. For private matters, she had chosen to be Mrs. James, but anything to do with work she still used Thompson. I simply responded with a smile, something I would do when I couldn't be bothered to comment.

"Why didn't you decorate the place yourself?"

June had a talent for creative things. I remembered that she used to draw. Not everyone who can draw knows anything about design, I knew that, but I thought June might enjoy decorating her own place.

"I had no time." She shrugged. "And Mom said my time is better spent doing the important things."

Sometimes I forget that her mother was a bit of a tiger mom like mine.

"Which is?"

"Looking after the hospitals and the patients." I noticed that she said hospitals and I wondered if she had been given more responsibility since the last time I saw her.

"What hospitals?"

"Oh, Link didn't tell you?" She checked for an answer before continuing, "My dad hasn't been very well, so I've been taking over his role for a little bit until, you know, until he gets better."

"No, we haven't spoken to each other lately. What happened to Dr. Bennet?"

I hadn't really been in touch with anyone over the last two years. I had so much to deal with back home, and I literally had no time to do anything else. When I finally remembered to call, it was either midnight for me or for my friends. I hated being in different time zones to them.

"Covid." June tried to force a smile. "Then cancer."

"No." That was exactly what I dreaded. Bad news. If I didn't know, I could pretend it didn't happen. That wasn't how the universe worked though. Just because I temporarily logged out, it didn't mean that the world stopped spinning.

I knew subconsciously I was avoiding calling anyone – that was my coping mechanism. Ignorance is bliss.

"I'm sorry to hear about that. Is he okay now?"

"He's doing another round of chemo, then they'll see." An electric shock jolted through my stomach as I noticed tears on her face.

"And that's why you've been looking after all these hospitals?" June nodded lightly. Poor *princess*.

I knew that the Bennet Medical Group owned quite a few hospitals, but I had no idea how many, or how they operated at all.

That explained it. I thought that the incident this morning had exhausted her, giving her that pale and frail appearance. But perhaps she was burnt out lately from working too much.

"Are you getting any help from your brothers?"

I didn't care that Link was my best friend. He should have helped her. What about her other brother, Liam, whom I didn't know all that well. Wasn't he helping? I seemed to remember that he was working in the same hospital as her?

"They do. But they have their own things going on." *Okay, fine.* Maybe they did help, but I had stopped caring. They should take on more, a lot more, so she didn't look like she was running out of battery. "Have you heard? Chloe is pregnant. Link is really excited about their baby."

Great news for Lincoln.

Again. I didn't give a fuck. It wasn't like Link had to physically carry the baby, go through the morning sickness, all the hormonal changes in his body. He had time and energy to help his little sister.

Baby sisters were meant to be spoiled.

Spoiled rotten.

Her brothers should be ashamed.

"You should get some rest." I jumped up to help June up from the sofa.

"I'm not tired." A yawn betrayed her as she said it. "Okay, I lied. But I need to finish some paperwork for tomorrow."

"Listen. You have had quite a day. You should go get a nap."

I think I needed one too. I was exhausted from sitting in the other car while she had a gun to her face, worried sick over her.

"Maybe you're right," June agreed, "but I'm too tired to move. Can you pass me a blanket from over there."

June pointed at the throw hanging on the other sofa just behind me. Instead of getting her what she wanted, I leaned down in front of her. Our faces were only inches away from each other and I could smell her mango flavored lip balm. "What are you doing?"

"Looking after you." She answered softly, her eyes wide as I leaned in just a little bit closer.

I reached out both of my arms and lifted her up from the seat.

"Put me down." June insisted, but I didn't. Instead, I held on to her tighter.

"You said you're too tired to move. So *don't* move." June struggled for another two seconds before giving in entirely.

June wasn't skinny like those women my mother made me date. She wasn't overweight either. I was no good at judging how heavy she was, but the curves of her body made it easy to have her in my arms.

I shook my head at how cliche my thoughts were, but she really fit perfectly to my body. Was it her body shape? Or were we just perfect for each other? Pfft, I refused to believe in such a thing. If that were true, divorce rates wouldn't be so high.

I reminded myself that she was nothing but my best friend's baby sister.

And I was just performing a big brother's duty on behalf of my friend. To make up for my absence and lack of communication these last few years.

I carried June to her room without much problem. Her room was the first one down the corridor. Inside, the decor matched the rest of the apartment, apart from the bed, which was surprisingly pink. Maybe pink was her favorite color. I had never seen her using or wearing anything pink. Having said that, wasn't her bed at her parents' house pink as well? I only ever saw her in her bedroom briefly so I couldn't be sure.

I put her down on her soft and fluffy bed and she climbed beneath the duvet.

"Should I read you a story?" I teased her as I picked up the book on her bedside table, *Haunting Adeline*. But June snatched it from me like I was going to steal a precious family heirloom. "Sleep tight."

I made a mental note to find out what the hell *Haunting Adeline* was about.

This wasn't the peaceful, relaxing trip that I had originally planned. Over the last two years, my mother had been on a mission to find me a suitable wife. I tried to brush it off by saying none of them were suitable. However, my mother made me go through a series of things to do with them before I could declare a hard pass on a candidate. According to Mom, if I could do everything on the list she provided with the woman she had chosen for me, and still feel nothing, then we really weren't meant to be.

Don't ask me where she got this list from. Probably from a magazine somewhere about dating. I could imagine an article titled, Ten Dates To Engagement.

To be fair, the women *selected* for me weren't bad looking. They were of a *high standard*, of a certain class – my mother's words, not mine. First of all, they all had to have studied overseas at a good reputable university, be from a wealthy family with a good background, be well mannered, and beautiful. Yes, beauty was part of it because she wanted to make sure that she had beautiful grandbabies.

The thing was, I found them all the same, and boring, and they all tended to look and behave in a certain way. Like my mother expected them to. Despite my busy schedule, I had to fit dating into my calendar, or my mother would never quit nagging at me. In fact, Mom had often made Andy, my personal assistant, schedule my dates without even asking me.

People are often curious why a man in his thirties would let his mother walk all over him like that.

I often wondered that myself. But I knew that it was pity. I felt sorry for my mother. First, my dad had an affair and then started another family with that woman. In recent years, my dad had been openly taking his mistress – instead of the official Mrs. Li – to events. And last year, at his birthday party, Dad introduced his illegitimate teenage son to all their guests.

That was what triggered all the madness in Mom. She wanted to make sure that I, as the true heir of the Li family, would inherit the family business when the time came. I didn't really want to meddle in my parents' business, but I couldn't help but feel sorry for Mom.

My phone buzzed and it was a simple good night message from the last woman I was dating.

Lucy Zhang.

The only one that didn't bore me.

The only one that didn't annoy the hell out of me.

The only one that I didn't want to finish the to-do list with.

Because I didn't want to prove my mother right. The list was a powerful one and I couldn't see any man not falling for Lucy after going through the list.

This trip wasn't just to escape Lucy. I needed a break from my mother. From my power-hungry family.

My thoughts shifted back to June. It still baffled me, why June would need two bedrooms when it was just her. I knew that she worked hard in her career and deserved anything she wanted in her life. But did she want a roommate?

After a short discussion with Clare and Dave, I had decided that I would use the yoga room. The duo would share the second bedroom – since they had to take turns keeping watch at night anyway, so they wouldn't both be sleeping, or sharing a bed, at the same time.

I didn't think that we should use June's home office at all – there might be sensitive information or data about the business that she might not like anyone to know. I personally wouldn't let anyone into my workspace without permission. My workspace was sacred and I hated it when people disturbed me when I was working or brainstorming business ideas.

Dave had sent instructions to my PI to find out as much information as possible about the residents living in the building. To me, it was just a routine check. Ever since I was kidnapped, my parents had made it part of daily life to background check every single person that I might meet. Just to keep me safe.

You never think that it's necessary until bad shit happens. Much like insurance.

I took a peek at June's room and made sure that she had fallen asleep before calling Lincoln. I didn't feel comfortable knowing that June might be awake while I talked about her in her own home.

Lincoln didn't seem too bothered about my lack of communication over the last two years. My best friend had visited China before and knew what it was like for me out there. But Lincoln was convinced that if my mother knew about my little fetish and found me a sub, I would say yes to marrying anyone.

I laughed at the idea.

Lincoln couldn't be more right about me – but that was years ago – what Lincoln didn't know was that things had changed ever since I saw how in love he was with Chloe. How he had risked everything to find her when she was missing and did whatever he could to protect her.

When I told Lincoln how I ended up staying with June, he was not only shocked, but furious about the incident that happened this morning. He wanted Mack to be violently tortured and I knew he meant every word. Through his wife, Lincoln had come across some rather powerful people that he would otherwise never have had an opportunity to meet. Chloe's cousin turned out to be the only daughter of a dead legendary

Mafia boss and she had the final say in everything in a very powerful organization.

Our conversation took a little over fifteen minutes and I was satisfied with what was being said – because I hated mindless chit chat. I'd informed Lincoln about my return. Told him about my stay at June's. And told him that I would be taking over the big brother duties while he was miles away from her.

Somehow, I found it weird that Lincoln had never heard about Mack, or where June might have known him from. I was curious what other secrets June was keeping from her family.

But both of us had agreed whoever this Mack person was, he might come back or might have an accomplice or two. June shouldn't be left alone right now and me staying with her was possibly the best way to keep her safe.

I laid on the Lululemon yoga mat trying to ease the headache starting to form due to my jet lag. I hadn't slept since I left China, and I was beyond exhausted now. The kind of exhaustion where every nerve in your body is on strike, like they've decided that you will never ever find a position comfortable enough to fall asleep in again.

Perhaps a proper bed might help with that situation. But there was no way I would take the guest room. I owed my guys too much – they signed up to this shit job, risking their lives to protect me 24/7. Making sure that they were properly rested was the least I could do.

I could buy a mattress, or futon, and have it delivered. June wouldn't mind, would she? *Nope!* That was too weird. What kind of guest brought their own mattress? Maybe that's what some people do, but not me. No way.

A knock on the door disrupted my monkey mind and my failed attempt to nap.

"Sir, the building is secure now. Everyone came back clean," Dave reported.

I sat up as Dave continued telling me everything concerning our security. Dave also took initiative in setting up security for Jenny, as his intel told him that the Law Family were scouring Europe at the moment looking for her.

We both knew that it was only a matter of time before they searched America. When it came to Jenny, most people thought that she was the vicious one who would kick and scream in public when she went mental. No one really understood that she had her triggers, and her husband had used that to control her for many years.

"See if you can find out what medicine she takes back home. And try not to alert anyone. I don't really know what she takes. Maybe some sleeping pills, or Prozac."

"Prozac? What Prozac?" June stood outside the door, her jaw now almost on the floor.

5

———

June

I couldn't stop crying. No matter what my brothers did or said, there was no way the tears would stop streaming down my cheeks. My best friend in life had died.

Lincoln tried to convince me that she was just missing. But how was that possible? When the media and the police themselves were convinced that Chloe was gone forever. Besides, my best friend was not someone who would run away from home. What could possibly make her want to run away? What couldn't we get through together?

Unless she was abducted against her will. But without her parents to pay for the ransom, she was as good as dead. Would Daddy pay for her ransom though if the kidnappers got in touch? I could pay him back in installments once I started working.

Anyway, it had been six months, and I hadn't heard anything.

And I couldn't believe that I still had tears left in me. I never knew that I would love someone so much. I didn't even know that I had that much space in my heart.

Sure, Mom, Dad, and my brothers were different. I loved them no matter what. Even when my irritating brothers were just being annoying, I still loved them. There were times when I didn't think I did, and I would react rudely or say something hurtful, but I would feel so horrible afterwards.

Chloe's death made me realize something. My grief was related to my love for her.

If my grief for Chloe was so strong, I couldn't imagine ever losing my parents or my brothers.

When Kai walked through my bedroom door on my 18th birthday, everything changed. My crying stopped. For a bit, but still.

To say that my heartache stopped would be a far stretch, but he most definitely had brought some light back into my life, like I finally saw light for the first time in a pitch-black tunnel that I kept falling deeper and deeper through.

THREE YEARS AGO, when Kai stayed in New York briefly for his new business venture, I thought that we might be going somewhere. We had grown closer after my brother's kidnapping – a story for another day. We had spent hours together, not doing much, but simply hanging out and connecting. It felt like what it would have been like if we were a family, if we were some kind of old married couple, playing house.

When Kai left the country without a proper goodbye, it broke my heart.

It was very selfish of me to think that he would stay for the lockdown, leaving his family behind in China. I should have been happy for him that he got special permission to enter China on his private jet.

I stayed in the U.S. working on the front line, helping patients. I could have died, and he wouldn't have known. He wouldn't ever know that I'd had a crush on him since I was eighteen years old. Though I doubted he felt the same way about me.

Perhaps that was the reason I was so angry at him now. In truth, I was angry at myself, for never having the guts to confess my feelings for him. I might not have feelings for him anymore but after going through Covid-19, after seeing so many deaths, it messes with your head. If the pandemic had taught anyone anything, it was that life was precious, and we ought to be mindful and grateful for everything at every moment.

"June, I'm sorry. I don't know what to tell you, but Kai has left the country." I could still hear Lincoln saying those words over the phone in my head like it happened two seconds ago. It hurt just as much as it did when my father told me about Chloe's death. I knew it was only an unsaid goodbye, but there were so many uncertainties in life, and we were losing so many people left and right. What if he died and I never kissed those lips?

I had my suspicions of what I might be suffering from. Although I didn't go into psychology, I had studied these things at some point in my career, in my life, and I even took an online test. Apparently, I was struggling with some kind of anxiety, grief and PTSD.

If my patients showed up and told me about their self-diagnoses, I would... Well, I'd want to roll my eyes, or scoff at them, but I wouldn't because I was taught to be polite. So, when I saw the results, I couldn't help but scoff and roll my eyes at myself.

But I had never sought out a professional. Because the thought of having a proper evaluation scared me. All I knew for sure was that it caused me pain when people I cared about left me. So, I just had to make sure that it didn't happen.

I woke up after my nap and Kai was no longer in my bedroom. My book, *Haunting Adeline*, had been opened and my pulse quickened. This wasn't a book for a good girl like me. Well, not the good girl that I appeared to be. Did Kai know about the book? Did he know how dark the story was?

Picking the book up, I scanned through the pages that were left open and felt a little relief. It didn't get too spicy on those pages. Unless he read the whole thing and just randomly left an uninteresting page open on purpose to throw me off the scent.

A long yawn creeped into my mouth, and I wished for a few more minutes in bed. Despite the interesting morning I had, I'd managed to rest well which surprised me greatly.

Knowing that I had guests in my apartment meant that I couldn't stay in bed though. Well, I could. But I wouldn't. My head wouldn't let me. I had an urge to make sure that they were taken care of.

Feeling a little self-conscious about bad breath, I gave my teeth a quick brush then wandered my apartment on tip toes. The guest room door was closed, and I decided to leave it – someone was probably resting in there. So, I continued to explore, feeling like a stranger in my own home.

Then I heard something, right outside of my yoga room.

"Prozac."

"What Prozac?" I could have held my tongue and listened to the conversation. He might say more and if I could've just been patient and a little bit more calculating I would have got a broader picture of what Dave and Kai were talking about. But I couldn't help myself.

Both men turned around as I sort of burst into the room.

"Don't you know how to knock?" Kai exclaimed. It was weird to see Kai sitting on the floor – and having to look down at him – on my pink Yoga mat.

And before this, it didn't occur to me that Kai would snoop at all. Even though it wasn't hard to find, he must have looked through my wardrobe to find those mats. And my meditation cushion which I just noticed underneath Kai's delicious bum.

"The door wasn't shut and it's my own home," I protested, "You should have whispered if it was a secret! It's nothing to be ashamed of though."

I had known Kai to be a proud man. So proud that he didn't like showing his emotions. When Lincoln went missing, he had a little bit of a meltdown. He might have thought that I only witnessed it because I was at the wrong place at the wrong time, but I thought otherwise. It was nice to know that I could hug him all night and make the pain go away.

"Why are you looking at me like that?" His face turned away, avoiding eye contact.

"I can refer you to a friend who can prescribe you the medication. How long have you been taking it?" I used my children's TV presenter voice, sometimes it helped with not stepping on people's toes.

Kai got up from the floor and walked straight at me, cornering me on the bookcase with his six-foot something frame. "Do I look like I need drugs?"

I coughed lightly and let out a pathetic "no".

Kai turned and exchanged a look with Dave.

I knew Dave would never say a word, he was the most loyal person to Kai on this planet, so I fixed my eyes on Kai's face – only inches away from mine. A part of me hoped that I would shoot out some truth confessing laser any second now.

"It isn't for me."

I let out a sigh of relief when he finally volunteered that information.

Still, I wasn't sure if I should believe him.

It was nothing against him, but I had learned that many people hide things. Patients for example would often hide their conditions from their loved ones. Some of them even tried to conceal information from their own doctors.

"You don't have to tell me if you don't want to." As much as I wanted to know, I knew he had no obligation to share. I was nobody to him after all.

"I–" He reluctantly opened his mouth, then after a long deep breath, "You can't say anything to anyone."

I rolled my eyes upward and was back to staring straight at his face. That was my way of saying "of course" and hoping that Kai could read my peculiar body language.

"It's for my cousin." That was when he took two steps back, then returned to the meditation cushion.

I nodded. Right. I still had my doubts.

"But you really shouldn't tell anyone about her." The way he looked at me, with a hint of a glare in his eyes, made me want to roll my eyes at him.

Shaking my head lightly, I sighed then tried to reason with him. "Who can I tell about your cousin? I don't even know her. Unless she's some kind of superstar, but still, what good would it do me to gossip about her, huh?"

"Fine. My cousin Jenny is running away from home. We found her at my apartment today. And you know what, she is kind of famous back home. She has millions of followers on her social media."

It suddenly made sense to me. Cousin Jenny was the woman he said was at his place earlier. So that meant he wasn't hiding a girlfriend in his apartment then. That information had somehow made my day.

"Is she in danger?" I asked as I noticed a cloud of sadness on Kai's face that wasn't there earlier.

"Not in real danger. But kind of in trouble." He didn't need to say anything more than that. "I think that she's been struggling for quite some time after having her first baby."

"Have you told anyone about this?"

"No. Her family is very private. But she's known for throwing her tantrums. Sometimes, she'll lose her temper in public, and her husband's men will drag her away with her still kicking and screaming. It's hard not to notice these kinds of things."

"And you think she needs Prozac?"

Kai shook his head. "I don't know what kind of medication she takes. It's all speculation. I suspect she had postpartum depression, but with the way she's acting, I believe there's more to it."

"And there's no way of having her medical records sent here?" I could guess the answer, but I thought I'd ask anyway.

"No, we can't do that. Because whoever is looking for her would know her whereabouts." Yep, Kai just confirmed it.

An hour later, we arrived at Kai's apartment. One that I had never been to.

He told me he'd bought this property a few years ago and had a housewarming party that I missed. I remembered the date because I was summoned by Dad to go to Hong Kong, to discuss an outbreak that could impact the world. We also discussed the possibility of opening a fertility hospital in Asia with me as the CEO. I even thought about getting something nice for Kai when I returned.

The thing was, I hadn't managed to get out of my quarantine to give him the present before he left the country.

My apartment was expensive for me. But it was nothing compared to Kai's. Though I came from money, I never used anything that was my family's. I had earned everything that I owned with the money I made myself. It had taken me years to be able to purchase my current place, and I was proud of my achievements.

Some of Dad's friends had urged him to give me a better

position, to skip a few steps when I started. But he didn't – he must have known that I would say no anyway.

A lot of people couldn't believe that I had to work really hard for everything.

My friend, Dr. Linda Rose, answered my call for help and arrived at Kai's five minutes before us. She waited in the hallway. Kai had made a call to the reception for the staff to receive her and let her in the building. Dave and Clare escorted us to the door, making me slightly uncomfortable. I couldn't ever get used to having people follow me around all the time.

 Kai whispered something to them, and it was clear to me a second later that he wanted them to stay outside for his cousin's privacy.

We entered into a wide hallway that led to the living room with a very tall ceiling. Needless to say, it was much taller than mine.

I wanted to know how many floors this apartment had. And if he could park his cars inside the building. But now didn't feel like an appropriate time to ask for a tour. The floor and walls were covered in cream and golden marble next to the floor to ceiling windows. Beyond the living room was a dining room and a kitchen, with a spiral staircase next to it.

It was a shame that the living room was covered in so much garbage. Take out boxes, papers, Kleenex, bottles, nut shells, and snack wrappers were a few of the things that I could make out. The good news was that Jenny had been eating though.

But there was no sight of her.

Dr. Rose and I followed Kai around closely and gingerly in search of Jenny. Like we were hunting for baby Bambi.

"Jesus," Kai shouted as he walked into the downstairs bathroom next to the kitchen.

A woman was passed out on the floor, facing down in her own filth.

"Be careful," I instructed as Kai went to turn Jenny around then I reached out my finger and placed it under her nose. "Good. She's breathing."

I needed to check even if it might have upset Kai a little.

Kai shook Jenny lightly, calling out a few different names in Chinese that she might respond to. Among them, I recognized words like sister and Mrs. Law. She finally opened her eyes, but only a little. She seemed to recognize Kai but didn't say anything before passing out again.

With some help, Kai had managed to put Jenny in bed. Dr. Rose and I took turns examining her, while Kai made some calls and arranged for a team to clean up the place and stock up the fridge for her.

"What's the verdict?" Kai walked into the guest room after finishing his calls.

I let out a small smile, the one that I put on when delivering good news to my patients. "She's okay. Maybe I had a little too much to drink."

"Goodness, I forgot she has issues with–" Kai didn't finish but I guessed what he was about to say. And I had no doubt Dr. Rose had guessed it too. It was obvious.

"Does she need to be in the hospital?" Kai asked, and continued without waiting for an answer, "She cannot go to the hospital, her husband will find her."

"No, she's fine and safe here." I looked to Dr. Rose's face for agreement, and she returned it with a nod.

"What's going on?" Jenny mumbled. "Who are these people, Kai?"

Jenny started off sleepy and weak but within seconds, she was ready to jump off the bed and fight off anyone who went near her. I remembered what Kai said about her temper earlier and wondered if she would need sedation.

Kai slowly sat next to her and wrapped his arms around her.

He whispered a few words in her ears and like magic, she calmed down. I was glad that she settled down quickly.

"This is my friend June. You've met her brother, Lincoln Young." Jenny nodded lightly. "And this is Dr. Rose, she's here to help you."

"I don't want to be locked up," Jenny blurted out without a second thought, her eyes immediately filled with horror.

"I won't do that," Dr. Rose chimed in, "I'm a psychiatrist. But I think of myself as more of a friendly therapist. And I want to get to know you."

With a warm smile, her speech was now pretty convincing. But I knew that was the reason Dr. Rose was so good at her job. Not only was she a kind and caring person, but she was also just genuinely trying to get to know all her patients so she could provide the help that they deserved.

"How are you going to help me? No one can help me." At first, it sounded like Jenny was challenging Dr. Rose. But I realized she actually sounded hopeless, like all those infertile patients that came through my door.

"Can we have the room to ourselves?" Dr. Rose turned to Kai and then me. "So we can talk privately. Is that okay with you?"

Her eyes were soft on Jenny's face as Jenny mouthed out a yes.

Kai and I waited silently outside the room. I could tell that he didn't want to leave his cousin's side. His brows were knitted closely, the usual brightness in his shiny brown eyes were now covered in darkness. I had an urge to lean in and hold him, but I held myself together.

"She'll be fine. I'll make sure of that." That wasn't something I would normally say, not to any patient for any procedure. At best, I might say that I would do my best, simply because there were no guarantees in medicine. But for Jenny – someone that

Kai cared so much about – I was determined to give my all to help her.

After what felt like a very long wait, Dr. Rose came out of the room. Kai had Clare keeping watch while he led us into his study, which was two doors down from the other room.

"I think she shouldn't be left on her own," Dr. Rose said as soon as we entered the room.

We sat down on a set of cream-colored sofas facing each other, next to a large glass bookshelf. Kai stood up, remembering his manners and offered his guests a beverage. "What can I get you? Whiskey? Vodka?"

"I'm okay, thanks," Dr. Rose said.

"Me too. Come sit down next to me," I offered, trying to prepare Kai for what Dr. Rose might say after. He could do with a friend right about now.

Kai poured himself a glass of whiskey and downed it before joining us. "You can tell me the bad news."

"Okay. Jenny seems to think that she is running away from some kind of danger."

"I wouldn't call that danger," Kai interrupted.

"Mr. Li, whatever situation she's in might not seem dangerous or feel like any kind of threat to you, but in her mind it is. And one should not judge her for feeling that way."

Kai nodded, because Dr. Rose was right.

"How can I help?" I chimed in.

"She needs to feel safe. And the good news is – she feels that here. That's why she came here in the first place. However, Jenny hasn't slept for a long time. She's constantly worrying that someone might come and get her in the middle of the night. I need to carry out a proper diagnosis when she's more herself. I believe she's at risk for self-harm and possibly even a suicide attempt."

"She told you that?" Kai hit the coffee table in front of him.

"Her exact words were that she wishes she could end it all," Dr. Rose said softly.

"Did she say who's causing her pain?" Kai sounded a little angry as he demanded an answer.

"No. But I suspect it was someone very close to her. Please gather yourself before I say this." I could sense another surge of anger flowing through Kai. "I think it would be best if I examine her to see if she's been raped."

6

———

June

The man I knew as Kai left the building as soon as Dr. Rose mentioned the word "rape". What was left was just a body without a soul. His eyes became a scary void, an emptiness that could suck out all the happiness from me if my gaze lingered there too long, so I looked away. I knew that no matter how hard I tried, I couldn't take away the pain he was feeling right now.

Rape was a terrible thing to go through. I had helped many sexual assault victims over the years, so I knew some of what they went through. The worst part was a lot of them were violated by people that they actually knew and trusted.

I shuffled a little closer to Kai and wrapped my arms around him gently. I had no idea if that would make him feel better. Actually, I was pretty sure nothing in the world would make him feel better right now. It hurt my heart to see him like that.

I realized then that a very small part of me was jealous that Jenny had someone like Kai, someone who cared so much about her. He had the kind of smile that could brighten up a room, it had even helped me find my own smile once.

When we eventually found Chloe three years ago, alive and well, with a new name and a new life, I was so happy. Until the feelings of betrayal creeped in. Did she know how much sadness she had caused me? Why did she think she couldn't share her little secret with me? Had I ever not been a good secret keeper for her?

The worst thing was when I found out that Lincoln knew all this time but didn't tell me.

They owed me those tears; those years I'd mourned her. They owed me six months of my life when I practically couldn't function.

"I'll be there alongside Dr. Rose during the procedure." My voice was slow and soft, the same one I used with my patients. "If Jenny wants me to be."

I hadn't performed many of these tests before, but I was trained as an OB-GYN, now as a fertility specialist, so I knew the procedure very well. The thought of actually performing the test turned my stomach upside down. I never liked it. It was just something I had to do. My duty to help victims.

Although I had only just met Jenny, it would be extremely hard to do the test on her with our personal connection through her cousin. But the process wouldn't be nearly as hard for me as it would be for her, of course.

Kai finally moved. The movement was so tiny that I wouldn't have noticed if he wasn't in my arms.

"Thank you." He mouthed the words quietly as if the act of talking itself was too tiring. I assumed that Kai wanted me to be there for Jenny, even though he didn't actually ask me.

Kai opened his mouth again, but this time nothing came out. Was he lost for words?

He sighed lightly and repeated the act once more.

I knew that he must have questions for Dr. Rose. It wasn't uncommon to be found speechless at a time like this. Trust me, I knew.

"What makes you think we should do a rape test?" Maybe this was what Kai wanted to ask but couldn't find the words or courage to. I decided to shoot Dr. Rose a few questions to ease Kai's frown.

Dr. Rose exchanged a glance with me, seemingly confused. These were the questions that were typically asked by the victim's loved ones. Not by a doctor. As a doctor, I knew the protocol, and the reasons behind those tests.

"First of all, Jenny was very frightened. But she did calm down after a few minutes and allowed me to inspect some of her body." Luckily, Dr. Rose played along. She swallowed hard before continuing, "Her body is covered in scars and bruises. Some old and some new. The newest ones haven't healed properly, and I suspect they are no older than one week."

"I see. Thank you." I knew that no matter how many times a doctor had dealt with situations like this, it would never be easy. Perhaps a robot – or a psychopath – would do a doctor's job better, because they couldn't feel and could never get emotional regardless of the situation.

"Is there a possibility that she might not have been raped?" This question blurted out from Kai's mouth.

Dr. Rose and I both knew that this one in particular was one of the most common questions asked, also one of the hardest to answer. After all, it wasn't something easy to accept.

"Totally. That's all the more reason to do the test." Dr. Rose cleared her throat. "Listen, as hard as it may sound, Jenny's scars and injuries have been there for a long time. At this point, we really should keep a record of her current situation, regardless of whether she has been sexually or physically abused."

Kai shook his head.

"How are you going to make sure that the test isn't going to cause her more pain?" He made a good point here.

"It will be hard." My voice was stern. "I'm not going to lie. But this may be the only opportunity she has to gather evidence against whoever did this to her."

I knew how hard it would be for the victim. I had been there. Intense emotions were going to get stirred up, tears were going to pour, the body was going to shake. But women are strong, and with the right support they could do it, they could do anything.

"And you'll make sure she's okay?" This was the first time Kai made eye contact with me after we sat down. I knew the man behind the body in front of me had returned, but I wasn't sure I completely recognized this version of him.

"I swear on my best friend's grave." I said, knowing he'd get my allusion to Chloe.

Kai rolled his eyes at me but didn't laugh at my dark joke.

But I knew that it had at least tickled him a little. His lips quirked, even if it was only just a little.

Kai stood up, headed to the drinks cabinet and poured himself another whiskey. This time, he didn't bother to offer anyone else a beverage. Not that we wanted one.

"The bastard should pay for hurting Jenny." Kai inhaled the whole glass of golden liquid.

Those words sent a chill down my spine, because it sounded so aggressive. And it was said with so much conviction that I believed every single word. He seemed different, darker as if he was under a shadow. Perhaps it was nothing but the lighting.

In a short time, he had transformed into someone that I didn't recognize. This man right here was definitely plotting something in his mind. He suddenly seemed like a man on a mission – to destroy his enemy.

"Can you do the test now?" His voice was hoarse from the

burn of the whiskey. He sounded calm but that was probably not the case.

"She hasn't actually given consent. I think we should give her some time."

"Stupid girl." Harsh but somehow full of compassion at the same time. Exactly what a caring brother would say to their foolish sister. And I thought that because I knew. "I don't care. If she wants to remain my cousin, she will do it."

"I see. Conditional love, huh?" I teased a little and he threw me a sideways glance. He didn't seem to appreciate it. But how else was I going to check his emotional state?

"I think we should order something to eat, let her get to know me. Perhaps that will help her relax a little around me. Then I'll try talking to her about the test again. Does that sound okay?" I offered, hoping he'd agree, for Jenny's sake.

Kai closed his eyes momentarily. Then he raised his hand and pointed at me, "I'll make her if I have to."

"I guess my job now is to tell her she has no choice but to do the test. And that her cousin is going to make her whether she likes it or not." I summarized the situation for him, telling him in no uncertain terms that he was being a dick.

"Fuck. Now you're making me sound like a real bastard."

"Yeah, you bet. The last thing she needs is to be forced into doing anything she doesn't want to." I said, seeing I was having an impact on him.

I couldn't help but feel warm and fuzzy inside. His love for Jenny was like the kind Lincoln and Liam had for me. It also reminded me of the times my brothers force-fed me vegetables. Now I ate my veg on my own, thanks to them.

"Calm down, Kai. This test isn't like forcing some healthy vegetables on a rebellious child because it's good for them. Please, you have to understand. Let me talk to her. Woman to woman." *Victim to victim.*

That was right. I was a victim of a sexual assault too. When I was too young to know what to do, I let someone handle everything for me. In the wrong way. It was something I had still regretted up until today.

WHILE WE WERE WAITING for the food to arrive, Kai took the opportunity to have a shower and change out of his suit. Like a lot of Asian men, Kai wore his trousers shorter than most western men, showing off their ankles. A lot of them either wore those tiny invisible socks or didn't bother with any. To me, it was an odd and ridiculous fashion trend. It somehow looked good on him, though.

Clare and Dave appeared from nowhere and started helping out with setting up the table, whispering quietly to each other as they worked. Dave let out a laugh so loud that it shook the table. Who knew that a 6 ft ex-military tough guy who could kill with a look had such a great sense of humor. No one would have guessed that they were bodyguards at all.

There were fourteen rooms in this apartment.

Fourteen.

I thought that my little apartment was too much for just me. Mom had repeatedly said that I could have stayed at Dad's, or with Liam. And that I was taking away a home from some homeless person.

I knew it was nonsense, but I couldn't help feeling guilty for ages after I made the purchase. My conscience kept reminding me that there were starving and homeless people in the world who would die for just a fraction of the space I had.

Kai came from money. That was no secret. Although I had met plenty of rich people in my life, I had never seen rich like

Asian rich. They simply knew how to spend their money. Or not to.

"You like?" His voice startled me as I stared at a remarkable painting in front of me, hanging proudly on the large wall in the living room.

"Yes." It was a beautiful painting indeed, but I was in fact staring into nothing.

"Leonardo, I think," he said nonchalantly.

"Da Vinci?" I couldn't believe what I heard.

Well, I shouldn't be surprised.

Actually, could people buy a painting like that?

"Yes, who else? Not from the Wolf of Wall Street I hope." He answered with a twinkle in his eyes.

I smiled. Not because the joke was funny. Or that I was impressed by the painting – even though the painting was genuinely impressive. But seeing Kai relax was such a relief.

"What is it called?" I might know a few famous paintings, but I knew very little about art, and I wasn't about to pretend. I had dedicated my life to medicine, and I wasn't going to apologize for being uncultured.

"Who cares."

I didn't have a clue what Kai meant. When someone owned such an expensive item, they should at least know what the heck the painting was called. "Didn't you buy this?"

"Not quite."

"What? Please, don't tell me you stole this?" I couldn't believe what I was even asking. "Oh, wait."

"Kind of."

Oh no, I thought I was going to faint.

A painting like this must have been worth hundreds of millions, right? I wanted to check on my phone and find out which Da Vinci painting had gone missing. But then if it was indeed stolen, it would be all over the news. There must be people out there hunting for it.

"I stole it from her lover," he *sort of* elaborated.

"Fuck, can you please stop talking in riddles. It isn't funny to joke about these things."

"I won it in a bet from a friend, I think. Or I might have had someone win it for me in an auction. To be honest, I don't really remember. All I know is that it looks nice on my wall."

Phew, I felt a relief as I dried the cold sweat that had started to form inside my palms.

"I gifted it to you, asshole." Jenny dragged her tired body down the stairs. Nobody could see her from the living room, but she had one of those voices that traveled well even in a large and crowded space.

"Are you sure? Did I not win a bet with your husband-" he stopped. It just occurred to him that mentioning her husband might be triggering.

"I don't think so." Her sight fixated on the painting.

Kai opened his mouth, but nothing came out until seconds later. "It's a great painting."

Jenny marched into the living room, eyes still glued to the painting.

"Because I chose it." She let out a small sigh. "I wanted to keep it for myself. But it's better here."

Her appreciation of art was unquestionable. Her stare reminded me of a hungry puppy drooling over a bowl of meat.

What possessed her to part with something she loved so much?

Luckily, the doorbell rang and saved us from the awkward silence. Jenny finally peeled herself away from Da Vinci's greatness.

Escorted by the doorman, four men came in with massive

bags of food, and headed to the kitchen. On the outside of the bags was the word "Gucheng".

Gucheng wasn't like your usual Chinese takeout place. Each month, they shipped out one of the best chefs in China to cook here in the city. And they only cooked what was available at the local organic farm that they sourced from. That meant their menu was very rarely the same. The price point was crazy high, and it would cost someone at least a month or so of salary just to dine there. Even if you had the money, you couldn't necessarily get a table there. It wasn't a place where anyone could just call them up to get a booking. There was no website, or any other way to contact them at all.

So how did one get to eat there?

You waited for their invitation, according to one of my clients, who had been there before. Apparently, they would get in touch first thing in the morning for dinner that was happening later that day. Then you had an hour to RSVP. If you couldn't make it, you lost the invite. But the good news was, you knew you were on their radar.

"My god, that place is so impossible to book!" I exclaimed. "And I didn't know that they would deliver! How did you manage that?"

Within five minutes, a table full of beautiful dishes was laid out. This was the first time I had had takeout where the staff would come and set up everything.

"They don't normally deliver. But for their boss, I guess they do," Kai said proudly, his face smug.

Why was I even surprised?

"Right. It makes so much sense now. Did you come up with the invite-only idea?" He raised his eyebrows slightly. "Stop pretending like you don't know what I'm talking about."

"Yes, of course. People love feeling special. Exclusivity sells."

"Evil genius."

"Why not? You make them wonder if they'll ever get invited to such a restaurant. And when they do, they can't wait to take out their wallet and pay big bucks for it. They're begging to dine at the restaurant, not the other way round."

As ridiculous as it sounded, it was very clever. But only someone like Kai could pull off something like that.

We sat at a massive black granite table with golden veins. It was probably made to seat 20 people. The dishes covered every inch of the table. I doubted that we would even come close to finishing it.

"I see. I didn't know you owned this one as well." I knew that Kai was in the food industry, but I couldn't assume every restaurant that I walked past was owned by him.

"I didn't used to. I bought it a little while ago from a friend who lost a bet."

I didn't know how to react to that statement. "Are you addicted to gambling or something?"

"He doesn't gamble," Jenny cut in. "He bought this one to save a friend of mine who was in a lot of debt. He paid too much though." She shook her head. "But within weeks, he turned it into something else. It went from losing money to huge profits just with a flick of his fingers."

"That's considered as some kind of witchcraft. At one point in history, they used to hang and burn people with skills like that," I joked. But deep down, I was impressed with what Kai had managed to do. "I've been curious about that restaurant for ages, but I had no idea how to get an invite."

"Next time, just tell them you're my guest and they'll seat you anytime you want."

"Really? How? I've heard the place is always packed." I asked, more than a little curious about the place.

"There's a private room upstairs, reserved for VIPs only – at the moment, it's just me. But you're welcome to use it."

"Thanks. But I think I won't be eating anything for a while after this meal."

Dr. Rose really missed out by not staying with us for dinner. I couldn't wait to boast about what we had this evening.

Dave and Clare didn't join us for dinner, either. Most of the time, they seemed like they were doing nothing other than standing around. In the background though, I knew they had to collaborate with another team – the invisible one that made sure things run smoothly for Kai's day-to-day.

Dr. Rose had gone home to tend to her daughter whom she had adopted with her partner. She tried to help her patients as much as she could, often even after working hours, but if the situation allowed, she would always try to have dinner with her family. I respected her for having her principles. Still, I wished she'd joined us for dinner tonight. Kai had ordered way too much food.

I made chit chat with Jenny over dinner and found out that she went to a boarding school in Britain, then went on to study at a university in London, then France. We didn't talk about her husband at all. Although there was no reason to suspect her husband was the person who caused her those injuries at this point, I preferred if Jenny brought up the topic herself when she was ready.

"I see now why my cousin is never satisfied with any of his dates." She changed the topic of the conversation, tired of talking about herself.

"Oh? Why is that?" Kai stopped chewing, intrigued by what Jenny was going to say next.

"Wouldn't you like to know?" Jenny punched Kai on his forearm as Kai childishly flicked her on the arm. Then she pointed at me like I was the fucking answer.

7

Kai

Jenny's words came as a surprise. Was she right though? June was unquestionably different to most of the women that I've dated, but in what way? I didn't have an answer.

"You mean American girls?" June chimed in. She didn't seem surprised at all. If anything, she seemed kind of happy about what Jenny implied.

Jenny smiled cryptically and didn't answer. I hated when she did that – left things unsaid. It drove me mad, and she had done this to me all my life.

It was nice to see Jenny warming up to June so quickly, interacting like they'd known each other for a long time. Jenny wasn't a difficult woman, but she'd had a very sheltered life. Her parents had been planting this idea in her head her whole life that people only befriended her for her money.

To be honest, her parents weren't wrong about that. Over the years, I've met plenty of gold diggers. Not everyone wanted to marry me of course. They befriended me for any kind of monetary reward – from something as small as a free meal, to something as big as a business partnership for those who were really ambitious. The ultimate prize was of course, marrying the trophy and inheriting their fortune.

Growing up, I never believed people would do things like that – until I got kidnapped. I could only remember part of the terrifying experience. In the immediate aftermath, I couldn't remember anything. But eventually, fragments of my memory came back to me when I least expected them.

I found out later that it was my best friend's mother who collaborated with the kidnappers. So, at a very young age, I had learned that some people would do anything to get money.

"American girls are *really* nice," I teased.

Jenny was kind of right. I did like western girls. They were generally more open-minded and not constrained by the unspoken social rules and emotional blackmail of their over-bearing parents.

"What's the difference? You just want someone pretty to fuck, right?" June tried to sound nonchalant. But her face turned the color of a tomato, as if she was a virgin.

"Think about your upbringing, June. Didn't they tell you nonsense about how to behave? Women shouldn't do this. Women aren't allowed to go to certain places. Women shouldn't say certain things. Women shouldn't think in certain ways." Jenny let out a sigh.

"Excuse me," I interrupted, "it applies to men as well."

Jenny rolled her eyes at me. I knew it wasn't quite the same, but I was not in the mood to argue with her. She had no idea how many times my parents expected me to perform so I could carry on the family torch, simply because I was their son. There were plenty of ridiculous rules that men had to follow too.

"And the pressure to be stick thin." Jenny coughed out those words.

June coughed in agreement. "Exactly. Although it might be

impolite to talk about it, it is implied. But things are changing now."

"Some people are obsessed with ancient teachings. But you know what, Confucius was a sexist pig who divorced his wife because she stopped him from being successful in his career. You know what, I think he was a closeted gay. And he much preferred to spend all his days hanging out in his boy's club, with his all male students – rather than going home to his wife and kids."

I nodded. I never thought about Mr. Moral in that way. There was no way of knowing Confucius's sexuality now that he had been dead for thousands of years, but a lot of his teachings were dated. It made me question whether the man should be worshiped like he is in some countries. Kind of like how slave owners shouldn't be looked up to in this day and age.

June was eating her dinner like she was snacking in the cinema. Clearly having fun enjoying the banter between Jenny and me.

"It can't be that bad being a woman, can it?" I asked, not seeing how being burdened with upholding the family name and being raised to be the heir was less than what women endured.

"Yes, it can. Ask Jenny." June replied, causing me to turn to look at Jenny.

Tears welled up a little in her eyes and I knew that I'd said the wrong thing.

"I'm sorry. I know it's been hard for you growing up. You should have talked to me about...stuff. And, uh, just let me help you. Whatever you need."

I stuffed a mouthful of abalone in my mouth and shook my head. "It's all about you right now."

I mouthed out the words as best as I could, as I'd do when a waitress came asking about how my food tasted when my mouth was full – which was somehow all the time.

"Thanks, *Didi*." *Didi* meant little brother in Mandarin. Even though Jenny was only a month older than me, she never missed an opportunity to remind me that I was the younger one. "But you have enough on your plate."

It was figurative as much as literal. Jenny had hardly eaten anything. I was oddly pleased about what she said. I knew things hadn't been easy for Jenny back home. But it must have taken her a lot of courage to talk about her personal thoughts.

"Isn't it amazing to be surrounded by your own culture, though?" It was faint but I could hear the bitterness in her smooth tiny voice. Jenny played with the food in front of her but without any intention, it seemed, of putting any of it into her mouth.

"Yes, I guess it is," I admitted. "I do miss China when I'm here for too long. The food, the people, just the way people do things."

"What was it like growing up here?" Jenny put down her fork, ready for a story from June.

"I don't know, I guess I don't think about it too much most of the time. But sometimes, I feel like I don't really understand the other half of me. My Chinese side that is." June flicked her wavy black hair.

"Your mother never brought you to visit China?"

"No, my mother is actually part Chinese and part British. My grandmother is Malaysian Chinese." She chuckled. "That means I'm only a quarter Chinese."

"Oh, that sounds so interesting. Is your mother very Asian? I mean, is she a tiger mom?"

June lifted up her hand to cover her chewing mouth.

"Yes, she is." She swallowed her food and continued, "Oh my

gosh, I didn't know that it was a thing until that *Tiger Mom* book came out! I thought I just had a super strict mother."

"To be honest, we don't really have tiger moms. Me and Kai." Jenny sounded sad. "Our parents weren't always there, I mean they were *never* there, really. We were brought up by our house-keepers, drivers, and other staff. And when we did see them, it was mostly to report our performance at school, and all these *fun* activities that they thought would make us great when we got older."

"Fun, huh? What kind of activities?"

"Fencing. Violin. Piano. Karate. Kung Fu. Tennis. Swimming."

"My god, that is a lot."

"And finance, fashion, ballet, traditional dancing, calligraphy, painting..." Jenny kept adding the list.

"I didn't have to do ballet, or traditional dancing." I knew it didn't help but I just wanted to point that out.

"That's because you were a boy," Jenny clarified. "But your violin was surprisingly good for a boy."

I rolled my eyes so hard that I swore I could hear them hit the back of my skull. "You're not allowed to say that here. Not in America. No sexist BS here."

"Wow, so you can do all that stuff you just mentioned?" June tried to keep track of what Jenny had told her. "You guys must have been busy growing up."

"Well, if it was something I liked, then I paid more attention. Otherwise, I just pretended to be useless," Jenny offered that information. "My little cousin here is good at everything. Even the things that he pretended to hate. Unlike him, I dropped out of most of them apart from fashion, painting, and traditional dancing."

I noticed that June's eyes sparkled, like a child who just

figured out a new feature of her favorite toy – that made her golden-brown eyes even more *irresistible*.

"That's still pretty impressive. I don't have any hobbies." June took a sip of her sparkling water. "I used to dance around with Chloe, my best friend, when we were little. I would go to her house and watch her do ballet in her studio, then I would copy her dance moves here and there."

"Oh? Why didn't you take lessons if you enjoyed it so much?" Jenny asked the question that I had always wanted to know.

"My mother wanted me to focus on my studies." She laughed awkwardly. "Become a doctor, follow in my dad's footsteps and all."

Typical Asian parent.

"You mean you were never allowed to do anything for fun outside of school?" Jenny sounded as if she enjoyed the after-school activities that she hated so much.

"No, not really. I guess hanging out with Chloe was kind of fun. Plus, when you grow up with two older brothers, you can have all kinds of unexpected fun that they swing your way."

My heart ached. I knew that Lincoln was a good brother. But he had no common interests with June at all. Apart from their love for Chloe. He loved swimming and was captain of the swim team at university. And he was free to pursue whatever career he wanted – other than medicine. It was so sad that June's mom held a different standard for her.

"But you're a doctor now and that's amazing." I didn't know what else to say.

"Yeah, but sometimes I hate it."

AFTER DINNER, a team of cleaning staff came round and tidied up. It took them less than five minutes and it looked as if we didn't even have dinner at all. I liked my teams invisible and unseen – most of the time. All the time if possible. Though my staff kept telling me that it wasn't possible.

There was a team that took care of my daily needs: groceries, cleaning, and laundry. They popped in to do the chores when I wasn't around. For rare occasions like today, when I had guests, they would pop in and out of the apartment within a given time frame. There was a smaller apartment downstairs that accommodated them.

Then there were two security teams: the visible one and the invisible one. Clare and Dave were obviously the visible ones. And the duo organized the other team that kept watch on me twenty-four-seven. I did think that it was unnecessary at times. But this was like insurance, people only realize how important they are after they've been in trouble.

My teams were often hiding in plain sight – like in the movies, where the undercover officers dressed up as hotdog sellers, street cleaners, the old man on the bench in the park, etc. Everyone on the team was tracked, and Dave kept watch of their positions on his tablet. The building across the street from my apartment was their base, where they watched for any suspicious activities around the neighborhood.

Dr. Rose came back, and she seemed a little more refreshed. Even her smile had a makeover. Happier, and more genuine. I was glad that she had had a pleasant break.

Jenny agreed to the examination after June had a chat with her after dinner, while the staff were clearing up. I was a little surprised by that. Jenny wasn't known for her decisiveness. Especially when it came to decisions that could sabotage her life or her future. It was like June had put some kind of spell on her. Or whispered some sense into her.

I didn't know how long the exam would take. I knew I had no

say on this matter anymore. June had sort of taken over. Thank fuck.

Waiting was the only thing I could do.

I paced up and down the hallway. Mainly outside of Jenny's room.

Every step I took heightened my anxiety even further. Yet, I couldn't stop.

When I first bought this apartment, I had promised Jenny that I would reserve a room for her. Why not? One room out of the fourteen for my favorite cousin was the least I could do. I thought it would end up being another guest room, and never thought that Jenny would ever show up and actually use it. She had been so busy with her life and kids, I just couldn't see her traveling here at all.

Now, I was glad that I stuck by my promise to her.

I was glad that she came, that she trusted me enough to come. There was hardly any trust in my family, which made this special bond between us more precious than gold.

I was glad that June was here too, because I wouldn't know what to do without her. When I saw Jenny right after I landed, it didn't even occur to me to find out what happened to her. My stupid instincts told me to leave her alone. And I listened to them. It was a good thing we came back and nothing bad happened to her. If Jenny did something stupid, just because I decided to *leave her alone*, I wouldn't have ever forgiven myself for that.

Self-harm.

Suicide.

The things Dr. Rose said about Jenny echoed in my mind. The thoughts gave me a shiver.

Forty-five minutes later, or what felt like forever, June appeared in the hall. She seemed a little surprised to see me there. Did she think I would just leave at a time like this?

"How is she?"

"She's fine. There's no significant signs to support rape. But she is covered in scars." Tears welled up in her eyes. "I'm sorry, that was really unprofessional. That's why I normally make it a point to not be too friendly with my patients."

I pulled her into me and whispered a thank you into her ear. Her hair smelled nice, a combination of coconut and vanilla. June collapsed in my arms. "And uh, there's something you should know."

More bad news?

I tried to pull to look down at her, but June shook her head. "No, I really needed this. Please, one more minute."

Just like that, I held her tighter, and we stayed glued together for another minute. We said nothing to each other. I knew that I needed a hug as much as she did, and I wished that we could stay like that forever.

June slowly peeled herself from me and opened her mouth like she was in a slow-motion video. I leaned in and kissed her. I had wanted to do that ever since I met her. I'd almost done it when she was 18, but that would make me some kind of creepy guy, because I was older than her and it was her 18th birthday.

She had the most kissable lips. Either that, or I was too stressed right now to make any judgments.

Even though I had met girls with plumper and more luscious lips, hers reminded me of a cherry, but tasted nothing like it, just a hint of honey.

"Kai–" June seemed to struggle with words. Was that how she dealt with her patients? It must have been hard for someone as sweet and kind as her to deliver any bad news.

"You can tell me." I planted a kiss on her forehead hoping that would ease her anxiety.

"She's pregnant."

"Jenny?" I realized that I had just asked a really stupid question. Who else?

"Yes." If it were her brother, he would take the opportunity to mock me. I was glad that she didn't as I wasn't in the mood to deal with any mocking.

"Is that bad news?"

I didn't know what else to say. People see pregnancy as good news most of the time. The way June delivered the news though, meant that there was more to it.

"It depends. Jenny was very angry when she found out and she started throwing things and it took a while to calm her down. She isn't sure if she wants to keep it."

I had made all the rooms soundproof and that was why I didn't hear a thing while waiting for them. My plan was to be able to have fun with any of my female guests as loud as we wanted without disturbing the neighbors, or anyone else in the apartment. Perhaps my decorating team had done too good a job because I hadn't heard any smashing – and that was a bad thing. If things ever did go south in the apartment, nobody would notice, no one would hear anyone crying for help.

"What are you thinking? You can tell me anything." June needed reassuring. "I won't get mad, I promise."

Her smile confirmed her reservations and concerns. "However it happened, I suspect she didn't even think that it was rape. Some partners force themselves on their other half. Just because they're married, it doesn't make it okay – consent still matters."

June paused to rub her palms on her skirt.

"Are you sure it's her husband?" I knew this was a sensitive topic, but it needed to be discussed.

"I hope I didn't offend her at all. But when I asked if she had any other partners outside of her marriage, she gave me this look, then she shook her head. Unless she was lying – that means the baby is her husband's. And given how she reacted so strongly about keeping the baby..."

"Got it." I pieced together the picture. The son of a bitch raped her.

"How long has this been going on for?"

This might not be something June would know. Her old scars indicated that whatever had happened between the two of them had gone on for quite some time. Scenarios were flying through my head with all sorts of things I wanted to do to that bastard. Names of bad scary people floated in one by one, and I wanted to hire them to make him suffer.

"Are you okay?" June stroked the side of my arm.

I leaned in to kiss her. That was unfair to her, but I couldn't help myself. I wanted an escape, and she was right there. I had always liked her, but she was my best friend's little sister. Now she's all grown up, oh so gorgeous, sexy, and smart – so much smarter than the women I usually dated. She deserved the best of men. *Not me.*

Not me.

She deserved better.

I pulled back and I knew I needed to apologize for my rudeness. "I'm so–"

She jumped on top of me and our lips locked.

8

———————

June

hat the fuck was that? My head was spinning the whole way back to my apartment.

I kissed Kai Li.

No.

Technically, he kissed me first.

Not just kisses on the forehead.

But proper kisses.

And oh my god, he was a good kisser.

It was how I had always imagined a perfect kiss would be. Lustful. Sensual. Hot. Passionate. None of those words could actually describe how perfect it really was. His kiss was so tender, like he was handling a fragile china doll.

I would have prompted him for a full on make out session if Dr. Rose hadn't walked into the room and interrupted us. The universe always knows how to play a joke on you. Perhaps it was a good thing, to have a small taste of whatever this thing between us was. It gave us a chance to think if that was truly what we wanted.

Did he have feelings for me?

It couldn't be, could it?

He had plenty of girlfriends and he was into different kinds of girls. Women that had more experience in the bedroom, doing the kinds of things I knew little about.

Lincoln got into the whole bondage thing because of him. Okay, that was unfair, Lincoln wouldn't enjoy any of that kinky stuff with any other woman than Chloe, and Chloe knew her fair share of that world. I'd thought about experiencing it, but the thought alone freaked me out for some reason.

Kai had offered to let me stay over at his place, so I didn't have to drive back alone at night. I understood his concern, his real concern. But I didn't need his protection. My apartment was secure enough that Mack or anyone else wouldn't be able to get in without alarming the building security.

He couldn't and shouldn't leave Jenny alone. Not after we found out what she had been through. It must have taken a lot of courage for a mother to leave her kids behind, let alone travel to another country without them. I wasn't an expert in psychology, but I'd picked up a few things here and there over the course of my career. From my observations, it was obvious that Jenny was running away from danger.

On the other hand, I was glad that I didn't have to accommodate Kai and his team in my little apartment. It would have been nice, being able to wake up seeing him, but having his team there was just a deal breaker. Sharing wasn't really my strong point and that was the reason I'd bought my own apartment in the first place. I needed somewhere that was mine and no one else's. Including my parents. *Especially* my parents. If they'd sponsored a dime in anything that I owned, they would feel like they had the right to take over everything.

Back when I was living in company owned accommodation – although it was larger, more modern, and comfortable – my family would dictate how I lived. How I should decorate. How often I should get it cleaned.

Well, I hated it so much that it drove me to buy my little apartment.

I entered my home and selected a lively playlist on Spotify. As music filled my apartment, I danced to the remaining sensation of Kai on my lips. I knew it was pathetic, but this was what the eighteen-year-old me had been dreaming about. After about ten minutes of uncoordinated bouncing, I went to my study for a walk down memory lane.

Inside the room filled with walls of light wood bookcases, there was a hidden safe behind a painting. Like the ones in every heist movie. It was silly but *so* cool.

When I requested to have one of those done, I didn't expect the decorator to say yes. Surprisingly, many of her clients had one, or at least thought about getting one. My decorator didn't actually recommend having one though. It was so common nowadays that most thieves were aware of it and would look there first. All they needed to do was find one and they would try anything they could to break into the safe. Of course they didn't always succeed in breaking in, but the damage from trying alone would cause the owner a massive headache.

From my safe, I took out a pastel blue Tiffany bag. I pulled out a pile of hundred-dollar bills and counted them one by one. Ninety-eight. I repeated again and I got ninety-nine. And one more time just to make sure that it was indeed ninety-nine. Putting the cash back in the bag, I pulled out the note that was left on my bedside table the morning after my birthday.

Hey little J. Wishing you no more heartache for the rest of your life. It made me happy that my party helped cheer you up. I would throw one every year just to see you smile. Your friend, Kai.

The note was from Kai thirteen years ago. For a long time, I wondered whose idea the party really was and who put in all the work. My brothers would never think of doing something so sweet. But why would Kai do something so kind? Did he really just want to be friends? I wanted to believe that there was more between us.

He had shown up to some of my other birthdays over the years, but he wasn't always there like he promised.

I put everything back where it belonged and climbed in my bed –unmade from my earlier nap – and passed out, falling into darkness in no time.

Then I heard footsteps approaching my room. I was too tired to open my eyes but given the day I've had, I knew I had to.

"Don't get up." A figure landed in my bed, his weight pressing on me. I didn't have to open my eyes to know that it was him, Kai. His large frame had almost no weight on me – like a warm fuzzy cloud that gave nothing but warmth and comfort.

"I thought you had to stay with Jenny?" I whispered.

"I couldn't stop thinking about you," he whispered back.

When I opened my eyes, his gorgeous face came closer to me, and he kissed me again. His hand cupped the side of my head, then lightly he trailed his finger down my neck and down to the bottom of my pajama top, pulling at it until it came off my head. I gasped softly when he found my bra, and with a flick of his fingers, he parted the front clasp and pushed the material off my shoulders. His lips followed his hand as he cupped my left breast and sucked at it with a force that made my hips arch up in need.

I moaned, unable to stop myself. "Kai, I don't do this."

"You want me to stop?" He breathed the words into my ears. I shook my head vigorously and *pathetically* – no. He dropped to his knees, his hands sliding up my hips and down went my pajama bottoms, leaving me in my lace panties.

"Hmm." His groan had literally made me soak through my panties.

"I'm going to. Need to. Keep these," he murmured, pausing in between words as his nose moved between my legs, smelling me through the thin lace.

"If you say so." I gasped, savoring each skin-to-skin moment as he removed my panties, the only piece of fabric left on my body.

"I'm so sorry I've made you wait this long." He popped his head up and watched me from between my legs.

Fuck.

I was in heaven.

My spine arched back as he leaned in, kissing me in the special place only I was allowed to touch. A shiver shot through my entire body.

He leaned in for the second kiss. His tongue went deeper and found its way down to the most sensitive area of my body. As a doctor, I knew exactly where my own clitoris was and that there was no shame in touching it. That didn't mean men generally knew how to find it. I squirmed as an erotic moan that I didn't know I was capable of escaping my throat.

He drew me to the edge of the bed, closer to him, and ran a finger along my thigh then to the tip of my pussy. I felt my back arch as his finger invaded me, filling me in a most delicious way. His hand worked that middle finger of his deeper inside me before pulling out, gliding through my juices until my thighs and his hand were completely soaked. I was so ready for him, and he knew it.

Kai's pants disappeared, like he was some kind of magician, before he climbed back up the bed, pinning me underneath him and rubbing his thick cock against me.

I wasn't sure how I was going to survive actually having sex with the sex god of my dreams.

"Oh Kai!" I moaned. My legs clung onto him tighter, bringing him closer, ready for the thrust that I was sure would send me to Mars. Then I heard it.

My 6 a.m. alarm. Damn! I knew it was too good to be true.

Every morning, I went to the gym, showered, then worked. It had been the same routine for the last few years of my boring life. That included Sundays.

It was sad, I knew that much. Though I had made it a rule not to step into my clinic at weekends, I still ended up with piles of paperwork that I didn't manage to complete during the week.

But today, I just wanted to stay in bed.

I turned off my alarm and went back to sleep. Sadly, there was no Kai this time. The dream had been so real that it was kind of freaky. I'd had sex dreams before, and a lot of them involved him, especially after my 18th birthday. But this one was different. This one was kind of emotional, and intense, and I really thought I was going to come. Was he really that good that even my subconscious was fooled?

Perhaps kissing him the day before had made my dream more vivid. That was the only explanation I could come up with.

I had dated a few men in my life. Dannie Wu was the only one that I had been intimate with. The men that I dated after Dannie, never even got to sex. I was basically in-charge of my own needs with the sex toys I'd invested in.

My desire to sleep in was out the window. My body (and mind) just wouldn't participate. I had gotten so used to waking up so early every day now that my body refused my brain's choice of additional sleep. How ungrateful was that?

I opened the podcast app on my phone and listened to my

favorite true crime show. I was intrigued at how addictive these podcasts were. At first, I was kind of against the idea of it – listening to the details of people getting murdered – it really didn't sound very appealing. Once I started the first episode, I couldn't stop. I even used it to fall asleep like a bedtime story. My family probably thought that I was some kind of psychopath.

Loud and urgent ringing made me jump. Then I remembered what that sound was – the new doorbell I'd had installed not too long ago. Some fancy bell where I could see the person at the door from my phone. I felt old for falling behind on the gadget trends – I simply did not have time to play or explore.

Who would come by at 6:30 in the morning? I put on a robe and turned on the doorbell app on my phone. I wasn't going to answer the door without knowing who it was at this time of the day. My new doorbell gave me the option of doing that. One point to technology.

Then I saw him, Kai waving at the camera, holding a paper bag up and grinning like an idiot. I had a strange feeling inside me, butterflies in my stomach I think, or perhaps I was having a heart attack, just at the sight of him.

I checked in the mirror quickly, no bed hair. Then I headed to the door. I couldn't help but curse him for visiting at this time of the morning, me without my makeup and pretty clothes on.

"What are you doing here?" I asked through the app as I rubbed some Vaseline on my lips.

"Let me in. I brought breakfast." Kai showed me a brown paper bag.

Sex with Kai – even if it was just a dream – followed by breakfast. Would that count as a win for the day?

"It's 6:30. Go back to your own house."

"Jet lagged." He begged again, this time whining like a little bitch. No one could resist a puppy whine. But I was going to let him in sooner or later anyway.

"I'll be right out."

I decided to let him wait as I got dressed. Turning around back to my bedroom, I quickly changed into comfortable loungewear. Although leaving my pajamas on was very tempting, especially after what happened (or didn't happen) last night. But I wasn't really convinced it would work with my Hello Kitty pajamas.

Kai walked straight past me like he was the master of my home. Playing with switches to turn on the lights he preferred in my apartment. Touching things as he walked past every piece of furniture. Was he examining my place for its cleanliness? Or was he plotting to buy my place? Both thoughts were ridiculous, I needed some coffee.

His formal attire of suit and tie was gone. He wore only a simple t-shirt with a designer logo across the chest and a pair of blue jeans. It made him look younger and boyish. Like many businessmen that I knew of, Kai was one of those people that rarely dressed down, unless you caught them at the gym or a sporting event. In which case, they would dress like they had been sponsored by some fashion company for a magazine shoot.

"Do you know how early it is?" That was my hello. I couldn't afford having him know how much I had missed him.

I grabbed a Starbucks coffee cup and started sipping like my life depended on it even though I had no idea what was in the cup I had just picked up.

"Yes, Dave told me you were up," he said nonchalantly.

"What?" I nearly spat out the sweet tasting caramel flavored latte.

"Yeah, he said your light was on. So, I came."

What did he mean by that? I needed my coffee to kick in right now to make sense of his words. I downed another large sip of the sweet coffee and pulled a face as the hot liquid flowed down my throat. "You mean you have him watching me?"

"No, not right now, silly. He's gone to rest. Clare is watching you now." I spun around but there was no sight of Clare. What was he talking about? "She's across the road."

Did I hear him right? I rushed and stood by the large window in the living room, whose curtain was automatically drawn open every morning at 6 by another smart gadget that my assistant had helped me set up.

There.

In the apartment across from my building, I saw a female figure with binoculars waving at me. I didn't wave back.

"What happened to the people living in that apartment?" I had heard about Kai's security team – that they were a little bit unconventional and over the top.

"They moved out of course."

"How?" His words didn't make sense. This Starbucks coffee was either very mild or decaf or I had turned really stupid overnight.

"Easy. Just write them a check for twice the amount of what their home is worth, and people will move right away. I was ready to triple the payout, but they took the first offer. Wasn't that easy, Silly?"

I had no idea when he started doing it, but at this moment I wasn't a big fan of the nickname Silly.

"Why would you do that? Are you crazy?" I opened my mouth and hoped that a series of very rude swear words would flow out of me effortlessly like some gangster, but nothing happened. I stomped on the floor instead. "You–you idiot."

"Look! I had a dream about you last night."

No! Did he mean 'you had a dream about me last night'? Can he read minds?

"What are you talking about?"

"In my dream." *Oh god, please tell me we shared the same dream.* "You were shot by that bastard."

Oh. Different kinds of dreams.

"I would never forgive myself if I let something happen to you. So, I sent Dave to sort out your neighbors. Wait, can you still call them neighbors when they live so far away from you now?"

Gosh, he seemed very chatty this morning. And I was in no mood to answer him.

"What happened to them?" This was the most ridiculous thing that had ever happened to me. I knew that some crazy rich Asians behaved in a certain way that my western ass could never understand. But I never thought that I would see it happen first-hand, right in front of my eyes. "Is this how you do things back home?"

"Oh, I have no idea what happened to them. Knowing Dave, he would have allowed them fifteen minutes to pack and leave before the deal expired. My guess is that they would either go stay with friends and family or go to a hotel."

"And what about their stuff?" I demanded, wondering if Clare was over there digging through their things. When she didn't have the binoculars trained on me, that is.

"Wait, I haven't answered the second part of your question. Yes and no, that's not how we usually do things back home. Usually, we would have more time to plan." I stopped caring about the answer, but he didn't seem to be able to shut up. "But if we were desperate, then yes, that's how we work. As I see it, staying alive and being safe is the most important thing in the world."

He tip-toed lightly next to me and gave me a hug. "I know you don't approve of the way I do things, but I was worried sick about you all night."

My heart melted the second I was in his arms. Was I touched by his crazy and unreasonable behavior?

"What about their stuff?" I repeated.

"Dave offered to have it all shipped to their new address, but they didn't want it. I guess their stuff wasn't all that valuable or precious to them."

"I guess. It is just stuff at the end of the day."

"Yeah, just some Ikea rubbish. Nothing is more important than your safety."

9

Kai

I turned sideways hoping that it might help me sleep. It didn't. I turned again – for what felt like the hundredth time – and stared blankly at the high ceiling. The ceiling that I'd thought about having a mirror installed on because the playful side of me was curious about how I looked when a woman was riding me.

Immature. That was me.

But I had decided against it for occasions just like this. When there was no one but myself that I could stare at during a long, lonely, and sleepless night.

Sad miserable idiot. That was also me.

The ability to sleep seemed to have left me. No matter how much I tried it just wasn't coming. My body was beyond tired, and it needed rest. But I couldn't find a comfortable enough position to fall asleep. There were times when I almost fell asleep but I'd immediately wake up when I heard a strange sound that wasn't even there.

My plan for a relaxing trip in New York had completely gone

out of the window. It seemed like, from the moment I'd arrived, things had gone sideways. Now, I couldn't even relax enough to get to sleep. My mind wouldn't let me.

I'd known that I had to see June at some point, and I'd planned on it. I owed her an apology and an explanation for why I'd left her the way I had years ago. She didn't seem to hold any grudge against me for leaving without saying goodbye three years ago. That was the June I knew. The understanding, loving, caring kind of woman you would bring home to meet your mother.

Dr. Rose had suggested another diagnosis, a proper one, for Jenny when she was a little more settled. At this point, she didn't want to just prescribe her anything simply because she showed some symptoms of anxiety. I could see why June opened up to Dr. Rose in such a short span of time. Her gentleness and attention to detail were worth paying her the premium rate she charged. June did say that Dr. Rose could do this for free as a favor to her, but there was no way I would let myself owe anyone any favors.

My thoughts drifted to my security team. Clare was left in charge at my place tonight, while Dave was out keeping watch on June. She would have to learn how to be in charge sooner or later. Dave planned to retire in a few years, but he hadn't completely made up his mind yet. He wouldn't know what to do to pass time, so he might as well stay in the job – his words. I knew that he wanted to spend more time with his daughter before she went to university. The problem was, he didn't know what to say to her when they were left alone together.

Wendy had called earlier at about 2 in the morning. I'd told she could call me anytime if she found out anything about Mack and we both agreed that we should avoid involving June for the time being. Mack had been released on bail. No one knew how. But someone powerful had given the order to let him go. That was why I needed to send Dave, my favorite and most trusted bodyguard, to protect June while I couldn't.

I had no idea why I cared so much about June. I just did. Perhaps it was the way she'd been so heartbroken over the loss of her best friend on her 18th birthday, face awash with tears – and I couldn't help but promise to myself that I would try my best to keep her away from any more hurt and heartache. That was why I always tried to show her my better side – the positive, can-do, everything-is-okay side. Regrettably, I had let my not so positive side out tonight when I received the news about Jenny.

Jenny, on the other hand, she was family. She had been through the same family crap that I had to go through. We were in the same boat, and I couldn't help but want to keep her, and our boat, afloat.

So, without having to announce it to the world, I had kind of vowed to keep both of them safe. Nothing would ever happen to them under my watch.

I instructed Clare to arrange for more help from our security agency – I wasn't sure how my usual team would be able to cope with keeping three people safe. That was the thing, I could look like the Prince of England and have ten bodyguards and two large cars following me wherever I went but I thought that just made me look like a dick. I might have been raised to be an entitled bastard, but I just couldn't act like one. Not openly.

The smart way was to employ a much larger team but undercover. It attracted way less attention. But the downside was, you wouldn't know if they were actually working.

I rolled over, punching my pillow into a new shape. My brain wouldn't shut up and I let out a frustrated groan.

Then there was the kiss. Another mistake.

I haven't been good today. I'd been jet-lagged. Burned out. Whatever...

Regardless of what my brain told me about not doing it, her

lips were too much temptation. My self-control didn't seem to work with her.

She was my best friend's sister – the thought of that itself was a turn on. It might have helped if she was a crazy ugly bitch, but she was the complete opposite. How could I stare at her lips and not kiss them?

I had no idea what to expect when I first saw her when we were kids. Lincoln had told me that his geeky little sister wanted to meet me. When I asked him why, he said that she had read a book about crazy Asians and wanted to meet one. Those words still made me chuckle. I wasn't about to admit that I was crazy – but in this day and age, who wasn't, at least a little? Only a crazy person would say that they are sane.

When I saw her on her 18th birthday, face all puffy from months and months of crying, my feelings for her changed as my heart melted. I wanted to give her a bear hug and kiss her all over to make things better for her. I wished that I could take away all her pain. I loved women, all kinds of women, including the crazy ones because they were usually really good in bed. But never had I had an urge to kiss someone without thinking about sex first.

If Lincoln hadn't warned me against making a move on her... that would have been a different story. *Crap! He did make me promise not to hit on her.*

I guess it was too late. I kind of did hit on her earlier. But he can't blame me for this. Didn't he fuck and then marry his sister's best friend? It was kind of the same, so who was he to lecture me on this?

A night like this shouldn't be wasted staring at a ceiling. I was here to relax and have fun after all. How could I enjoy myself if my mind was filled with June's face? With a heavy huff of annoyance, I got out of bed and searched through the laundry basket for my pants that hadn't been sent out to the cleaner yet.

Fishing through the pockets, I found a piece of paper that the sexy flight attendant slipped to me under my coffee. She had made her intention clear that if I ever needed someone to show me New York…Well, let's just say that I wasn't interested in seeing New York at this time of the night.

I picked up my phone and sent a message.

"How are you doing?" I imagined Joey's voice from Friends as I stole his pickup line. It was late but I didn't really give a fuck, I texted her and decided to leave the rest to fate.

A bubble popped up on my screen. I knew she was interested and typing a reply.

Can't sleep? I could do with some company.

Straight to the point. I liked her more already.

But it was also way too obvious. Why else would someone text at 3am in the morning, the smarter side of me snapped. I stared at the screen and tried to think of something clever to type – I typed something but deleted it right away. I stopped when I saw that she was typing again.

I can come to you. Send me your address.

Again. Straight to the point. I liked her more and more. But what was her name though? May? Mandy? Something beginning with M.

Truth be told, I was too exhausted from everything that happened over the last few days, but I needed a distraction. And I needed to get June out of my system.

I texted the flight attendant my address. No emoji.

I put on a pair of sweats, not caring how unsexy they felt on me. From my bedroom, I trailed along the hallway until I reached a locked room, scanning my fingerprint on the lock to gain access. The door opened to my playroom.

I had one of these in every property I owned.

It was a kink that I picked up, as I was introduced to a secret high society, where wealthy and powerful people sought joy and pleasure. Where desires were explored without judgment.

Though the playroom wasn't really my favorite room in the apartment, it had brought me many moments of calm. Letting me unwind and forget – with a fun playmate of course!

I walked past all the leathers and ropes displayed on the wall, then the four post bed until I reached another locked door. It was another smart lock, and I pressed my thumb onto the reader, unlocking the door to a spiral staircase that led downstairs.

I SAT in the apartment downstairs waiting for my *friend* to arrive. This apartment was a lot smaller with only three bedrooms spread across one floor. Much humbler compared to upstairs, but it was perfect for what I needed it for. A place I could use to meet strangers that I didn't want to invite into my home. Only Dave knew about this place, so if anything were to happen to me, at least one person on my security would know where to find me.

Fuck. I really wasn't in the mood for this. Never had I ever thought that this day would come. The day where fucking no longer interested me. What had gotten into me?

I got up from the peach leather sofa and quickly fixed myself a drink, and hopefully my mood. A good whiskey should fix everything for me. It usually did.

Twenty minutes later, the doorbell rang, and I opened the door and greeted the hot blonde who had served me on the plane. She still had her uniform on. Either she hadn't changed, or she put on the uniform just for me. I wouldn't blame her, a lot of people had fantasies about those in uniform – that was why dressing up as slutty nurses and hunky firefighters was so popular on Halloween. I didn't really care what she wore. Not now. Not today.

If I had to guess, she wasn't a real blonde. Even though I didn't know much about women's hair color, something about hers didn't seem natural.

"Care to give me a tour?" she asked. I answered with a nod and showed her around. No words were exchanged as she examined my place, analyzing my net worth, I'm sure. I wasn't in a chatty mood, not with her anyway.

"This way, May." It sounded like a demand, just as I'd intended. I wanted to draw her back to the living room. And to remind her to keep her nose out of my business.

"Melanie." She rolled her eyes, seeming annoyed that I didn't remember her name. I couldn't be responsible for remembering every woman that hit on me, could I?

"Ah, all English names sound the same to me." *That's right.* I shamelessly used our cultural differences to my advantage.

"Aww, so cute."

See. Works every time. It was a shame that she didn't get a job as some kind of investigator or inspector, she walked around as if she was one – investigating every corner of the place. The smaller apartment obviously wasn't as large as upstairs, but it was still situated in one of the most expensive and desirable buildings in New York. "I would die for one of these apartments."

Right, this was a very nice home for New York standards. And the one upstairs would blow her mind, unless she was Trump's daughter, which I knew she wasn't – not that I would be interested in bedding his daughter. As soon as she was satisfied with what she saw, she pulled me down hallways until she found the master bedroom and started undressing herself.

"Wait." I honestly didn't know why I wanted to wait. A woman with such initiative was usually a huge turn on for me.

She paused, leaving the last button of her shirt undone. Her face clearly said, "what now?"

"Let me grab you a drink." Finally, I managed to come up with something to say. I ran out of there so fast anyone would think she was going to rob me.

"Can I have a gin and tonic?" She raised her voice.

"Sure. Anything for you," I mumbled, not really caring if she could hear me.

As I reached the bar in the living room, I poured out a gin and tonic from a can into a glass for her. I heard that they weren't very nice, but that was what I decided to stock in this apartment. Besides, if the drink was horrible, then no one would ask for a second, which meant that there was nothing else to do in here but fuck or fuck off.

Melanie appeared at the edge of the living room, leaning her curves on the door frame, watching me.

"What kind of music do you like?" I handed her her glass before moving to my sound system. As simple as I wanted to keep this place, music wasn't something I would go without.

"What?" Melanie sounded surprised by my question. Maybe she was hoping for a quick fuck as much as I was. But the way she checked out my apartment suggested that she was perhaps after something more.

I tried to respect every job and every career choice. And being a flight attendant was a respectable job. But a lot of them did try to look for a wealthy husband while they were on the job – in my experience anyway. Not many succeeded though, because rich men knew about this and often used it to their advantage. Sometimes, if they were willing, they would end up as a kept mistress where all their needs and wants were taken care of. A few of my friends met their mistresses that way.

"Never mind. I'll just put on some jazz." Everyone liked jazz, right? It didn't really matter, I only had an old fashioned stereo there and I only had one record. I really should add more music to the mix. But then, what was the point when the only purpose of this apartment was to bring home my one-night stands? And if they managed to keep my attention, then I'd let them explore my playroom. That was it. They would never get to see where I lived.

"I wasn't expecting you to be so sweet," Melanie whispered next to my ear. I cringed ever so slightly. I wasn't expecting her to creep up next to me. I froze as I found her hand stroking my cock through the not-very-sexy sweatpants. "Have you ever had a girlfriend?"

What the fuck? Did she think that I was delaying sex because I was a virgin? But as soon as she leaned in and kissed me, I dodged like I was avoiding a bullet.

"Do I look like a freaking virgin to you?" That was really impolite of me to flinch. "I'm so sorry. It must be jet lag."

That's right, blame it on the jet lag.

A teasing smile escaped her mouth, and it just occurred to me that she was just joking. Gosh, I had no idea how tense I was until then. I could really try to blame it all on the jet lag, but I knew that wasn't it.

Jenny and June's situations had definitely affected me a whole lot, but it shouldn't have gotten to me so much. Years of conducting business had taught me to be calm during stressful situations. Trust me, we've been through worse in my company. The number of throats I had to cut to get to where I was was uncountable. As much as people loved me and celebrated my success in business, there were also a lot of people who hated me for kicking their asses in the field.

"I see. Come sit down next to me." When she held out her hand to take mine, I let her and luckily, I didn't pull back this time. She sat on the long side of the L-shaped sofa. Then she helped me lean on her legs while she massaged my head.

The massage was really comforting, and I started drifting into sleep. Then I heard her voice.

Not really her voice.

June's voice.

"Not all of us are gold diggers you know?"

I jumped a little as I opened my eyes and realized that I must have been dreaming. Melanie was still here. "We don't have to do anything you know."

"I'm sorry, I'm really tired." I felt like an asshole for inviting Melanie here for nothing.

"I get that. I thought you wanted to see me. More of me, you know."

"Of course. I wouldn't have texted you if I didn't." *I lied.*

I would text anyone with a pretty face and a nice rack. But I knew what I should and shouldn't say to a woman, regardless of what I thought.

10

June

It had been a while since I sat down and ate breakfast with someone. My normal morning involved getting ready really quick, heading to the gym, and being at the hospital before any of my team got there. Apart from my assistant.

She usually got there before me with my latte ready on my desk – my almond milk decaf latte. Why decaf? Well, I easily go through about five of them before 2 pm so ordering decaf was a way to keep my caffeine intake low – or at least controlled. Yes, most people hated decaf. It was disgusting. But I didn't really enjoy the taste of coffee anyway, it was only a tool to keep me awake and alive.

Oh and no breakfast – no solids until after midday. My morning routine was so busy and stressful, and breakfast often ended up in the wrong place before it even had time to settle in my stomach. So, I just decided to not eat anything until things calmed down at the hospital.

The salmon bagels that Kai bought were really nice. It occurred to me that I might throw up since I really couldn't remember the last time I ate breakfast but I felt fine afterwards. I knew that stress did horrible things to our bodies, but it was still amazing – from a doctor's point of view – to experience it firsthand.

"Is Jenny going to be okay on her own?" I had asked him a few times about this and he kept reassuring me that Clare was keeping watch for now.

"I have a surprise for her though."

I hated Kai's surprises to be honest. He had very skewed ideas about things sometimes, like how he thought it was okay to give an 18-year-old 99 one-hundred-dollar bills.

"I'm flying Jenny's best friend over so she can help look after her."

"Oh? Does Jenny know that she's coming?"

"It wouldn't be a surprise now would it, if she knew?" Yes, he was right. But sometimes, best friends don't necessarily know everything about each other. Chloe and I were a good example. She ran away for ten years, and I'd had no idea that she was still alive and kicking. It still bothered me that she didn't think she could trust me enough to drop me a line so I could quit grieving for her.

"I thought it would be a good idea." He stared at me blankly, as if he didn't see the problem.

"Maybe." I couldn't keep out the note of doubt in my voice and I watched with a twinge of guilt as his eyes went wide.

"Shit!" His voice was so loud I thought I felt the cutlery on the breakfast bar vibrate. "I, honestly, I thought it would be a good idea."

It was somehow adorable to see him care so much about his cousin. My own brothers cared a lot about me, but I think it pained them to show me that side of them.

"Do you know her at all?" I asked, hoping to find out if the best friend was at least trustworthy.

"What are you talking about? I grew up with her, we are family." Kai's brows drew together in confusion.

I stood up, stacked up all the plates from breakfast, and took them over to the sink to be washed. "I mean her best friend, genius."

"I see. No, I've heard Jenny talk about her, but I've never met her personally." Kai came over and tried to take over the washing up.

"Please, let me. You brought breakfast, at least let me do the washing up." He didn't need much convincing and let me carry on. "Maybe make yourself another cup of coffee."

"Great idea." Kai searched through my cupboard, examining my coffee selection. Not all of them were still drinkable, I must admit. "Cat poop coffee?"

"Kopi Luwak."

"Whatever. We call it *cat poop coffee* in China."

I chuckled. "Yeah, that was a gift from an Indonesian colleague. Although that might have expired."

As I suspected, not everything in my cupboard was still in date.

"You know I don't believe in expiration dates. For most things, it really isn't necessary to have one. It's just a business strategy to make you buy new things! And coffee is definitely one of those."

"Are you sure?" I raised my eyebrows as I questioned him.

"One hundred percent. Either way, I'm drinking this. You can't stop me."

Kai proceeded to make himself a cup of coffee with my coffee machine as I dried and put away the dishes. I did consider letting him do the dishes, because I was kind of curious if a spoiled Asian man like him would even know how. To be frank, the fact that he knew how to make coffee, to operate a coffee machine, was kind of remarkable.

My father, for instance, wasn't born Asian, but my mother had spoiled him during their short married life. She took care of him so well that he had forgotten how to do most things in the house. Washing dishes. Doing laundry. Brewing coffee. Even putting on his own slippers... and I wasn't even joking. Hopefully with his new wife, things would change a little.

"Just so you know, I'm not responsible if you get a stomachache from that."

He added a touch of milk to his *cat poop coffee*. His eyes closed as he sipped it slowly.

"Enjoying it?"

"Tastes kind of weird. But I like it." I didn't recall it tasting *weird,* but I wasn't going to find out for myself if the coffee was safe to consume. "Can you do me a favor?"

"Depends on what it is?" He took a few more sips of coffee but didn't say a word. The suspense of him not talking was killing me.

"Just spit it out." I instantly regretted my choice of words. "Not the coffee, the words, what do you want?"

"I was just thinking, give me a sec." He grinned at me.

I stared at his face – he had dark circles forming below his eyes, but he was still so gorgeous. Even if he looked ten times worse than now, he would still be welcome to visit me anytime, in dreamland or reality.

"Would you come to the airport with me to pick up Ting Ting?"

"Sure. Why so secretive?"

"The thing is, it's a high security airport, so you'll need to send me a copy of your passport. Just a photo should be fine."

Hmm... was that really a thing? I didn't recall ever having to send any documentation just to pick someone up from the airport. "This isn't a stupid trick so you can take a look at my passport and laugh at my photo, right?"

"No?"

"If you want to see mine, you have to show me yours. It's only fair." I felt my eyebrows raise unintentionally, and I knew my subconscious wanted to see something else other than his passport photo.

"No, this isn't a joke." His stern voice broke my little fantasy about seeing him naked. "The security at this airport is top notch and they will do a background check before they allow you entry."

Insanity. The world had gone mad. It's not like we were going there to pick up the president.

I really needed to reevaluate what I knew about Kai and his family.

"Can I wait outside?" The American side of me refused to hand over my personal documents just because a pretty boy batted his eyelashes at me.

"No, princess." *Princess?* No, not that word. It sent a shiver down my spine.

That word was the cheesiest word a man could ever use to call a woman. It was diminishing and I blame Disney for brainwashing us. My brother did that to Chloe for years – still does on occasion – and I hated it.

Somehow, Kai saying that word to me made me feel warm and fuzzy.

"It would look even more suspicious if you waited outside. Someone would come and escort you into a little dark room and interrogate you."

I swallowed hard. *Please don't take me to such a place.*

"Do you really *need* my company?"

"I was going to go alone. But after hearing what happened between you and Chloe, I have my doubts about this whole thing now. Jenny might not want to share this vulnerable side of herself with Ting Ting."

I nodded and couldn't agree more. "This is what happens when you decide things without discussing it with other people."

His decision came from a good place but teasing him tickled me somehow.

"Well, she's arriving in an hour. I can't send her back." He put his palms together as if he was praying.

"I'm sure you *can* send her back. Just tell her you made a mistake." I could see his Adam's apple drop – swallowing hard at my words. Kai wasn't the kind of man who would easily admit that he had made a mistake. I knew the kind, I grew up with one.

"I could…"

"You don't have to." I announced. "I'll help you."

Fortunately, I always kept a picture of my passport on my phone. It was easier so I could send it to agents that helped me manage all the traveling that was part of my job. I made a few taps on my phone and Air Dropped the picture to him.

Evidently, I wasn't so precious about my personal data after all.

"Sent. Don't look."

"Sorry, it's impossible not to look, I have to forward it to Dave." He took a peek and then chuckled. "Cute. And I promise I'll show you my passport photo later."

Or more? I wouldn't mind.

WHEN KAI TOLD me about picking up Ting Ting, I had no idea he meant we had to leave right away. Dave picked us up pretty much straight after I sent my passport photo, allowing me only ten minutes to clean up and get dressed. Thank God I had a shower last night and didn't smell too bad. I spritzed extra perfume on just to be sure.

What surprised me most was the fact that security took so little time to clear. I never thought twice about things like this, but I guess it wasn't impossible in the age of the internet. IT was never really my strong suit but as long as they were sure that I was a trustworthy person to be around their guests and promised not to shoot me while I was there, I wouldn't think too much more about it.

After about forty minutes of driving, we entered a secluded space with a large sign on display – the largest one I had ever seen – trespassers will not be tolerated. What did that mean? Would they be shot at? Or taken down to a little dark room and held captive until the police came?

I knew people got into trouble for trespassing, but it had never occurred to me how serious it could be. To me, those signs were just there to keep people out of unused land. Seeing the number of surveillance cameras and armed guards around the compound had given me a different understanding of those signs now. It took us another few minutes before we reached another compound, and inside the high walls were even more cameras, and guards, all armed.

There was a container looking building and, on the tarmac, parked several small to medium sized luxury jets.

"Are we here?"

"Yeah, we were here about fifteen minutes ago," Kai confirmed.

"Fifteen minutes ago?"

"Yes. It wasn't marked or anything. But the land belongs to the airport."

Funny how he called it an airport like it was just a regular bus stop or something. "You come here a lot?"

"Only in emergencies. I like traveling commercial. It's more fun."

Okay. He and I had a very different understanding of fun. I

hated flying and every time I thought about flying it just made me nervous. I wasn't afraid, but I hated the whole routine, checking in, security checks, the waiting, etc. I wondered if I would enjoy traveling in a private jet, not that I had the money to afford one – not even a sharing scheme.

"I think that's our plane."

Right in front of us was a white plane with three golden stripes, and some Chinese characters thrown in – probably saying *The Great Li Empire* or something like that.

"You own that?"

"No, this one belongs to one of my friends. My family owns one too, but I couldn't let them know that I brought Ting Ting over without them finding out about Jenny. They get notifications when I use it. That's the other reason why commercial is better, because they can't really track me." I doubted that was true. Someone could hack into the airline database and find him if they really wanted to. I'd seen it in movies – any ordinary geek downtown would be able to do that.

We got out of the car and waited, watching the plane pull up closer to us. The door was released after a few minutes. A lady in red, with a stick thin supermodel body walked out onto the steps.

Kai removed his sunglasses as if he was trying to verify how hot this woman was.

"Lucy?"

What was going on here? I thought we were picking up Ting Ting.

"Li Kai." She didn't seem surprised to see him, though.

"*Zen me shi ni?*" I could only assume that Kai was speaking in Mandarin, or some other dialect that I didn't understand.

"Does she speak English?" I snapped, interrupting rudely like the American that I was. No one should speak in any language other than English.

"Yes, I think she does." Kai introduced us quickly and Lucy spoke beautiful English with a hint of a British accent, very much like Kai's. Fortunately, they didn't spend too much time speaking in Mandarin before they switched to a language I could understand.

"Lucy and I–" He paused.

"We were dating and then he left the country." I could totally see that. She was definitely the kind of woman Kai would date. Beautiful. Supermodel body.

Her fingernails were so perfectly manicured I felt a little embarrassed when she shook hands with mine. Not that I didn't enjoy a little manicure at the salon, but I just didn't really have the time. Besides, I scrubbed my hands so much, there wasn't much point really.

"Blind dating." Kai felt like there was a need to clarify.

"His mother arranged it." The gorgeous woman winked, and I had no idea why she did that. Perhaps she was trying to say that she was the perfect candidate for Kai's wife, approved by his mother.

Kai sighed quietly. She noticed it right away and gave him a nudge. "Come on, we had fun."

Kai nodded and I could feel my heart sink. It was only when he looked up and stared right into my eyes that I realized I had been staring.

"Interesting. Uh, by the way, what happened to Ting Ting?" I had to clear my throat ever so slightly to speak – it had somehow seized up.

"Lucy's Ting Ting. I just didn't know her Chinese name until now." *Ah ha!* Their dating can't have gone all that well then if he didn't even know this about her.

"What a small world right?"

Really? "Did you know Kai was Jenny's cousin?"

"Not until yesterday." Lucy replied, her smile flirty, yet

somehow innocent. I narrowed my eyes at her, wanting to hate her, uncertain that I could.

"Why didn't you tell me then?" Kai asked and they went on to chat in Mandarin, and at times it sounded like something else, while I watched the airport staff get busy with unloading her belongings. My God, she had a lot of stuff. Was she planning to move to New York permanently? I couldn't hear a word that they were saying, not that I would understand.

My mind was everywhere. With the kiss the other day, I really thought that we were going somewhere. Perhaps it was all in my head.

Then Kai got Lucy and I in the back of the car while he volunteered to be in the front seat. Throughout the drive, he had his face turned towards us while having a conversation. Dave asked about switching the Porsche for a limo, but they didn't have time to do that.

Kai gave me a signal and I started briefing Lucy about Jenny's condition.

"Don't worry. No one knows why I'm here," Lucy reassured him. "But I told my mother that I was visiting you."

"Ah, I see." His face changed a little as he rubbed his fingers on his forehead.

"Was that a secret that you're here?" I chimed in.

"Well, I didn't exactly tell my mother I came." He laughed awkwardly. "Never mind, my mother would have found out sooner or later."

I had learned a lot about Kai from my brother, especially how amazing and brutal he was when he conducted business, but I didn't know much about his family.

"I'm sorry," Lucy said nonchalantly. I doubted that she actually meant it.

"I guess now my mother will get off my back about seeing you."

She laughed a sweet laugh, covering her almond-shaped mouth with her perfectly manicured but short nails, as if Kai had said something funny.

I felt like a third wheel.

"So, how long have you known Jenny?" I asked, hoping that this would change the topic of the conversation. I knew Kai had dated many women – beautiful, sexy women – but seeing what one of them looked like was reality hitting home. I didn't look anything like that.

"We went to university together."

"Did you go to her wedding? I would have remembered if you were there." Kai asked with a huge smile, his voice vague as he seemed to try to remember.

Jeez, was Kai flirting with her? Then suddenly, his smile turned upside down. I wondered if it was the thought of Jenny's unhappy marriage.

"No, I was stuck in Canada. Snowstorm. They canceled all the flights, so I missed it."

Kai didn't tell Lucy about Jenny's husband, or our speculation of what her husband did to her. It really wasn't our place to say anything. It was up to Jenny if she wanted to share the details with her friend.

"Have you been to New York before?" I tried to think of something else to say as Kai didn't seem to be in the mood to say anything.

"Yes, I have many times. But only for work."

"What do you do?" It felt rude not to ask after what she said.

"A bit of everything. I'm an artist but I model in my spare time."

Okay. She just confessed that she was an actual model. What did I say about Kai's women?

"Anything that I would have seen you in?"

"Nothing big really." *Phew.* "I had a contract with a prestigious lifestyle magazine called *Gao Shang.*"

Okay. I knew about that magazine. It was so prestigious that you couldn't just buy it. These magazines were gifted to the wealthy. It was their version of the Bible. Who was whom, what to wear, where to be – for the richest of the rich.

I was glad that our car journey didn't take as long as it did to get to the airport. Dave had the airport staff – who had been following behind our car – deliver Lucy's suitcases to Kai's apartment.

"Thank you for coming to the airport with me. Come up for a cup of coffee. I owe you that much." He said, though his attention kept drifting to the amazingly beautiful woman we'd picked up from the airport.

I felt my eyes narrow as he looked at her again, not even paying attention to whether I answered him or not. He owed me more than just a coffee.

Kai held my hands, and his eyes came back to me. This time, I could really feel how much he appreciated me being there. Even if, in the end, I was just another plaything to him.

11

June

Mission completed.

Kai wanted me to pick up Ting Ting, or Lucy, with him and now that it's done, I should leave them alone.

It would spare me feeling like a third wheel at least. Or fourth wheel with Jenny there.

I stood by the entrance of the tower to Kai's apartment, staring into the passing traffic looking for an available taxi. Perhaps I should just order an Uber. It would have been easier on a Sunday morning.

"Hey," Kai said as he came out of the building, "what are you doing out here?"

I shrugged. Talking felt like hard work.

"You're just going to leave me like that?" His voice sounded a little bitter. I couldn't tell where he was going with this.

"You wanted my company to pick up Ting Ting. We've picked her up and she's here now. What more can I do for you?" Now I sounded bitter.

"Oh–," He blinked a few times, then as if he had a light bulb moment, "were we rude? I mean when we were talking to each other in Mandarin. I'm sorry, it was just so much easier talking to her in the way we speak in Shanghai."

Yes and no.

Yes, that was a little rude, but I had gotten used to it as many of my patients were not from the United States. They would often discuss things with each other in other languages before telling me what they wanted in English.

No, that wasn't really the reason I was feeling a little down. My head started to hurt.

"Please. I need you." Kai gave me puppy dog eyes and I turned my face away from him. "I wouldn't know what to do, you know, what if Lucy and Jenny don't see eye to eye. You know, there's no way I can predict how Jenny is going to react."

His hand cupped my face softly. The warmth that radiated from him made my soul melt – I could never say no to him. And he knew that.

"Fine. You know that I'm a *very* busy person, right?"

My fake stern voice didn't seem to have any effect on him as he grinned foolishly at me.

"Of course, *my* princess." I hated him for saying that word, but it worked, as it melted my emotional armor. "I will make it up to you, I promise."

Gosh. I don't know what happened to me then. My mind suddenly had the dirtiest thoughts flying around at the speed of light in all directions.

I clenched my misbehaving thighs that wanted to creep up around his waist. I cleared my voice before I spoke. "Let's go."

Lucy and Jenny's reunion had no drama. Which was good. But a very small part of me hoped that Jenny might throw a tantrum. That was very evil of me for thinking that. Jenny was kind of my patient. Even though she hadn't officially registered under my service, she had verbally given me consent to look after her throughout her pregnancy – regardless of how short it was if she decided not to keep the baby.

The two women would talk to each other in Mandarin, with some Shanghai dialect here and there. Then they would switch back to English sometimes – for my benefit if I had to guess. Perhaps they wanted me to know that they weren't gossiping about me. Or they were just kind enough to include me in their conversation. They mostly talked about their university life, then caught up on news about themselves. If I understood correctly, Lucy and Jenny went to the same university. And Lucy was some kind of artist, or photographer because they were talking about some exhibitions. It was all very lovely and happy, and it didn't seem to me that Jenny disclosed much about her current situation in their catch-up chat.

In the beginning, Kai was pacing around them like a headless chicken. Fussing over their comfort. One minute, he would offer to adjust the air conditioning for Jenny and Lucy, then the next he would offer them some blankets. Then he would bark at his phone to have people prepare them lunch, then some snacks, then beverages. It felt never ending. It was adorable though.

He settled down soon enough as the house filled with all kinds of food and finally sat down on a chair that almost looked like a throne in the living room. Like he was the king of the place. I guess he was.

"I didn't know you knew Kai." Jenny's eyes alternated between Lucy and Kai.

Lucy whispered something into her ear, and they giggled like teenage mean girls.

"I didn't know she was your friend." Kai interrupted. "My mother introduced us."

"Match making you mean." Jenny corrected him.

Jenny made match making sound so old fashioned.

Matchmaking was back in fashion. That was why dating apps were so popular right now. And I personally had accounts across different apps, for when I had time to chill.

But it surprised me a little that Kai would let his mother organize dates for him. It just didn't seem like Kai at all. The Kai I knew didn't have a problem attracting women himself.

"Oh, you are very much Auntie's kind of girl." Jenny's words made me uncomfortable. I could just imagine Kai's formidable mother – played by Michelle Yeoh – screening through the list of girls for her perfect son to date.

"She was a hard one to please." That's what the movie poster would say. *I wouldn't expect less from Michelle*. Or Kai's mother.

"Please. Auntie is lovely. What are you talking about?" Now, either Lucy really was a people person, or she was just faking it. Wealthy and nice are two descriptions that don't go together for older Asian women – those that I know of anyway.

Kai chuckled. "You're right. She's actually very nice to you. A bit unusual for her."

I felt a bit uncomfortable. What would Kai's mother think of me? *Shit*. Why would I care what Kai's mother might think of me?

"Wow." Jenny went on and sang the wedding march, "dang, dang, dang, dang…"

"Oh stop." Lucy's face flushed the color of dragon fruit. It kind of made her even prettier, actually. Damn.

I got up and went to the bathroom.

My instinct was right.

I shouldn't have stayed.

Now I was an even bigger third wheel. The third wheel of their happy family. I stared at the mirror and realized that even my appearance was out of place here. Sure, I had some similar features to those Asian women out there, but in some ways, we weren't the same. I felt racist for thinking that all Asian moms might have prejudices against American girls. But that was what the recent Hollywood movie, *Crazy Rich Asians* led me to believe.

When I was dating Dannie back then... I pushed down the memory of my ex and focused on thinking about an escape plan. Maybe I could make up something about work. That would work.

I opened the bathroom door only to be greeted by Kai's chest. Technically, it was one of those awful cheesy slogan T-Shirts that said "kick ass or die" which I ran straight and buried my face into. He smelled really nice. His expensive woody cologne transformed into a scent of unique sweetness on him. "Are you okay there?"

Yes and no.

"I – um – have a work thing to sort out. I have to go."

"No, you don't." *Oops.* "Whatever it is, get someone else to sort it out."

He pulled my face up towards his and I could feel my feet pointing up on my tiptoes as my lips opened for his.

"You're doing fine." I whispered.

"I need you." His hand went up to push a strand of hair away from my face. I closed my eyes trying not to squirm. He reached down and our lips met.

I'm in so much trouble.

FOR THE FIRST time in my life, I realized that I was a poor sucker for *hypnotism*. True Blood has been one of my favorite shows of all time. In fact, I binged it all over again when it became available on my streaming service not too long ago. And I told myself that only people with weak mind control would be glamoured by those gorgeous blood suckers. I knew

I would be like Sookie Stackhouse, completely immune to them.

Perhaps I don't know myself as well as I used to.

I wasn't implying that Kai knew about hypnotism and that he was using that on me. But if he did, then I probably would hand over my bank account details along with the jewelry my granny passed down to me. However, Kai wouldn't care much about my little treasure chest.

The kiss confused me. I wanted to clarify our *relationship*, if there even is one. I had been on plenty of quick dates through swiping apps and had a few dates with men who all but had giant red flags waving behind them. None of the dates were anything I would be too proud of. But we were talking about my brother's best friend here. Clearly, there were rules about humans that were close to your life? Like, some kind of code about that.

A drunken night with a stranger is one thing. Your brother's best friend is a whole other matter.

I'd known Kai ever since I was a kid. We weren't best friends or anything. But he had been in my life more than some of my high school friends – during important events of my life anyway. He also kind of saved my life on many occasions. My crush and lust for him had always been there since day one. Unfortunately, he only ever saw me as the little sister that he never had.

Thanks to Lucy, our intimate session was cut short. It was Jenny who had interrupted us, however. She was simply too excited about the shopping event that Lucy had arranged for us.

In about thirty minutes, a crew of staff in tailor-made suits from Gucci arrived. Lucy's family had an account with Gucci, among other fancy luxury brands – mostly French and Italian. I figured when she meant accounts – or memberships, her words, not mine – she didn't mean the same lame kind that I get when I signed up to Costco, or Target. None of my memberships would have their staff bring the latest seasons of clothing and accessories for our choosing. They even brought their own sparkling wine.

Lucy said that Gucci was the only one available on such short notice. They weren't going to come in the beginning, but she had made a call to her guy in Italy to pull some strings. I couldn't help but wonder, what would it be like to have all these brands available to you at the snap of a finger?

I watched the staff giving us an introduction to their latest products. Lucy decided that every single one of them was made for Jenny. Either they went well with her eyes, or her hair color, or her skin tone. Don't get me wrong, it was very sweet of her to compliment her best friend. Retail therapy is a thing, and I know a lot of people do find joy in that.

Jenny was mesmerized by the introduction of each of the items. She studied every one of them carefully when they were passed around for us to see. I even saw her sniffing one of the dresses. I thought luxury items would be like everyday items to someone like her. Clearly, she really appreciated the craftsmanship of a good designer item.

Lucy occasionally pointed a few items my way, but I wasn't planning to shop on impulse. I make terrible choices when I do, and I wasn't familiar with this kind of shopping. I wouldn't know how to return an item if I didn't like it later.

"That gown would be perfect for you." Kai creeped up behind me a little while after he left us to have our *fun*. His words.

"I'm not sure." I gasped. The skintight wine-colored gown didn't seem like something anyone could just slip on. You would need a helper to get you into it. It was very much like a hold-your-breath tight mermaid wedding dress. That was what Chloe wore at her wedding, and I had helped her whenever she needed the toilet at her wedding.

"Good eye, Mister Li. This is a one-of-a-kind dress. This is the only one in New York." The brunette lady who seemed to be in-charge explained.

Kai nodded but didn't say another word.

I felt bad about not buying anything from them. They had brought up their entire collection to show us, minus the sold-out items of course.

"Pick anything you want." Lucy said nonchalantly, before looking back at the woman in charge. "Just add it to my account."

I shook my head hard and repeated the words *no* several times. "I haven't really seen anything yet."

"No, honestly. I haven't even finished my credit from 2019."

"Forgive me. What do you mean credit?" It might sound like a stupid question to her, but I really wasn't familiar with what she meant.

"Oh, can you explain Samantha." Lucy answered. I only realized then that Lucy and the lady in charge were on a first name basis. Though why Samantha couldn't come to us when Lucy called the first time, was a mystery to me.

Samantha smiled lightly – though I couldn't tell if she was just being polite or if she was laughing at me. "Miss Zhang's family currently hold the largest account in the world with Gucci. Every year, Mr. Zhang will top up an amount of store credit for Miss Zhang to use. Members can choose the desirable amount of credit to top up and that will determine the tier of membership they are in. Credits are not refundable and can only be spent with Gucci."

So, the first name basis thing was only one way. Lucy was still Miss Zhang to Samantha.

I remembered reading about this but didn't know that the membership tiers actually existed. "Of course, I know about that."

But I wasn't going to admit that this was the first time I'd ever witnessed it in real life.

I had known many billionaires in real life. My brother was one, though he made it very clear that his money was his – and Chloe's of course – and I had to make my own. But I didn't remember them shopping like this. I made a mental note to ask Chloe in the future – and if that was the way she shopped, and I wanted to know why I wasn't ever invited to one.

My insecurity had started to creep in. I could feel Samantha eyeing me up with judgment. I knew she thought that I wasn't able to afford anything. She wasn't wrong though. Although I was the head of the fertility department at the Bennet hospital, the whole Bennet Medical Group actually, the reality was that I had to be careful with money after spending a fortune on my apartment and my Tesla.

"I think I'll take that limited edition bag." I pointed at a pile of bags, at nothing in particular, wishing that I had chosen one of the cheapest of the pile.

"The Katerina Tote Bag?" Jenny asked, obviously knowing the brand very well. "Good choice."

I had no idea which one Jenny meant. But at least I knew it was a good one. Asking about the price seemed like a socially unacceptable thing to say here. Samantha never said anything about the price and the girls never asked either. The only things they would say were things like "I'll try that," or "I'll have that," before they'd move on to the next items that caught their attention.

"Do you have something smaller?" Perhaps it would be cheaper if I just got the smaller one, right? My common sense led me to believe that.

"That was the smallest we have," Samantha added. "It's fifty-nine thousand."

Suddenly, all eyes were on her as if she had just sworn at us.

"She didn't ask you." Lucy snapped. "Has money ever been an issue for me? Or for my friends?"

Samantha's head went down.

"I'm sorry. Your friend might–,"

Kai cut her short with a cough. "She will take the gown, the princess bag and one each of every item you brought along today."

Fuck. How much was that going to cost?

"Just add it to my tab." Lucy volunteered.

"No, Lucy. Add it to my tab." Kai also had a tab? I felt a little lost here as two nice, or very egotistical people continued fighting to pay for things that I didn't even want, while defending the pride that I didn't know I was lacking.

"Just stop!" Kai spoke with such authority that Lucy looked taken aback. "Over my dead body will I ever let a woman pay the bill at my house."

12

———

Kai

What happened yesterday with Gucci still angers me.

June wasn't poor. There was no reason for the Gucci staff to treat her like some second-class shopper. I wouldn't have that.

After the Gucci crew left, I had a stern word with the New York manager. Samantha had apologized and said it was unnecessary for me to make another scene with her boss. Lucy's family might have had a large retail account with them, but we had a business relationship with them. Not just New York but globally.

Pissing me off wasn't something they would want.

People in the west don't understand how Asian people think. We do not like to be looked down on. We have fought many battles over generations to be taken seriously on a global scale. And we are not about to back down when some sales assistant makes a stupid mistake like that.

With a few rounds of persuasion, June finally tried on the gown. It was perfect for her, as I'd predicted. I wasn't one of those men that could just tell what size dress a woman wore. Those kinds of men that buy perfect anything for their dates, they only ever exist in the movies. But somehow, I could just tell what would look good on June.

It sounded creepy. It was almost like I was playing with her as my own personal dress up doll. First, I would slowly and carefully undress her. Then I would put those dresses on her, caressing her soft skin as I did it.

My sultry thoughts were abruptly disrupted as staff from Dior started to march into my home. It seems Lucy arranged for Dior to come as well. The women continued to have fun, but I was exhausted. It was hard to pay attention when everything just seemed the same to me. If it was up to me, I would have my personal shopper pick out one or two items as and when I needed.

June didn't want anything from Dior. I had the manager pick up a few limited items for her anyway. I still couldn't tell if having Lucy there was a good idea. Jenny's mood seemed to pick up a little as her friend distracted her. I was hoping that Jenny would open up and talk about her problem with Lucy. Then again, they haven't had a chance to have a private chat yet, so maybe later.

June had some food delivered to us over dinner with the app on her phone. Pizza, fried chicken, burgers and chips. Standard American Food – not the healthiest food for their bodies. Sadly, the girls had the biggest smiles when the food arrived. These smiles were even bigger than those they wore when they saw Dior's exclusive off the shelf item.

Despite how unhealthy the food was, dinner was somewhat relaxing and it reminded me of my university days. I smiled as I remembered the days when I could just sit with a bunch of my friends, eating in front of the TV while binging on pretty much anything from sports replays to popular sitcoms like The Big Bang Theory. Those were the kind of memories I savored.

Dinners were never the same before and after those days.

Dinners now seemed to always be formal. It ranges from semi to very formal. And I had to dress accordingly. On the semi-formal days, a well pressed shirt was essential, coupled with a pair of *proper* trousers, that means denim jeans were deemed rude and inappropriate. Formal days on the other hand, were when my family had some kind of event, either at home, someone else's, or some kind of ballroom in some five-star hotel. Without a question, those were suit and tux kind of days.

Even when I was dining at home alone, when my parents couldn't be bothered to come home to see me, I still had to dress smartly. Which also meant being ushered to the dining table by the butler, Mr. Edwards. The most ridiculous thing was that my mother would demand evidence that Mr. Edwards, the Englishman that he was, would follow all her rules to a T. He would snap a photo of me holding onto the days' newspaper at the dining table. Fond memories huh?

I had to say that I did have a little bit more freedom after I graduated from the university, especially when I was abroad. Some days I would not eat, so that I could just skip the whole fuss. Mom knew that I hated being bothered with stupid questions like whether or not I had eaten. And she knew full well that I would simply just ignore her. These days, she would pester my assistant instead.

And guess what? Having basic Photoshop skills was listed as an essential skill for my assistant. Whatever evidence or photos my mom received, it was all fake.

We had a somewhat relaxing dinner with the girls. It was the kind that I had missed the most. We were surrounded with friends and joy. It wasn't a polite and civilized meal where we all sat around a table, using the correct fork and spoon kind of deal.

Food was just laid around the table, and people just picked up whatever they liked while continuing doing whatever they were doing.

The two best friends continued chit chatting about fashion while admiring and comparing their latest purchases. Soon after dinner, June made an excuse about work before going home.

I zoned out after she left.

The next day, Jenny and I waited at the reception area at Bennet Women's Hospital. The interior was mostly white – not hospital white though. The floors and walls were decorated with different shades and patterns of white marble, which gave it a very sophisticated look. It takes a lot of effort for things to look *simple*. That clean and minimalist look was actually more complicated than anyone can imagine. Especially when it comes to the upper-class way of simplicity and minimalism. Simple often means expensive in our world.

A lady in a dark blue dress approached us with a nice professional smile.

"You must be Jenny." She said, her eyes on my cousin. She didn't seem to know who I was. It made sense though. I wasn't the patient after all. And I wasn't in China. "My name is Siti. Please follow me. Dr. Bennet is expecting you."

Jenny wanted Lucy to come with her, but I insisted on coming instead.

Though I didn't really have a chance to talk to June after the Gucci team left last night, I knew something was on her mind. She looked as though she enjoyed the rest of the day, but I wasn't convinced that she was over the shock of how she'd been treated.

After dinner, she'd left in such a hurry I didn't have a chance to kiss her goodbye.

I'd thought about leaving the best friends to catch up alone to go after June, but Lucy needed some help with her guest room. I don't know why it didn't cross my mind to leave David or Clare to handle those two so I could chase after June.

And… there were no messages from her.

Since yesterday.

So, I'd decided I might as well go to the hospital with Jenny.

We followed behind June's assistant up the brightly lit elevator to the third floor. That floor was dedicated to consultation rooms. I glanced at a sign on the wall that listed the doctors' names and their specialty. June's name was at the very top, as head of department. That's my princess there, so smart.

Soon we walked past a long corridor and entered a glass room at the end. Inside the room, there was a waiting room that was much fancier than the one we walked past outside. Two couples sat patiently. One of the couples was having a quiet and serious discussion. The other pair were busy scrolling on their phones. June's assistant then knocked on a frosted door with a plate that read 'Dr. June Bennet' on it and led us in soon after it was answered.

Dr. Bennet was a little surprised to see us. Or me, that is.

She wore her hair in a neat bun today. No perfume or jewelry, apart from a smart watch. She removed the stethoscope from her neck and left it on her desk before standing up to greet us.

"Good to see you, Jenny." Her smile was as formal as the bun on her head. She looked exactly like the woman she posed as on those posters plastering the hospital walls. I had no doubt that that woman was a good doctor. But she wasn't my June.

"Hi." It sounded a lot goofier than I intended.

"I wasn't expecting you though, Mr. Li."

I wanted to tell her that I missed her.

But it wasn't appropriate with Jenny there.

Odd. I had been with my fair share of women before. Although there were a few that I had a somewhat close relationship with, I had never missed anyone before. Even when I really – how do I put this – *feel* the urge to get off, I never missed any of them.

"Have you made a decision about whether to keep the pregnancy, Jenny?" June asked without judgment.

"I have. I'm going to keep it." Jenny answered with a firm nod, her eyes on the fingers clutched in her lap.

It surprised me that Jenny had decided to keep the baby. Perhaps Lucy had helped her to come to that decision. I supported her decision but had my reservations. We could have made an appointment with the best OBGYN in New York, but Jenny decided that she wanted June to handle her case.

Picking June was a great and obvious choice for Jenny.

It also gave me an excuse to see her whenever I wanted.

After asking Jenny a series of questions and performing the standard health related exams, June escorted Jenny to a private room. Jenny followed June into a small room attached to the office, which could only be an examination room. I sat there quietly on my own, knowing it would be rude to follow. As much as I'd like to see more of June, I wasn't interested in seeing the inside of my cousin.

For the last few years, I've been following her work. I have to say that her reputation among the Chinese Elite was highly respected. She and the clinic had been recommended multiple times in digital magazines, and social media, among other articles and blogs etcetera, by wealthy couples who had been successful in their fertility treatments. Of course, being able to pay for her hefty bill was also one of the reasons those wealthy couples liked to brag about it.

That was one of the reasons why so many rich Chinese couples had chosen to fly all the way to New York to see her. They simply wanted the best fertility treatments the world could offer, with her.

My dad's company had been working on a proposal to bring the Bennet Fertility Program to China. My intel told me that the board wanted no one but June to be the person to oversee the program. Sadly, thanks to the pandemic, the project had been postponed until further notice.

Legally, I had no say on the board of Dad's company. I didn't want to be accused of meddling in my half-brother's inheritance. Dad suggested that I come and help him out. Lately, he'd become a lot more sentimental, and we'd been talking a lot more. Perhaps he wanted to mend our relationship. Perhaps the pandemic had really changed people. Still, I tried to stay away from family politics as much as I could. However, I have my ways if and when there's a need to sway any decision on the board.

At one point last year, I was really desperate to get the fertility program in Shanghai kick-started. Everything was ready. The funding was there. They even had the location of the medical center reserved – all they needed was a green light and the renovation team would start.

George Bennet, June's dad, had even signed the contract. I knew that June was more than ready to live and work in Shanghai. If it wasn't for the new woman health campaign that her brother Liam had forced upon her, she would have left the country already.

My phone vibrated. I glanced down and saw a notification – a message from Lucy. I unlocked my phone to see the full content of the texts in Chinese.

Lucy: Samantha just told me that June sent everything back to the store. Did she tell you why?

I couldn't say I was surprised.

June was complex. An American girl with a part Chinese mother. In some ways, she was very American. At other times, she seemed a little out of place, like she didn't quite fit in here in

America. It was hard to know her thoughts, or what she wanted, but that didn't mean I didn't try.

I searched through my phone for a contact, then stepped outside for a quick call. As I was about to head back to June's office, my phone vibrated again.

Call me. TC.

It wasn't a saved contact. Just a random number. I called.

"Tom Cruise is an alien." I said as the person on the other end picked up. Then the call was put through to a pre-recorded message. I listened carefully, trying not to miss any details, as these messages only played once before they were deleted. That was a very peculiar way to stay in contact set up by my private investigator. He would only contact me on a new burner number each time, so his work could stay confidential at all times.

Bad news.

Mack was missing. Someone in the police department had released him without charge. But I already knew that from Wendy. No one saw him leave the precinct where he'd been held. The guess was that someone smuggled him out. No one from the police department had contacted June about pressing charges against Mack. It was very naive of me to think that they would actually try to do their job.

The question was who had the authority to let him go? My guy couldn't find out who was behind everything. And what's more, he couldn't find any information about Mack in the United States, like it had been purposely wiped squeaky clean. Mack was either using a fake name or had been issued a new identity.

It didn't make sense though. People always leave some kind of a trace, that is how criminals end up caught. I was going to suggest having Mack followed, but no one knew where he was, no one had seen him leave.

My guy suggested we should look into him outside of America. Now that would involve more people – internationally. Though I wasn't keen on the idea, I knew it was necessary. But where do we even begin?

Oh princess. What have you gotten yourself into?

I HAD Clare escort Jenny home and texted Lucy to keep an eye out on her.

Jenny seemed alright – just a little on the quiet side – after her consultation with June. But I wasn't a mind reader, and I didn't know how she really felt.

Perhaps June could tell me more.

That would be my excuse to stay at the clinic.

Normally, June's OBGYN services were only supposed to be for her fertility clients only. She had made an exception for Jenny. She would probably do that for her close friends and relations but Jenny and her only just met. Needless to say, she was doing it as a favor to me.

"Can I help you with anything?" June's assistant asked as soon as I approached her office door. Her gray eyes questioning my intention like a guard dog.

"Yes, I was just here a minute ago with my cousin, Jenny Law. I would like a word with June," I paused as she cleared her throat and glared at me. "Dr. Bennet."

Her eyes X-rayed my body from top to bottom and she gave me a *one moment* hand gesture.

She mumbled a few words into the mic on her headpiece and spoke after what felt like a very long minute later.

"Dr. Bennet will see you now." Unapologetically, she added, "please make it brief, her next appointment has arrived."

I couldn't help but laugh inside. What on Earth was going on with people? Did she really just tell me to hurry the fuck up?

Was that part of her job description or was she just keeping an eye out for her boss? I couldn't be bothered to give her the, "do you know who you are talking to" talk. I could use the "I'm rich and famous and important card", something a lot of my peers would often do, but I knew that wouldn't work here. Not in America. Nobody knew, nor did they care.

Whatever. I gave her an eye roll and walked straight into June's office.

"Hey!" My rant about her assistant was about to start. But she looked a little under the weather, her eyes were watery from tears. "Are you okay?"

"Yes, I'm fine." She touched her eyes to wipe away any makeup smudges. "I got a little emotional, is all."

"I was going to ask you about how Jenny was doing, in there. Is this a bad time?"

"No, it's fine. She and her baby were doing fine. I told her about my concerns, and really you should talk to her. You know, patient doctor confidentiality."

Right, I'd thought there would be no secrets between us and that she would just spill all the details without hesitation.

I was wrong and I felt a little betrayed, even though I knew full well that she was doing the right thing.

"So, this concern that you have…"

"Don't you dare try to fish it out of me." She replied, her voice stern. "Look, if there's nothing else, you should leave. I have a busy day today."

Ouch. Cranky, huh? Something must have set her off.

"I'm here as a patient." *What for?* I pinched myself ever so lightly on the thigh. Having feelings for her was one thing, but I really hated acting like a lovesick loser. What was I going to say now, huh? That my lady parts needed some love?

"This is a women's health hospital." She gave me a look and believe me, I knew I sounded like a toad.

"Yeah, you know." I looked around her office, searching for an answer. Then I saw it on her notice board. "Sperm bank."

"What?"

"You know. I'm here to donate my sperm." *Not really.* I was there to make sure Mack didn't show up and twist her head off her neck. But I couldn't really tell her that.

"You want to donate sperm?" She sucked a breath in. "You? Mr. Kai Billionaire Li? Why would you do that?"

Why indeed.

"So that we could have more billionaires in the world." I cringed inside because I knew those words didn't make any sense, and it sounded stupid.

"It's a good thing, isn't it? My business mind alone is worth–" I couldn't come up with anything smart sounding. I wanted to say receive, or download – definitely not it, "purchasing my product, right?"

"You *said* donate, not selling sperm. I won't pay you anything for it."

"I don't need your money." I said proudly. "Just your time."

She shook her head hard and there was an unshakable smile on her face, followed by a flush as my words brought some color to her cheeks. "You will have to go to the reception and register."

"No, I need you to oversee this." I demanded. "I'm shy."

The sound that followed that statement was a weak groan of distress. And weak was right because I should feel weak for being an immature idiot.

"My next appointment is here, and they have been waiting for," she checked her watch, "quite some time now. Stop wasting my time, Kai."

"I'm serious, princess." No woman could resist me when I called them princess.

"Fine. If you're sure, then wait outside until I'm free."

Yes! That was exactly what I wanted. Free pass to stay as long as I want – for now. "And I cannot guarantee how long you'll have to wait. My schedule is very full today."

Double wham. That was even better. I had been given permission to camp out in her office.

I walked out of her office with a triumphant smile and found the best and most comfortable seat in the lounge to settle in. Believe me, I had time to test every single seat in there.

It was a good thing that Andy, my assistant, arrived today in New York. I gave her a call and had her set up my essentials right there in the middle of June's waiting room.

Within thirty minutes, I had turned a corner of the waiting room into my personal workspace. I had my eyes closed, meditating as well as trying to get over my jet lag. Andy sat on my side working away on her iPad. Occasionally, I would bark out some words at her. That was because during meditation, my mind would suddenly remember something. Sometimes it was important. Sometimes not. Then at times, it would create some problems. Problems that I didn't know existed in my life. At times, there were some answers that I had been seeking, usually something that had troubled me for some time. Many of my creative ideas during my meditations had benefited my business.

Andy was no stranger to this behavior. This was something I would do often. To other people, it may seem a little odd. June's assistant must have reported the situation to her as she peeked out of her little cave and gave me a strange look.

I grinned at her, wondering if she regretted not letting me skip the queue yet. Now her clients had to witness this weird man doing this weird thing in her waiting room. But I pretended to be in the zone and kept ignoring Siti, the *lovely* assistant, whenever she frowned or huffed in my direction.

Dave was out on his security assignment, a suitable vantage point across from June's office. Just a protocol – for her own safety. I did this even for myself and it had proven to be very effective. My team had successfully eliminated conflicts before they even happened many times.

Sometimes, it wasn't anything serious. Mainly opportunity seekers trying to sell their ideas to me in return for an investment.

Or stalkers that wanted to say how much they loved me.

Some just wanted to get a selfie.

The love of the public could be problematic, but my team kept them at bay.

Back home, people love to gossip about celebrities and rich people. Magazines, blogs, forums. They can't get enough. Some people literally cannot live without them. They love knowing what the celebrities do from day to day, who they are dating, what they are wearing, where they are hanging out.

It's exhausting trying to avoid them. And that's why I take every opportunity that I can to stay overseas.

"Ahem," Siti cleared her throat. "Here's your Americano. From Starbucks." Damn right, I had her order a coffee for me. I knew they had a coffee machine. I also knew that I had my own personal assistant who could just go and fetch me coffee. But I loved seeing people with an attitude put to work. If she decided to be rude to me, then she'd have to deal with me being difficult. Besides, I was sure that June didn't pay her well to just sit there and be pretty.

Lunch time came and there was no sign of June.

No one brought lunch in for her either. I had Andy check with Siti and found out that June often worked through lunch and would skip any food as part of her intermittent fasting regime.

Good thing that Siti and Andy got along. It was almost like they had a code among them as assistants. They talked about everything. It was like magic, as if they shared the same taste –

reading the same books, haunting the same cafes, e-shopping the same clothing brands. Andy's loyalty remained with me, however, and she would tell me later what she found out from Siti. I had no idea just how much information personal assistants know about their bosses until Andy came along. And Andy? She's very good at digging that information out of those personal assistants.

Five coffees and six hours later, Sit finally smiled in my direction with a condescension that made my blood boil. "Mr. Li? Dr. Bennet will see you now. And it's now or never. Her words."

"Thanks, Siri." I said, using the wrong name on purpose.

"It's Siti."

Whatever.

13

June

I frowned as I finally stole a moment to myself to check on my blood pressure. I couldn't say that I was surprised that it was higher than I expected it to be.

Making an emergency appointment for Jenny early in the morning was definitely a big fat mistake. She wasn't the problem. No, not her. I didn't expect her, and *him,* to show up early and catch me in the middle of trying to take my blood pressure.

I knew it could be worse. They could have walked in before Siti had a chance to tell me about their arrival. Before I had a chance to put away the blood pressure meter. Why was I so afraid of them catching me doing something so routine, though? Maybe I couldn't help but think it showed some sign of weakness.

Kai and his assistant setting up a small office in my waiting room didn't really help with my blood pressure. He'd spent all day here with some of his people coming and going. Some of my colleagues noticed the odd set up, but none of them asked me about it. I was glad about that. I didn't really have the headspace or the time to deal with him.

Until now.

"Dr. Bennet." A little too formal coming from Kai. Like the greeting came from a new patient. What kind of game was he playing?

"Yes, Mr. Li. Please have a seat."

Two can play this game.

He made a noise which, if I'm not mistaken, sounded almost like a strangled groan. "Oh, you have no idea what you're doing to me princess."

"Uh huh." So, he has a slutty doctor fantasy huh? "Here's *the* cup. Place the sample in the cup."

He looked up and down, at my hand then at my face multiple times.

"Chop, chop!" I barked the words at him, enjoying this moment of control.

"Okay, right away, ma'am," He snatched the cup from my hand and unbuckled his belt.

"What are you doing?" I tried very hard not to laugh. Collecting sperm had never been my job before and I didn't know what to say to this 'donor'.

"Taking my pants off." He explained, like I didn't know what he was doing.

"I can see that."

"How are you going to collect my sample if I keep my pants up?" His eyebrows rose twice. His voice and the rest of his face remained serious. And somehow, he'd managed to make it sound like I was the one being ridiculous.

"Hmm, you're right." Smiling, I got up and put on a pair of gloves that I snapped tightly for effect. I heard a soft moan behind me, but I wasn't sure if it was a sound of pleasure or worry. From the cabinet to my right, I retrieved a long needle and syringe, humming to myself as I attached the needle. I turned to face Kai, a smile that I knew was a little sadistic, firmly in place.

"What are you doing?" The smile became a grin as his eyes went round and wide at the sight of the needle.

"Extracting some sperm." I answered a matter of factly.

"With that?" He pointed at the syringe now in my hand.

"No silly. That's just to draw out the sperm. First, I need you to remove your pants, then I'll swab your testical with alcohol, insert the needle and draw out the sperm." His jaw dropped. And I couldn't help but burst into a laugh. "Your face! I wished I had it filmed so I could send it to Link."

"Don't you dare." He warned with his finger as well as his voice. "So, we're not doing the needle?"

Poor thing, I must have really messed him up.

"No, I was just messing with you. I'm sorry. You know, just the normal," I couldn't say that word that I had said so many times to other patients without flinching, not to him... "masturbation."

I coughed the word out.

"Okay. Phew. I thought you were going to stick that thing up my little..." he whistled two notes to replace the word penis. "Do you ever do that to people? Just curious."

"Yes, if they can't produce sperm on their own, then I've had to perform the procedure. It's testicular sperm aspiration." I said it like I was proud. But doing such a procedure with a lack of confidence would only make the patients doubt your professionalism.

"You're joking!" Horror came back to his face. "Tell me you're joking. Please?"

"No. I'm not joking. It's necessary to have sperm to perform many tests–"

"So, you've touched other men's penises!" He cut me off. "And saw a lot of penises."

"Just the normal amount a doctor would see. Well, not compared to a renal specialist, for example."

Neither of us talked for a minute. Maybe less. But it felt like the conversation had gone too far.

"Can you please get on with this? You can go down the hall to a private room to produce your sample. I've had a very long day, Kai."

Kai reached down to his fly and started to retrieve his penis. I gasped, more than a little annoyed now.

"Not in here, Kai! What the hell? Go to the exam room, at least." I pointed at the little room attached to my office. The one he had seen Jenny and I go into earlier. "There's an exam table and a chair in there. You know – whatever makes you comfortable."

He nodded.

"Got it, Dr. Bennet." Then he headed to the room next door. "Aren't you coming with me?"

"Why would I be coming?" I raised my eyebrows at his silly question.

"Well, don't you need to help me with it?"

"No." I screamed. "Why is this so hard for you to understand? You go to the exam room, jerk off into the cup, and then we can all go home, alright? Don't make me bring the needle!"

"Fine. There's no need to shout."

Wait. Did I just shout at Kai? No, I couldn't have.

"I'm sorry. It's been a long day."

"Got it."

He stayed silent in the room for what felt like days on end. Guilt surged through my veins as I waited for him.

I don't know when it started, but lately, it always feels like he's playing some kind of games with me. Like a cat and mouse game. He wanted me one minute, then he didn't want me the next.

There was no doubt that I wanted him. This game that we were playing really frustrated me somehow. My problem was, I didn't know if he was serious about this or not. Was this a fling, or the real thing? I wanted to know either way.

My mind began to wander as Kai took his time in my exam room. There was a couple today who had had twelve rounds of failed fertility treatments in their life, two of them with me. They were one of the loveliest couples I had ever met, who adored children and wanted their own child. Life hadn't blessed them with one. Their last treatment had given us high hopes, but a miscarriage eight weeks later brought nothing but heartache. The wife was in tears, right there in my office. They were on the brink of giving up trying. My professional advice was to try again, in six months, if they were still feeling up to it.

I studied their file in front of me. Had I missed anything at all? I prided myself on being one of the top fertility doctors in the country and nobody knew how hard I took it when I failed to help a patient. My stomach clenched as I thought about Mrs. Johnson, as if I could feel her sadness over not being able to have a child of her own.

"I need some help." Kai called out, whining again. It was kind of cute though, to be honest. I rolled my eyes at myself, someday someone had to invent some kind of vaccination for hot guys, so people would be immune when hot guys batted their eye lashes.

"You done?" I stood outside of the room. There was no answer.

"Please. I need some help."

"Are you decent?" I asked just in case. A loud clanking noise hit the air, something clearly had hit the floor. I panicked and rushed in without a reply.

No. He wasn't decent. He'd taken his pants off, but at least his tight, very tight boxer shorts were on. I saw a tray on the floor and along with it some equipment that had been on the tray. "What did you do?"

"That? I was just using the tray as a stand for my phone. And you know, it wasn't really helping."

I checked my watch and breathed out another sigh.

"You have somewhere to be?" He sounded so flirty it made me roll my eyes.

"I'm sorry princess." Not that word again, even if it came out innocent. "I was just trying to hurry things along by watching some videos on my phone. But uh, it wasn't working."

"You're watching adult films in my clinic?" Not unusual, but I was shocked that he had to resort to that.

"Yeah, I was trying to. But all I can think about is you."

"Oh sorry, did I make it awkward for you? I did tell you we have a room for sperm donors here." There was a room designed especially for that purpose, where male patients could produce their samples. It was a soundproof room equipped with the necessities from magazines to videos. Never had I ever let a male patient in my exam room.

"No. All I can think about is doing things to you." *Oh, that again.*

Were we back to the cat and mouse game?

I swear, I don't know what's going on. I could be a bit insensitive about things like that and I could never tell when someone was hitting on me. Beating around the bush didn't work with me. Firm and direct worked a lot better. Which meant that I had missed out on the fun quite often.

Kai closed the distance between us in the small room. "You left in a rush last night and you didn't even say goodbye to me."

"Did I not?" He shook his head. "I'm sorry."

I felt it, genuinely sorry. How did he make me feel things that I didn't want to feel?

He pressed his index finger to my lips and made a soft shushing noise. "Can I kiss you again? I've missed these lips."

He leaned in before I had a chance to nod. Our lips collided, hungry for each other. Our bodies moved around the small space then out to the main office as he pressed me on top of my desk, on my keyboard and a bunch of documents. It was really uncomfortable, but I didn't care. His hand trailed down to my breast as he inhaled the scent of my neck before his tongue started exploring my mouth.

His hand ran further down my waist and up my skirt before his fingers slid beneath my panties. I shuddered as his fingers slid down, opening me up to his touch. I made a sound, a noise of protest, when he pulled his fingers out of my panties. The second he got down on his knees, pushing my skirt up around my waist, I stopped protesting.

Kai's brown eyes came up to mine, full of things I never thought I'd see there. Desire. Need. Maybe even love, but I'm not sure.

"You're so ready for me, princess." He whispered before something ripped and my panties disappeared. I leaned back when I felt the heat of his breath between my thighs. Never had I ever imagined myself having sex in my office – on my desk.

We both jumped and gasped when someone knocked on the door. My legs clamped around Kai's head and my eyes went to the door, willing it to stay closed.

"Is everything okay, Dr. Bennet?" *Damn.* Siti was such a buzzkill.

"Uh huh," I squeaked.

"Should I come in?"

"No, I'm with a patient." My high voice was a dead giveaway, and I could only hope that she didn't figure out what we were doing in there.

Kai stood up and I could see his beautiful face again. "Should I continue?"

I shook my head awkwardly. As much as I wanted this to happen, I was afraid I had to cut it short. I saw how disappointed he was, but his disappointment couldn't match anything that I was feeling.

Kai didn't have a problem producing his sample after that. He was rock hard after that moment between my legs. That much I knew.

I quickly tidied my office before asking Siti to send the sample to the sperm bank. She would have to make up some kind of explanation since sperm donation wasn't a service my clinic offered. But I trusted that Siti would make up something worth believing.

Then, I dashed out of my office.

"What's your plan for the evening?" Kai asked, giving me those sad puppy dog eyes again. His look suggested that he wanted to continue what we'd started in the exam room.

"Well, I have to go home, get changed and then go to a charity event. And..." I looked at my watch for the millionth time today, "I have thirty minutes to get ready."

I wasn't lying when I'd said I had a full day today.

"I'd love to help. How much money do they need to raise? Can I come?"

Kai followed me out of the hospital.

"I would love for you to come, but unfortunately the tickets were all sold out."

"Can't I just be your plus one?"

That would have been nice. "Unfortunately, I asked Siti to come with me."

"That little mouse?"

I raised my eyebrows. "What? Yeah, my assistant. She said she'd never been to a gala before for fun. She's had to work at a few, but she's never been a guest, so I invited her."

"But she's still at work."

"Don't you worry about her." I had no time to think about Siti right now. All I knew was that whenever she had to work at an event, she had always managed to be there on time regardless of what else she had to do. That woman was like a time management wizard. That was why I couldn't do this job without her and in return I made sure that she was well compensated with plenty of bonuses.

I got into my car and drove home, distracted and tense. I needed a vacation from all of this stress, but I knew that wouldn't happen any time soon. When I got home, there was a large parcel that the doorman had collected for me. It was something from Gucci. I thought I had made it very clear to their manager that I wanted nothing from them. I wondered why it was so hard for these people to take no for an answer.

I brought the large brown box upstairs and found the wine-colored red dress tucked inside.

Seriously?

There was a message.

Promise me you'll wear this tonight,

Kai.

Kai had somehow managed to get Gucci to deliver this dress to me after I told him my evening plans. It annoyed me that he'd ignored my refusal of the dress, but that was Kai. I didn't have enough time now to call him, or to do much of anything else but get ready.

I made a mental note to send Kai a text later. That was when

I realized that I didn't say goodbye to him in the parking lot. I'd just driven away like a mad woman. Had my life become so chaotic that I'd blanked the man of my dreams? This event was no more important than the last one I organized. Regardless of what I told myself, I still couldn't shake off this bad feeling. The feeling that I had forgotten something, or worse something was going to go wrong because of that.

Fifteen minutes later, a well-dressed, fully made-up Siti stood outside my building with the town car I ordered. I had never questioned her ability to be there on time. Her college had really trained her well. Or she must have possessed some kind of superpowers that allowed her to do her job well, all while, also, being totally gorgeous at the same time. I thanked her for work and made her promise to enjoy herself tonight.

Tonight's event was really important to us. At the Bennet Medical Group, we emphasized and celebrated the importance of women's health. For the last year, I had been leading the group in promoting better women's health, not only for the United States but for the world beyond. We have donated millions to countries in need, to help women in poverty overcome problems, from small problems like getting clean period products to bigger ones like fertility and abortion issues. Our group was working on correcting the problems caused by the outdated and poorly executed experiments of the past.

The main problem with those experiments were the test subjects. In the past, most of the test subjects were mainly white and male. Now, the university that we worked with was creating larger sample sizes that comprised females with a variety of backgrounds. We wanted to know how a variety of people, with different races and backgrounds, reacted to certain drugs and treatments.

Now, I'm raising money to further those studies, and I was really pleased about how well the gala had been received. As I stepped into the building, I saw that many of the guests that I invited had indeed showed up. We had invited philanthropists, celebrities, politicians, journalists, social media influencers but my real aim was to get the government's attention, so we could help more people in need.

"Hey, you look great." Lincoln, my brother tapped me on my shoulder.

I turned around and gave him a hug. "You look nice too. Where is my sister-in-law?"

"She's just checking out backstage."

"What? Is she performing?" I couldn't believe what I was hearing. Chloe was a first-class pole dancer, and a very talented ballerina. When I invited her to perform tonight, Lincoln had rejected the invitation on her behalf because she was pregnant. But that was almost six months ago, and I didn't know about the pregnancy.

"Yes, she said she would if there's an auction large enough. And if they didn't mind her belly." Lincoln said sheepishly. In spite of everything, I knew how much he loved watching Chloe dance.

"No one would mind a little bit of her belly. She looks nice with a bit of a belly." I reassured him, my hand on his bicep to comfort him. He was so protective of his wife, and it was touching.

"Listen, Liam asked me to tell you that your item went missing."

"You mean the antique vase from the Ming Dynasty?" It was an antique replica that a client gifted me. Although it wasn't an original vase that was used by the emperor, it was a replica secretly made and traded during that time period among the aristocrats. It was still worth a fortune.

As much as I loved that vase, it didn't quite fit in with the rest of my apartment. I knew it would collect lots of money tonight, so why not donate it for a good cause?

"I have no idea. Just that your thing was missing." Damn, of course he wouldn't know what I had donated. Lincoln and Chloe had been living in Myrtle Beach and had no part in organizing this party.

"Did someone steal my vase? What happened to it?" I whispered loudly to him, looking around me as if I'd see someone casually walking off with my vase.

"Junie, how many times are you going to make me say this?" It was too tempting. Link couldn't resist giving me a lecture whenever there was a chance.

"I handed it over to someone from the auction house, alright." I hesitated. "I'm *pretty* sure."

My big brother rolled his eyes at me, and I totally deserved that. I couldn't remember who I'd handed the vase over to now. Writing a note was the last thing I could recall doing for that vase, whether or not I sent it off... *Shit!* It was probably still sitting in my apartment somewhere waiting for someone to collect it. I had no memory of me making any sort of arrangements for it to be collected after the note.

"You forgot to send it, didn't you?" Lincoln asked, and I could hear another lecture was on the way from the way he sighed.

"Spare me the lecture." I scolded, though I was the one in the wrong.

"Calm down Junie," his voice softened.

"Calm down? How do I come up with something for my auction on such short notice?"

"You don't have to give them anything." He was now using his daddy voice. Having a daughter definitely had made him a better brother. A softer, more compassionate one, I hoped.

Link had a point. I didn't have to give them anything.

But no, it didn't feel right.

"It would look very bad on me if I didn't. Do you even know that *this face* was the face of this event? Have you seen the posters, no I mean the *wallpaper* around here?" I emphasized the word wallpaper.

Link chuckled lightly, I wanted to put my fist in that little socket where his pretty brown eye twinkled at me from. The left one. The good side.

"I could donate something instead." He paused, his eyes checking my face for approval. "But I know you wouldn't want my help."

One of these days, I really should consider taking face acting class, if there's such a thing. I swear that people – especially my friends – can always tell what I'm thinking. And I always lose in poker. Winning at poker every now and then would be awesome.

"You could donate your services instead." Lincoln suggested, looking around as if he hadn't just saved my ass.

Suddenly, my urge to punch him eased.

"Keep talking."

"Isn't this benefit about women's health?" I lifted an eyebrow prompting him to continue. "And you're a doctor, right?"

"Wait... You mean like, free IVF treatments? Like ten of them or something?"

"No, that was just depressing." Yes, he was right. Who would even want to openly bid for that and let the whole world know that they had fertility problems, huh? "Maybe a year of private consultation with you on anything women's health related. A lot of women would go for that. In fact, go for longer, like five years."

"One is enough. I couldn't commit to anything longer than that. I don't know where I'll be next year."

"Why? Where are you going?"

"I've been working on a project for ages. You know that" I replied, glaring at him a little.

"Oh, right. The one in China."

I met his eyes, and saw an acknowledgement that he knew about what was happening in my life. Last year, I almost went to China to set up a fertility clinic for the Bennet Medical Group. Our potential partner had requested me to be their chief, and without me there would be no deal. Though I was eager to take the project on, there was still a part of me that had reservations about it.

"Fine, let me go speak with the auction director about the mix up and then I'll go say hi to Chloe. You mingle and keep my guests happy. You're good at that." I kissed his cheek and left him standing in the crowd. After I spoke with the auction people, I headed to the area behind the stage.

Lincoln was more than happy for me to deal with Chloe right now. Even though she had been performing for a long time, for some reason, she didn't do well having Lincoln with her backstage. Anything Lincoln did was deemed a distraction to her getting ready.

When I saw Chloe at the back, I realized that her belly had gotten larger than I had expected.

We gave each other a quick hug, before I leaned back a little to look at her. "Is everything alright with your pregnancy? You seem a little..."

I didn't know how to phrase it in a way that wouldn't hurt her feelings. Inevitably, I end up sticking my foot in my mouth when I voice my concerns. I'm not very diplomatic, sometimes, and it's gotten me in trouble before.

"We're expecting twins." Chloe's grin relieved my worries that I'd stuck my foot in it again.

"Phew." That makes sense. "Congratulations. Why didn't you tell me earlier?"

"Well, please promise you won't stress out." I knew I would worry but I nodded anyway. "I have gestational diabetes and with me carrying twins and all, the doctor wants me to be extra careful. And Link didn't think we should worry you about this."

I nodded along, pinching the side of my thigh to keep my mind clear and calm. I couldn't give her my advice without knowing the full picture. And I knew for a fact that they wouldn't let me handle their case anyway. Chloe said it was too weird and also too much pressure on me.

"You're with Rebecca, right?" Rebecca Simpson was an outstanding doctor that I'd met at a conference. I wouldn't say we were best buds or anything. Let's just say that Dr. Simpson and I happened to go to the same school, different year, and had a very similar outlook on the way we treated patients. We often recommended patients to each other.

"Yes. You recommended her, remember?" Of course, I remembered, but people don't always go with the first recommendation they received.

"Rebecca is a great doctor. She'll take good care of you. Do you mind if I talk to her about your health? You know, just to see if she needs a second opinion, or if she needs any help."

Chloe reached in for a big hug. "Please don't worry."

With that, she meant no. My best friend and now sister-in-law still didn't want me to worry.

"But you can talk to her *only* if that makes you feel better." Chloe said and I nodded. Talking to Rebecca would definitely make me feel better.

14

───────

June

Despite what Chloe told me, she seemed fit and healthy. There was nothing I could do about it right now. She wasn't comfortable with me treating her. I took it rather hard at the beginning, wondering whether it was my brother or her, or both, that didn't want me to treat her. I'd been tormented wondering if they thought that I wasn't a good enough doctor.

But now, for the first time, I saw the downside of being my best friend's doctor. Her case wasn't really that complicated. Many women had gestational diabetes, and I had helped plenty give birth to beautiful babies healthily. The worry I would have for my best friend, and my future niece and/or nephew, would be a heavy burden if I was to be responsible for Chloe's care.

I quickly sat her down in front of the dressing table. Her face was glowing even more under the mirror lights. Pregnancy really looked good on her. I fired a series of questions at her, all about her discomfort and concerns.

"I heard that Kai is here." Chloe said instead of answering me, clearly not willing to talk about the topic with me.

"Yes, so?" I was eager to get back to our previous topic, not wanting to talk about me or Kai.

"Well? Do you think something is going to happen between you this time? Three years ago, you guys nearly...you know?"

I sighed lightly, for two reasons.

One, I was frustrated with Kai.

Two, I knew that Chloe wasn't going to let it go until I talked about it.

"We nearly what? Nearly slept together? Or nearly got together? I'm not even sure what happened back then. We kissed, but that's all."

The last time I was with Kai, I was emotional about seeing Chloe. I thought she'd been dead for a long time. At first, I was happy about having her back. Then I got really angry that she couldn't trust me enough to contact me in all that time. For ten years, she let me think that she was dead. She let me grieve for her. When I found out that my big brother was the one helping her disappear and lying about her being alive, I couldn't help feeling betrayed all over again.

I had never told Chloe or Lincoln about my feelings. I'd never mentioned how they had betrayed me on some level. Or that I still felt that pang of betrayal over them keeping that secret from me.

Kai distracted me for a while. If it wasn't for him, I'd have gone completely crazy. He helped me to contain my feelings, to focus on keeping them both safe, without making demands on me. He'd been there to feed me, talk to me, and keep me in one piece.

There were moments when we could have taken it further. Kai could have taken anything from me he wanted to, and I'd have let him. But I think we'd both known we'd regret it, and we'd both maintained control, even when we didn't want to. The timing just wasn't right.

When Lincoln stupidly got himself kidnapped, whether it was his fault or not, Kai had taken it as some kind of failure on his part. I'd blamed Lincoln, even if I shouldn't. I'd been so upset about it all that my emotions didn't make sense to me.

And poor Kai. Lincoln's kidnapping triggered something within Kai that no one could understand. Even though he had never seen a shrink about it, I knew for a fact that he struggled with some kind of PTSD. Really bad. I had hinted that he needed professional help, but he just shrugged it off. A lot of people do that. Clearly, the best way to cure a disease is to simply imagine that it wasn't there in the first place.

Chloe brought my attention back to her with a sound of delight. "Well, finally, you admit something happened. Tell me more."

"There's nothing more to tell. Just a few kisses." I felt my face going red.

"You know what he's into right?" Chloe asked, a hint of worries in her eyes.

I nodded. I'm curious and I'm not a complete idiot. I knew what Kai liked.

"BDSM, bondage, or whatever you cool kids call it these days." My face was practically melting now. I'd all but admitted I knew what she and my brother were into as well as Kai.

"And you know he has a reputation?"

I shook my head, no. "What reputation?"

"Oh, sweet girl."

"What? Tell me!"

She took a deep breath in. "It depends on how you look at it."

I could tell that Chloe was trying to find the right words, a nice way to put what she was about to tell me.

"You don't need to protect me from him. I'm a grown up you know."

She tilted her head slightly, giving me a sideway glance. Slowly, she nodded. "I mean a lot of those rich boys are the same, they kind of sleep around, you know."

That didn't really surprise me.

What surprised me was my brother's devotion to her. I knew it was disrespectful to think of my big brother as a man slut, but I couldn't help knowing full well that he was. Or used to be one.

"Unlike Link." I smiled, but it wasn't very nice.

"Yeah, but your brother is a weirdo. But I also heard that Kai's looking for a bride." Her eyes cut to me, soft and gentle, despite my cattiness.

My little heart did a little dance knowing that he was finally ready to settle down.

"And I met his potential bride. Lucy something." I didn't know what possessed me to say that. But it was a fact. And that also killed the little dance in my heart.

"Miss me, bitch?" Shouting at the top of her lungs, Wendy barged into the room without even checking who was inside. Chloe got up from her chair and hugged Wendy. Her eyes squinted as she looked at me, telling me that we weren't done with our conversation.

I stood up automatically to welcome Wendy, and she gave me a hug even though we were never the hugging kind of friends.

Grabbing another chair for Wendy, all three of us sat in a triangle, like we were in some tight knit gossip circle. I wanted to stay with the girls as long as I could, and I had no intention to head outside.

Out there, I would have to do mindless chit chat about my campaign. Luring and sweet-talking people into parting with their money to support us. It was all for good cause, there was no doubt about it, but I found mingling tiring – and I had hired campaign managers for that.

Chloe went on talking about her pregnancy. Mostly the news of her carrying twins but nothing about her diabetes. Like me, Wendy wanted to hear everything that was happening in Chloe's life. I knew that Wendy and Chloe were close, and I reminded myself that there was nothing to be jealous of. Wendy had helped her when I couldn't. Wendy protected her from troubles back when Chloe was someone else. Roxie – the infamous pole dancing stripper. She seldom used the name Roxie anymore, except for her stage name. Wendy couldn't help calling her Rox every now and then though.

"June, what the hell are you doing backstage. Everyone is looking for you. You're up next!" Liam stormed into the room, hissing the words at me. I stared at the clock on the wall and realized that I had been hiding back here for half an hour. That's the thing, when you are with the right company, time flies.

"What's wrong?"

"What do you mean what's wrong? Your event is coming up. You need to be out front on the stage." Liam said matter of factly.

"No, I don't. The presenter will handle everything." I was no stranger to this kind of event. I knew that I didn't have to be there. Our presenter, Amelia Anderson, whom our medical group had been using for years, was very experienced in handling events like this and never once in all that time did I have to be out there on stage with her. That was one of the reasons I chose to hire her again and again.

"Yes, but not when you're selling your services."

"Jeez, Liam, why do you have to make it sound dirty?" Wendy chimed in. I wasn't sure if she was flirting with my brother, but it kind of felt like it. I thought she was dating my brother's other best friend.

"Oh! Hi Wendy, nice to see you." His tone changed

completely, to a giddy school boy. "You look very pretty by the way."

"You too." Wendy showed no sign of shyness as her gaze scanned my brother up and down.

"You need to show your face." Liam lowered his voice significantly, almost whispering or hissing at me.

Crap. I had completely forgotten that my auction item went *missing* and now I was auctioning my services. "I'll be right out."

The girls checked on my dress and make up before sending me out.

"There she is." I heard Amelia saying and I wasn't even on the stage yet.

Stage fright was a real thing for me. Flipping my hands vigorously, I tried to hide the shaking, which gave away how nervous I was. The spotlight stalked me as soon as I was on the stage. The strong light made me flinch and I felt really exposed.

"Do we have ten thousand?" Amelia began before I knew it. Before I had a chance to compose myself.

"Ten years of Dr. Bennet's consultations. Ladies, you know that's a bargain, right?" She walked around and pointed at the bidder in the distance., "Thank you madam, fifteen, anyone?"

Amelia pointed to someone else. "Twenty? How about twenty?"

"Wait, Amelia, there's been a mistake," I said, trying to grab her hand, but Amelia walked away, eagerly pointing at new bidders.

Did I hear her right? What was she talking about? I didn't agree to ten years of consultation. That would be insane. I'd only agreed to a year, how had Lincoln gotten it so wrong? I'd told him about my goal to get to China to start a program there.

Fuck. This had to be Lincoln's fault. He either thought that it was a fantastic business strategy to sell me off for ten years, or he hadn't understood what I'd said. My guess was the first one. Business always comes first for him.

"Two hundred and fifty thousand." Amelia repeated after someone shouted a bid.

What had just happened?

Someone was willing to make that kind of donation for my time? Did they know that they couldn't lock me up and have me treat them 24/7 for ten years?

There was a flaw in what they were selling.

It was false advertising.

If I had to offer ten years of service, it would be a few sessions each year. Did they know what they were bidding on?

I tried to find the person who bid next, but the spotlight had made it impossible to see more than 5 feet away from where I was standing.

"Wow, that was a very generous bid." Amelia's sweet tone suggested that she was more than thrilled about the amount, but then she should be. A mere ten treatments from me could add up to that amount, especially the IVF treatments. "But sir, are you bidding on behalf of your wife or loved one?"

I took a small step forward, trying to see the audience clearly.

"We aren't sure that Dr. Bennet could take care of your womanly needs." The crowd laughed at Amelia's comment. "Two hundred and fifty thousand going once."

I could tell that Amelia was eager to close the deal. First, people were probably as confused as I was and had no idea what they were bidding on. And secondly, 250,000, was as good as it got, for something as vague as ten years of consultation with me.

It better not be Lincoln behind this bid.

I hated it when he thought he could help me by just throwing money my way.

The audience's increasing chatter was proof that they had started to lose interest in this auction. Who could blame them?

"I'll double it if she would swap that for ten dates instead," someone in the crowd shouted.

I recognized the voice.

It can't be.

Kai didn't have an invitation to this event.

"Have we got a secret admirer for Dr. Bennet here?" Amelia chuckled and the crowd laughed with her. "And sir, I'm not sure you understand how an auction works. You just placed a bid against yourself. But I have to say, if you're doing this on purpose, it has to be the most romantic way on earth to ask a girl out."

Blank. That was the only way to describe my mind right now. The spotlight had somehow managed to pierce through my eyes, straight into my brain, and had erased everything.

Amelia turned around and whispered to me. "Dr. Bennet, ten dates in exchange for 500,000 dollars. What do you say?"

I stood there for a good minute without saying anything. Was that really Kai? Or someone who sounded oddly like him? Ten dates weren't much, but a lot could happen in ten dates. Hell, even three. Or one.

A man in a tux approached the stage area and our eyes locked.

"Just say yes." He mouthed the words at me.

"Yes, definitely." I answered. Loud and clear. And I was amazed at how confidently the word came out of my mouth.

Had I just sold myself for half a million dollars?

The whole thing felt like a dream. I headed off the stage and left as the audience whispered among themselves. The girls were as shocked as me. Chloe had her concerns about Kai and his games, but she knew that I've had a crush on him forever.

Wendy couldn't stop talking about how romantic the whole thing was, and what I should do for Kai in return, in bed. Wendy had a way dirtier mind than the innocent, oh so serious look that she projected to the world. Chloe had never really said anything dirty to me, even though she was a stripper at one point of her life. Did I fail to mention that she was also part owner of a sex club? A prestigious and secretive one that only the elite knew about. I was sure Kai and my brothers were members.

Kai came through the back and the ladies made some strange teasing noise – oohing and aahing – at us.

"I think he's come to claim his prize." Wendy couldn't stop herself from saying.

I took a deep breath, squared my shoulders, and prepared for battle. In the dress that he bought me. I smoothed my hands down my sides and waited.

"How did you manage to get a ticket?" I asked as we sat down at my table. My jaw felt tight, and I wasn't sure if I was angry or pleased, but I hid it. For now.

"I made your assistant an offer she couldn't refuse. I offered her $100,000 for her ticket, but she refused it. When I saw a giant vagina costume being taken into the back, I offered to donate the same amount if she stood outside taking pictures with your guest." Kai opened the button on his tuxedo jacket as he settled back in his chair, looking rather pleased with himself. "She accepted the second offer."

I was surprised that she rejected the money and chose to have the money given to charity instead. But then, she does support our charity work and is good at her job.

"I can see why she doesn't like you." I said nonchalantly.

"Ouch, I thought we were best buds." He teased me. "She was just jealous that I've got you."

Picking up my hand, he pressed it to his lips.

I frowned at his remark. "What are you saying?"

"That girl is in love with you." He said it as if it wasn't an earth-shattering idea.

"What?" I gasped, pulling back.

Really? Siti was in love with me? I had no clue. I had a peculiar *curiosity* about hot female celebrities – Angelina Jolie and Scarlett Johanssen were among my favorites, but I had never explored the other side of my sexuality. If there was a scale for my sexual preference, I would still prefer men, ninety-nine percent of the time.

So, yes. There was one percent chance that I could be gay. It had to be someone as hot as Angelina or Scarlett though. Unfortunately for Siti, I didn't feel the same way about her.

Kai stayed with me for the rest of the evening while I handled the mundane tasks, greeting and chatting to my guests. He waited patiently while I encouraged them to donate. He started to look a little bored when I thanked those that already had for their generosity.

Lincoln and Chloe headed back to Myrtle Beach right away on their helicopter. My brother was very serious when it came to parenting. He'd promised my niece a story before bed and that was the reason he was determined to be there. It was amusing to see him getting annoyed with Chloe and I – as we took our time to hug it out and say our goodbye.

I snickered as I remembered the way he glared at me. The big brother glare. But I couldn't say I got the message he was trying to deliver. Was it a warning? Concern? Good luck? Or I know what you did last summer? I'd shrugged at him, hoping that he could get my simple message – your message is as clear as mud.

If I had to guess, Lincoln was trying to say something about the auction. I had kind of announced to the world that I would be going on ten dates with his best friend. His best friend, a bigger man slut than he ever really was.

I knew one thing though. I couldn't handle him doing his big brother thing right now. His stern gaze would have no effect on me. Not today. I had wanted Kai for all this time. And now that he had made his move so clear and obvious, I had no other excuses to walk away from it.

Even if it was for ten fun dates.

I wasn't the naive girl who dreamed of marrying Kai anymore. Ten fun dates could be the way to go. To fuck him out of my system. Forever.

By the time I was ready to leave, it was past midnight. I went back to our table and sat next to Kai – who was busy doing something on his phone.

"I am hoping that I can claim the first date with you tonight."

I wanted to believe that what happened tonight was all real. With the kisses that we shared in the past, there shouldn't be any doubts that there was chemistry between us. However, part of me still couldn't believe it. "You can't be serious right?"

"Why not?" He brushed a misbehaving strand of hair off my face. "I've wanted to ask you out since you turned 18."

"Wait... Do you mean thirteen years ago when you came to my birthday party? When my eyes were swollen from months and months of grieving and my face was covered in snot?"

"Precisely." His glance was soft. Perhaps the champagne had gone to his head, or my head rather, he seemed really dreamy right now. Like we were in an airbrushed dreamy scene in a movie. "It upset me to see a princess so sad. And back then, I wanted to kill the person responsible. Then when I found out the reason you were crying, it broke my heart even further."

He leaned in and I welcomed his lips with mine.

"My brothers aren't going to like it." I mumbled, still kissing him.

"Yeah, I can handle that."

"How?" Another mumbled word. His lips left mine and I immediately missed them.

"Thirteen years ago, I wanted to ask you out. Of course, I asked Lincoln, you know, bro code and all. We made a pack that I could date you on three terms. One – when you're all grown up, working, and have your own career. Two – when I'm all grown up," He chuckled to himself, "have my own career, business, empire or whatever I saw as a career path."

Did he really mean that? My overprotective brother gave his consent to date me? Liam, sure, he made it a point to stay out of my business, and I out of his. But Lincoln? He would never leave any of us alone. Even my mother was scared of his meddling.

"And three?"

"When I'm ready to settle down." Butterflies, a warm sensation filled my belly. That was followed by doubts as Chloe's words about him looking for a bride came back to me. Was I his last hoorah before he settled down with Lucy? Or did he mean me?

There I was, ready to have ten dates, some good sex, and fuck him out of my system. And he just casually hints that he sees me as his future wife? Fuck. He had a way of messing with my heart.

"What about your girlfriends? Your supermodel dates? Your *special* hobby?" I emphasized the word 'special' with a raised eyebrow. I didn't want to say the obvious. It certainly wasn't public knowledge what Kai Li was into, but him being my brother's best friend, I'd learned things about him.

"That was exactly why Lincoln had term three. Your brother wanted me to date all the women I wanted. Any kind. And if I still felt the same way about you, he wouldn't stand in my way. If you'll take me, that is."

What feeling was he talking about?

How could he feel the same thing about the same person after all these years?

I admit that I've had a huge crush on him since I was eighteen. But I was naive. I was barely past believing that Santa was real. As much as I wanted to believe that Santa was real, my scientific mind would just kick me back to reality.

But Kai was my Mr. Right. My soul mate. The one I wanted as my forever love. All these were just some abracadabra made up words, as I'd come to believe over the years. Sitting at our empty table, the large empty ballroom felt small, as the world started to close in on us.

"How did you know that I would date you?"

"Oh princess." He kissed me on my forehead. "I had ladies, young and old, eyeing me up from the day I became a young man. So, trust me when I say I know who likes or dislikes me. My radar has never failed me."

Cocky. But no one could blame him.

He was right. I would always date him. But I wasn't sure I trusted my heart with someone like him.

"How about the other thing?"

"Supermodels? Oh, you know, a lot of them are nothing but good clothes racks."

"Don't be mean." I punched him in the chest.

"Sorry. Yes, I know some of them are very smart but not those that I dated."

"And the *other* thing?" I started to think that he was dodging my question.

"Oh, that–" He took a deep breath. "That world was fun. But it gets boring when you're not into your partner. I'm sad to say it, but I haven't felt any excitement in that world for a while. And I'm ready to give it all up."

"Don't." My voice was small.

The sparkle in his eyes told me that he heard. "Are you serious?"

"I would like to get to know that part of your world." I whispered as liquid fire started to dominate my lower body.

"Oh princess, you have no idea what you're doing to me."

I had a small taste of just that when he kissed me.

15

Kai

I couldn't believe what came out of her mouth. Dirty thoughts flashed through my mind at a million miles an hour, or whatever unit brain scientists used to measure brain activities. Suddenly, I saw life in my much-neglected playroom. The very same one that I thought about transforming into some kind of Zen meditation room. Fuck mindfulness.

She really did surprise me. My impression of her – the innocent good girl – really needed a re-evaluation. I grinned like a giddy teenager who had just heard the word boob for the first time.

At the same time, I felt like an old computer, unable to process the information presented in front of me. I didn't know how best to handle this woman.

We sat on the sides of the chairs at our table, facing each other. A jolt of electricity went through my body, from the bottom of my feet to the top of my skull. That was when I realized that June wasn't wearing her heels anymore. Her toe was stroking my ankle as light as a feather.

The little game of footsie she was playing sent blood flowing straight to my southern regions.

Her pupils were dilated, and her eyes were the darkest shade of green I had ever seen. That was a signal. Strong and clear.

There was something else in her eyes, and it felt like a challenge. Daring me to rock her world. I looked around the room. Most of the guests had left. There were a few drunk stragglers left wandering around the other parts of the venue, but we were alone.

I lifted her chin and planted my lips on hers. That was when I knew that I had done something dangerous.

Her kiss was hot, wet and urgent. Gone were the innocent little pecks that we'd shared before. A purring sound escaped her mouth causing my cock to harden.

She had been a regular guest in my fantasies. My fantasies and my dreams. More often than I would ever admit.

All the women that I had fucked, however filthy and animalistic it got, didn't compare to this moment with June. Every one of my escapades in the past lacked the sensual and intense lust that I found with her. My fantasies of June had always been better than my real-world experiences. In my fantasies, lust and sensual sex was achievable, and there was no other woman who made me feel that way.

I would have never guessed that she was curious about my hobby. My cock got harder as images of what I wanted to do to her flashed through my eyes. The throbbing was so hard that it started to hurt.

My fingers would no longer take instructions from my conscious mind. They traced along her leg, starting with that naughty toe. I drew small circles with my fingers until they reached the bottom of her dress. But the fabric that clung greedily to her couldn't stop me. My palm pressed into her skin, bypassing her dress and swiftly up her outer thigh, feeling her supple soft skin and surprisingly toned muscles.

At the corner of my eyes, I could see shadows lurking. As much as I wanted us to be alone, I knew we weren't. Her gaze remained on my face, and there was only me, only us in her world right now. Everyone else was irrelevant.

No one had ever looked at me like that.

Like I was their whole world.

I had wanted her since yesterday. I wanted her three years ago. Thirteen years ago. For what felt like my entire life, I'd wanted this woman.

Her crush on me was clear to me from day one. Though I hid mine from her, my crush was no less powerful than the one she had for me.

The timing was perfect. The timing was now. There was no reason to hesitate now. Yet, I, Shanghai's number one playboy, failed to act at the moment. I didn't know what to do now that I had her in the palm of my hands.

Her mouth slightly opened, letting out a gasp as my fingers flattened on her thigh. Or was it a sigh? The pause on my part had finally got to her. Before I knew it, her hand found mine. June guided my hand between her thighs and I watched her face as the muscles of her inner thigh clenched, relaxed, and then went into a slight tremble.

She wanted me to touch her. And she showed me how.

Fuck!

It was sexy as hell.

My body ached. My mind wanted this, wanted the relief she offered, relief that I had refused myself for so long for her.

The heat that radiated from her inner thigh tore away all my concerns and worries. I didn't care who was left in the building, watching us or not.

There was only one thing left on my agenda for the rest of the evening.

Worshiping June.

An urge to please her overcame me. I wanted to claim what was rightfully mine.

Her moans and screams. Her shakes and trembles. Highs or lows. Good or bad. I wanted to be the reason for all that. Tonight. And from now on.

As if she could read my mind, she smirked, silently asserting her control. She reached for my tie, yanking me closer until her face was just inches away from mine. Her fingers twirled the silk, and when she released it, her touch trailed down, following the fabric all the way to the zipper of my trousers. Her fingers worked quickly, undoing the zipper slowly, popping the button, and then I felt her warm, silky hand on my length. My hand on her thigh tensed, making her breathe out a sharp sound that knotted my stomach with hunger—for her.

Out of nowhere, I felt her wetness. She wasn't wearing anything beneath her dress. No trace of underwear. That was when I understood the real reason she'd gasped. She grinned, clearly pleased by my discovery, and then surprised me: her other hand slid down, boldly caressing my swollen cock. It felt incredible. So damn good. I couldn't help myself. I rubbed against her hand greedily.

With her other hand still over mine beneath her dress, she guided two of my fingers into her opening. She was wet, oh so hot, and silky. I knew exactly where this was going—a place consumed by lust. But even though I thought I knew the destination, I felt lost—in her gaze, her scent, her touch. Everything I'd learned about her over the years seemed to vanish in an instant. I no longer recognized the person in front of me.

Her body began to move, riding my fingers as her other hand rhythmically stroked me in sync. I hadn't gone long without a lover, but this felt like I was discovering something entirely new, as if I was being *touched for the very first time*. I shook my head, chuckling to myself. She was something else. All the experience I've had over the years melted away, leaving her completely in control of my body and soul.

"Are you going to claim this as your first date?" she whispered, her eyes wide and innocent but her voice breathy and insistent.

Here? In public? I'd had sex in public before—dark cinema rooms, alleyways, in the open acceptance of a certain type of club—but never in a grand ballroom in one of the world's most prestigious hotels.

My hesitation was enough to make her impatient. She yanked my tie hard, our faces now inches apart.

"It's now or never, Kai" she breathed.

"You don't mean that?" I asked, although I was enthralled by what she was doing. This was my kind of play: daring, pushing boundaries, seductive.

Still, I was hesitant—not because I didn't want it, but because I wasn't sure I'd be able to stop if we started. Especially not with her. A part of me tried to resist, but the part that wanted her was winning.

"You don't know what you're asking."

Her lips parted, and she breathed, "Yes, I do. You have no idea how much I've thought about this."

"This?" I challenged, pulling my face back slightly to deny myself the kiss I craved, forcing her to tell me exactly what she wanted.

"Yes." She pushed me back into my chair, lifting her dress just enough to keep her modesty as she climbed on top of me. "Do you know how much I wished I could be one of those women you bring to these events? The one you'd go home with and...take completely?"

A tear slipped down her cheek, and I swallowed, wanting to apologize, but she pressed a finger to my lips.

"It hurt that you never asked me," she whispered, her fingers now combing through my hair.

"Oh, if only you knew how much I wished I had."

"Really?" She seemed doubtful. I wished I'd been ready for her sooner. I'd wasted so much time.

"Believe me, I wanted this as much as you do."

I hadn't exactly imagined her confessing her feelings and riding my fingers in public, but I'd fantasized about her, us, in countless other ways, each scenario filthier than the last.

"Prove it." Dr. June Bennet challenged me, a look in her eyes that invited me to prove her wrong, dared me to do it. Still, something in her tone was playful yet insistent, as if she didn't quite trust my words alone. This wasn't the obedient girl I thought I knew, the one who'd do everything her family expected of her.

My mouth crashed into hers, and lust took over. I fumbled under her dress, found her even wetter, impossibly hotter, and definitely ready for me. She gasped against my lips, her hips grinding on me, and her hand found me, sending pleasure surging through me.

For a moment, the awareness that we weren't alone tugged at the edges of my mind, but I shoved it away. She sank down onto me, making me realize she'd already freed me. I pulled her close, burying my face between her cleavage, groaning as her walls gripped me, her hips moving in a rhythm meant only for us. My hand on the toned globes of her ass guided her movements, urging her closer as she moved faster, occasionally leaning down for hot, messy kisses. The chair creaked in protest, but we ignored it. Her green eyes darkened, shining with ecstasy, a hint of gold flickering within them. She arched her back, her head falling back, moans spilling from her lips as I felt her clench around me.

Like a teenage boy, I followed her, eager for the same pleasure she'd taken from me. She gasped, moaned my name, as I surged into her, her fingers in my hair, her lips at my ear. She held me as I exploded deep inside of her, clutched at my back as I shuddered beneath her, urging me to take what I wanted with her lips at my ear.

"June," I groaned her name, gasping as she pulled away to look into my eyes. She grinned down at me before she collapsed on top of me, giggling as she peppered my face with kisses. It was over too quickly for my liking. I never thought I'd complain about a quickie, but with her, it wasn't enough. I wanted more.

I wanted all of her.

I NEVER REALLY UNDERSTOOD THE appeal of watching someone sleep.

Until now.

There was something really serene about it. The whole world was muted, and I wanted it to stay that way. The urge to keep that silence was strong.

A crack of lightning outside the hotel suite window made me realize that the silence was about to be broken, and there was nothing I could do about it.

The Thompson hotel didn't use cheap interior designers. The walls were thick and laid with luxurious wallpaper that was changed well before it started to look tired. But the walls and windows were not entirely soundproof. Not enough. Not for what was about to happen.

There. The loud sound of the thunder made June fidget ever so slightly. Though it sounded stupid, I couldn't help but wonder if the thunder sounded louder on the top floors of buildings this high.

June rubbed her half-opened eyes and blinked lazily. "What time is it?"

Supporting my upper body with my elbow, I leaned in and kissed her forehead.

"It's 4:20. Go back to sleep."

"But I don't want this night to end." A yawn took over and she fell back to sleep right away. She had left her hand casually on my upper thigh.

"You want more, princess?" I whispered as I stroked her hair.

After our rather public display of affection, we came up to the suite reserved under the Bennet Medical Group. It was a complimentary room given by the hotel as a token of appreciation for booking their grand ballroom. Although, with the connections that June had, she could easily get any room she wanted for free.

However, I couldn't imagine June doing that. She would never take advantage of her friends, or their businesses like that. It was a common practice in business, to use your connections to get things done. Of course, a little deal here and there that benefited everyone, wasn't so bad. That is how we keep the world going round.

I was surprised that the staff that worked the gala had actually used the room. As we came into the room, frantically touching and kissing each other, we kept bumping into things that were just laying around the room. We'd tripped over some open boxes, then bags of unknown items, and what looked like extra promotional materials.

There wasn't any time to rearrange the room. We both wanted to be absolutely naked together, to have more of what we'd had in the ballroom. A lot more. In the end, we had three or four more sessions until June practically dropped dead.

The sex was simple and vanilla. There wasn't anything overly kinky. Well, apart from some spanking here and there. But I definitely loved every moment of it.

My heart was in it. It wasn't like all the other times, when I was merely seeking a thrill and the need to get off.

Frankly, it scared me a little. I knew who I was fucking. My best friend's sister, the one I wasn't supposed to be fucking around with, unless I was willing to offer her the keys to my castle. And when I called her princess, I meant it. Every single time.

I wandered into the mini bar area and found a fridge. A full-sized, fully stocked refrigerator, apart from raw items, which make sense as they didn't have the facilities to cook in the room. I settled on a bottle of Perrier then unscrewed the lid. The fizziness from the water was loud in the quiet room. It wasn't something I usually noticed. The chaos in my head wouldn't allow me to notice the little things in life.

Then the rain started. That was something I did notice, every now and then. I enjoyed the gentle sound of rain, even when it came as a heavy downpour.

"Water seems like a great idea." Her voice startled me. It was still sleepy and tired.

I turned to see her right behind me, a sleepy smile on her face.

"Did I wake you?" I asked, brushing hair back from her face.

"No. Well, kind of."

"I'm sorry." It wasn't sorry that I was feeling. But I did feel guilty for not letting her rest more.

"Well, I'm not." She snatched the bottle from my hand and sipped. "That felt nice. I love the taste of fizzy water."

I tilted her chin and brought her lips to mine.

"Who knew fizzy water could taste so divine."

"Are you calling me plain and simple?" She pulled her face back from mine.

"No. Of course not." That wasn't what I meant at all. Did I say something I didn't mean to by mistake? I had known that women interpret things differently than men. I've never bothered to explain myself to the women I dated – I didn't give a shit.

Her side glance and a raised eyebrow told me that she'd been joking, but I couldn't be sure. I couldn't tell what she was actually thinking anymore.

"I'm just kidding." June finally said, with a cheeky grin. What a massive relief.

"Phew..."

"But I want you to show me..." She bit her lower lip. Now that totally worked for me. It was so fucking sexy my cock was ready to go again.

The lip biting thing was something I didn't quite understand before. Why were Americans obsessed with women biting their lower lip? It wasn't a thing in Asia. Now, seeing June do it, I finally understood.

"Show you what?" I wanted to pretend I knew what she meant but I really couldn't. But I sure as hell hoped that it had something to do with sex.

"You know..." June leaned back on the fridge and like a magnet, my face followed her, leaving only an inch between us. "I want to know what turns you on."

A knot formed in my throat. My dick was dangerously close to breaking out of its cage – my boxer shorts.

"You."

She shook her head, like a schoolteacher disapproving of a lie. I had a feeling that if there was room between her head and the fridge, she would move it further back to punish and starve me from her sweet cherry lips.

"I don't want the standard answer you give to your dates." June replied with a pout to those luscious lips as she spoke.

"It's true."

"Do you like it rough?" She bit her lower lip again.

"Do you?"

"It was surprisingly arousing when you spanked me." That didn't quite answer my question, though I realized that I'd answered her question with a question.

"Did it hurt?" I stroked her soft jawline.

"A little." She cast her eyes down to the floor, innocently, and somehow, that made me even harder.

"I'm sorry princess." I wanted to stroke her cheek, but I was too worried it would change the moment. We needed to have this conversation, so I held back.

"But I liked it." She gave me a pout that sent me to crazy land.

Suddenly I got it. I understood how those silly things like biting their lower lips and pouting, made American men lose their minds. This timid, shy display from *her*, was fucking beautiful. And suddenly, I couldn't wait to have her on her knees, or on my table in my playroom.

Her naughty confessions, combined with her lip biting were all she ever needed to turn me on. The rest were all brownie points. Speaking of brownie points, I could see her starting to move, then I felt her hip dancing, brushing on my painfully hard cock, hungry for the sweet tight pussy that belonged to her.

I lifted her up with one arm. June moved gracefully, like she'd done this before and wrapped her legs around my waist. She was going to let me take her wherever I wanted. And do whatever I wanted to her.

The bed was too far for us right now. The way she settled her lips on my neck, sucking hungrily at a place below my jaw, told me that she agreed with me on this. Reaching for the nearest surface, I put her naked ass on the desk by the window.

Removing my shirt that she'd put on, I could see that she was ready and had been ready for a while. Her pussy was dripping wet, so wet that the sides of her thighs were moist from it. The redness and rawness of her pussy from our last few sessions didn't stop her from wanting more.

Without wasting another second, I found her folds and thrust so hard that the desk moved a few inches.

"Now we're talking..." She squirmed as she mumbled those words.

I chased the desk and stroked into her a few more times. Objects from the desk fell off one by one as my thrusts shook the whole surface. She clung to the edge of the desk hard to steady herself. I couldn't control the need I felt for her, the need to claim her with powerful strokes that kept pushing the desk until it bumped up against the floor to ceiling window.

But our game of chase wasn't over.

June crawled backward until she was back-to-back with the window, a teasing, inviting smile on her face that I couldn't resist. I climbed on top of the desk, left knee first, then my right. Then, like the seductress that she was, she climbed on top of my lap and rocked.

I held on to her back as she ground down onto my cock, bringing us closer with each movement she made. Our eyes locked together, and she leaned in to run her tongue along mine before she pressed her plump round breasts into me.

I heard her gasp when I pulled back and cupped her right breast, bending neck to take her nipple into my mouth, sucking at it hard. She moaned a sound then that made my dick grow even harder, harder than I ever thought it could be.

She must have noticed the way my cock swelled inside of her. Her eyes lit up, then she wrapped her arms around my back.

Our bodies were tightly fused together as her rock turned into a mix of rocking and bouncing.

She was fucking me. Her movement grew aggressive and faster. I matched her rhythm thrust for thrust. Then her tight pussy spasmed around me and I knew she was coming. The way her walls gripped me, the strangled sounds of pleasure she made, sent me over the edge. I didn't even care that her nails clawed at my back, I was coming deep inside of the only woman that ever mattered to me, and it was heaven.

16

———

Kai

You should not live your life for your family, I thought in a half-awake, half-asleep state.

The word family had different meanings in my life over the years.

Mom hated Dad's guts for cheating on her and our family. But they never failed to post a happy family image for the media and social media whenever it was necessary. They pretended all the arguments and disagreements were nothing but rumors. To the world, we were this picture-perfect family without a single skeleton in our closet.

I have no idea how much I could do to protect Jenny from our world, our lives, but I would try my best. After all, she was the only person that I deemed as real family. The only person that I could talk to. Really talk to. And without having to bury or bend any truths.

Her pregnancy had to be kept a secret, for now.

For her own sake.

Her husband wouldn't give up looking for her. Not because

he loved her dearly, but rather because he would see her disappearance as a betrayal of their marriage, of his pride. However, in our world, betrayal was a one-way street. It was deemed as acceptable, even necessary for men to entertain the idea of affairs and mistresses. But for a woman, it would be frowned upon. And leaving your husband? That was a sin too far, even if he was a monster. Women weren't given the same consideration in our world.

A woman who cheated was often seen as a witch. The social circles we lived in would socially shame them. I bet they would be hanged like the witches of Salem.

Things were changing in China though.

Divorce rates were going up. People were allowed to leave their spouses if they decided that they were no longer suitable for each other for whatever reason. However, for the upper class and the wealthy it was still deemed as socially unacceptable behavior.

At least with June being Jenny's doctor, I didn't have to worry about the medical side of things. I trusted her judgment more than I trusted myself. And I was sure that June wasn't about to leak Jenny's information to anyone that could cause her any harm.

It wasn't hard to get someone to keep a secret though. You just have to offer them enough incentive. Money was one thing that people often cannot refuse. If they cannot be bought by money, then give them an opportunity – something that only you could offer, be it a limited contract from your company, some out of reach item they craved, or an introduction to someone they admired deeply.

When playing nice doesn't work, there are other means to get people to cooperate. Threats, extortion, and kidnapping were all possibilities. In fact, the possibilities are endless, if you have the right kind of imagination. This kind of dirty work isn't easy in the modern world, not when security has been tightened around the world. But if you offered enough money, someone would always pick up the job.

Jenny's husband had a disgusting habit. His good looks and charming personality meant that he was never short of any attention from the ladies. However, he liked to pay for his sex. I had known for years about his dirty little secret, and it wasn't hard to find out when his personal driver escorted different women in and out of his office on a weekly basis. Besides that, he also kept a couple of love nests with some B-list actresses.

How did Jenny end up with someone so disgusting?

She didn't choose it.

Her parents had arranged this marriage for her as soon as she graduated from her university. They wanted to strengthen their business empire through marriage. By marrying their daughter to the Chen Family. Jenny's dad could tap into different businesses, establish new relationships through their new in-laws.

My innocent cousin fell hopelessly in love with her husband Erik Chen, though. To be fair to him, he was sweet to her at the beginning. Jenny's parents kept her on a tightrope all her life and would control every person she met. My poor cousin had never really been with a man until Erik.

When Erik showered Jenny with presents and attention – be it the right or wrong kind – she gobbled it up like a starving stray dog.

There was no doubt that Eric was just playing his part in finding himself a good, proper wife. One that was approved of by his family. And Jenny fit into the role perfectly. They were seen as the perfect couple, both wealthy and gorgeous, a match made in heaven. Their marriage was often featured in the Asian tabloids as the dream couple of Shanghai.

I suspected his dirty little habits before they announced

their engagement. The rich Asian boys circle really wasn't that big. And people talk – men included.

He had the courtesy to invite me to his bachelor party, hosted by his secret club. The club often organized getaways on some private exotic island for an unforgettable weekend. Though I politely declined the invite, many of my friends went – it wasn't hard to find out what happened at the party.

I'd thought about saying something about Erik's disgusting habit to Jenny's parents. In fact, I was sure that someone she knew had mentioned something about it. But Jenny fell in love so fast with him that she wouldn't hear anything negative about him.

Lucy's presence reminded me about my own fate. She was handpicked by my mother – her favorite among all the women she wanted me to date. Was her being here solely because I'd asked her as Jenny's best friend, or was there more to it? She had not caused me any problems since she'd arrived though, and she'd been a good friend to Jenny. I would be forever in her debt for that.

I brushed the thoughts away. Second-guessing her right now did me no good. There was no doubt that she cared about Jenny and with her help keeping my cousin company I could keep watch over June.

I could keep my woman, my princess, safe.

My PI hasn't had any news about Mack since his disappearance. It would probably take a few more days if he were to extend his search worldwide. For now, we have to make sure that he doesn't go anywhere near June. However, having to secure her workplace had proven to be rather challenging. We had to make sure that every entrance to the hospital was watched. I wanted every person in and out of the hospital to be identified.

Siti was the one who woke me this morning in the hotel suite.

She woke me with a cough so loud that I worried about her lung health. Right after I opened my eyes, I had to block off a bunch of flying objects aimed at my face. The woman literally threw my clothes at me before leaving the bedroom.

June was nowhere to be seen.

There was no sweet note next to me saying "call me" either. I guess romance only existed in old movies.

I got dressed and saw that it was only 7 o'clock as I put my watch on. A team of five or six people were busy removing the materials they'd left in the suite the night before, while I took my time making myself a cup of coffee.

I wanted to ask Siti where June was. Judging by the grumpy look on her face, she was in no mood to talk to me about her boss.

If I had to guess, Siti came in and found June and I naked in bed. She then woke her boss and let her sneak out of the room with dignity so she could shame me with that dirty look of hers.

It was all speculation, of course, because I had no idea when June left. Siti didn't say a word to me apart from coughing and glaring at me here and there.

Part of me was sad that June left without telling me.

The other part was just mad for not noticing her leaving. How would I protect her if I failed at something as simple as that?

A quick phone call to Dave had eased all my worries. She was seen leaving the hotel not too long ago.

I was greeted by a mess at home. In the living room to be precise. The coffee table was covered in bottles of beverages and delivered food. And piles of expensive looking fabric laid on the floor. Lucy and Jenny seemingly had their own party going on last night. Picking up a bottle, I was glad that they were at least sensible enough to not drink alcohol.

"Hey, zao." I turned around and saw Lucy standing there in a long champagne-colored nightgown, the satin glued to her skin like it was part of her. She had no makeup on, and her hair was a little messy but still perfect. Damn, she was a sight that would cause an instant hard-on if I hadn't already had so much sex last night. And if she'd been June.

"Morning." My brain told me not to stare at her Pilate body. "Did you guys have a party last night?"

"Yeah, what about it?" She chuckled lightly. "We had a fashion show, and plenty of food, of course. Apparently, Jenny's baby loves American junk food."

"Is that so?"

"Yeah, pizza, fried chicken, burgers, American style Chinese food."

I shook my head at the list of things she'd just listed, but I knew that wasn't all of it.

"Shouldn't she be eating something healthy right now? Something more nutritious? You know I own several restaurants in New York, right? They could easily whip up something healthy for her, and you, of course."

"Of course. But we wanted the naughty food. Plus, I could hardly say no to a pregnant lady."

She was right. The only way to make Jenny happy was to satisfy her needs. Her cravings.

"Umm..." I forced myself to stop staring at Lucy below the neck. Regardless of how much sex I'd had last night, I couldn't help but stare at a body so stunning as hers. I was still a man, after all. "Do you want a coffee? I can make us a coffee."

She probably didn't really need coffee. It was just a line I used to get out of an awkward situation.

"It's okay. I should get dressed and maybe take a nap." Lucy answered, looking down at the mess she and Jenny made the night before.

"Wild party, huh?" I said, wincing at how stupid I sounded.

Of course, we'd already gone over all of this, so I knew that was lame.

"You could say that." Lucy turned around and went back to her room, leaving me in peace, at last.

On the way to my room, I found Jenny's door ajar. The soft snoring that came from inside felt remarkably comforting to me. I could never say that I understood what my sweet cousin had been through, because I knew I never would. I was just glad that she thought of me when she needed shelter and some peace.

Having Lucy here has been a great help. A fast food party and pretend fashion show was definitely not something I would think of to do to cheer Jenny up.

I couldn't help but wonder what would have happened if I hadn't come on to New York. If I followed through on the dates that my mother planned for me and Lucy, would I have fallen for her?

About an hour later, just as I stepped out of the shower, June called. The call made me ridiculously happy, and my dick clearly remembered our night and it was eager to say hello to her too. Disappointment quickly overrode my happiness when I found out that the phone call had nothing to do with me. She wanted to have Jenny come into the clinic for a blood test and another consultation. Still, it made me giddy thinking that she had chosen to make the call herself rather than having her grumpy assistant do it.

Fuck.

I had fallen so fast for her.

As much as I liked her, I hated that I had no control over how she made me feel.

At eleven o'clock, Jenny, Lucy and I were back again at June's office. Lucy and Jenny sat in front of the doctor's desk. I stood next to Jenny as there wasn't another chair for me.

Some nurses gave us an odd look as we entered, and I

couldn't blame them. We were an odd combination of people as we came through the clinic. Mother to be, with her straight male cousin, and her best friend, that hardly seems right.

"It's good to see you again." June stood up and shook Jenny's hand, then Lucy's. A little too formal if you ask me, like she'd purposely put up a wall between us. The doctor and the patient. I gave her a nod but didn't shake her hand. My body ached to be close to her, a hug would be sufficient. But now just wasn't the right time.

"I just saw you yesterday. Is everything okay?" Jenny's voice was small, but her concerns were not.

"Do you want to do this in private?" June's eyes paused at Lucy and then me. The hint was loud and clear. As much as I wanted to know everything that was happening to my cousin's health, I respected that she might want some privacy. I turned around, ready to leave the room.

"Please stay. I can't do this alone." Jenny pleaded, "and you too, Lucy."

She grabbed Lucy's hand.

"Okay. I believe Dr. Rose has told you about her diagnosis. We had a discussion about the prescription you'd been taking. And those that Dr. Rose recommended that you take." June paused for a second, acknowledging my stern stare, begging for her to tell us more.

"Yes." Jenny's voice is soft and weak.

"I'm concerned that the medications may cause complications for your pregnancy, for you and your baby's health. It could cau–"

"I want to keep the baby." Jenny blurted out, interrupting June and the information she was telling us. "I don't care. I want to keep the baby."

Jenny shook her head no, contradicting her words.

And I wanted to know what was going on. What was the diagnosis?

"Are you aware of the increased risk of miscarriage, birth defects, and stillbirth with your medications?" June pressed firmly. "And–"

"Yes. Yes. Yes." Jenny was at the border of shouting. "I know. I read about it all."

Suddenly, I realized that Jenny would be risking her health for something that had barely formed. The baby was a cancer, an unwanted cancer that should be taken care of.

"Qing Qing." I called Jenny's childhood nickname. "You want to think about this?"

Erik Chen and his stupid children had caused Jenny enough heartache. I had no idea why she would go through another pregnancy.

"I'm sure." Jenny said, avoiding eye contact with me. "I want to keep this baby. If God doesn't bless me with a healthy baby, then so be it. But if I can carry this baby to full term, then I'm going to raise the baby alone." She paused for two seconds, "Kai, I know you hated Erik from the beginning. And you hated my kids."

"I don't hate your kids."

"Then what are their names?"

Trouble and Smelly.

"I–" There were no words. I couldn't remember her boys' names. I only wished that Lucy wouldn't jump in and volunteer. It would only make me look worse, though.

"I don't blame you. But I can't say that I am not disappointed." Lucy handed Jenny a tissue from her brown leather bag.

"I'm sorry." I truly was. I could never stand someone crying. Especially someone I cared deeply about.

"I know you are. But your words are meaningless to me."

I agreed. My words meant nothing to her. I should have tried harder in the first place.

"I needed you to be a better cousin." Jenny continued, "I love Erik so much. But I need a divorce. Not want. I *need* one."

"It's okay, sweetie." Lucy rubbed the side of Jenny's arm as she struggled to talk now.

"But I'm weak. I can't do it." She sobbed, "He won't like it. It will ruin what he, what *we* stand for. And I know me, I'll change my mind if he starts to beg. I don't really know what he will do to me, or my kids."

"I won't let him near you." Divorce wasn't something her family would support. Not mine either, that was why my parents were still legally married. "Whatever you want, Qing. I'll support you no matter what."

I put a hand on top of her shoulder.

She looked up and tears streamed down her cheeks. "I don't want to lose my children. Don't let him take them from me."

"The fucker can try." My tone came out much more brutal than I intended. "He will have to walk over my dead body."

"Okay." June's voice softly interrupted us, before this meeting turned into something else. "I would like to monitor you closely throughout your pregnancy. Is that okay?"

Jenny nodded again, this time with a small smile.

"Is it okay if we get a blood sample from you?" June asked, her voice gentle and reassuring, just what Jenny needed right now. I respected her more for that.

"That's fine." Jenny gulped in a breath of air before she sobbed again, her tears falling faster now.

June handed Jenny another tissue for her tears.

That was pretty much the end of the consultation. Jenny was escorted by a nurse to have her blood drawn. I signaled for Lucy to go with her while I stayed to have a chat with the doctor. None of them suspected my real intentions.

"Hey you!"

I popped back into June's office after a quick check on her next appointment in the waiting area. They hadn't arrived yet. I grinned wickedly because that meant Siti didn't have a reason to stop me from staying a little longer.

"Hey! Shouldn't you be with Jenny?" Her eyes ran over me hungrily, letting me know that she wanted to see me as much as I wanted to see her.

I swiftly approached her chair behind her desk – not giving her an opportunity to get up. I planted a deep kiss on her lips. Fuck, her kisses were intoxicating. Her lips were not thin, but full and plump, making it a very nice kiss.

"Did you miss me?" I asked, needing to know.

"Wow. When did I get myself a clingy boyfriend?" She asked and I felt the masculine side of me leave the building. Strangely, I didn't give a fuck because she just used the word boyfriend.

She let out a chuckle, a very short one when she realized what she'd just said. However, I wasn't going to let it go. "So... interesting. You think I'm your boyfriend?"

She pushed me away from her and sat up straight. I was surprised at how strong she was.

"You heard it wrong. I said–," she paused, and I waited for the word to come out of her mouth when she finally made up her mind.

"What?" I shook the handle of her swivel chair which was a bad idea because it only moved her further from my face.

"Brother." She said finally.

"Brother?" Oh? Did I hear it wrong?

I had wanted to be someone's boyfriend for quite some time. I wasn't one to believe in romantic love. Can you blame me though? My father cheated on my mom, while my mom's life was nothing but plotting against him and his other family. There were so many families like that in China that it jaded me against that idea.

When I found out about Lincoln's mission to find Chloe – the presumed dead girl – simply because of one memorable night he had with her, I thought it was the most laughable thing I had ever heard. But when he found her, and risked everything including his life for her, and she finally loved him back... it made me believe in love again.

Me, believing in love. Who would have thought?

"Yeah, you have always treated me like your little sister, right? You told Lincoln you needed to step up for him and play the big brother role. He told me." June teased me mercilessly.

That was true. I said those words. Mostly to make my feelings for her go away. To make me feel wrong for having feelings for my sister. But my mind couldn't be fooled. It knew that she wasn't my sister.

For years, I had treated and protected her like my own sister. But I'd always wanted more with her.

I leaned into her again, putting more of my weight on the chair arms this time, not giving her another chance to push back.

"Does a brother do this?" I pressed another kiss on her. I groaned as she opened her mouth, letting me explore her with my tongue.

"No." She mumbled, and her tongue was now in my mouth as hungry as mine.

I pulled my mouth away and her face followed mine for more. She sealed her lips tight, pouting as I pulled further away.

"And can your brother do this?" I pulled her neck closer and inhaled her scent. She smelled intoxicating. I trailed my hand down her body as her legs uncrossed, welcoming my next move.

I continued drawing my hands up her skintight skirt and found nothing but her wet center.

I couldn't believe it. She really did have a habit of not wearing underwear.

I checked her face, and she raised an eyebrow with one corner of her mouth.

"You naughty girl. You do this all the time?" I scolded, feeling a little angry. With her going commando under the skintight clothing, it left nothing to the imagination. Any guy could see what was mine. And mine only.

"Isn't it better than showing pantie lines?" She challenged me. And I wasn't sure how I felt about it.

"I don't want other men smelling your scent."

She rolled her eyes, "That's crazy talk. No one can smell me."

"I can. And it drives me crazy." I wasn't lying. She wore a perfume that I wasn't unfamiliar with. It was a very popular perfume made by Vera Wang. But it smelled different on her. The mix of the perfume with her own scent was enough to make me want to jerk off.

"I don't want other men smelling you." I repeated my words, this time with a sterner voice.

"How does wearing a thin piece of fabric help mask the scent?" She was getting bold with her teasing.

"It's better than nothing." I nipped at her earlobe, "and I should spank you for talking back at me."

She made a soft noise that I wasn't expecting. It sounded almost like a moan causing my dick to throb in my jeans.

She reached for my belt buckle and whispered in my ears. "What are you doing tonight?"

I nearly moaned as she tugged at my belt, her cold soft hand caressing my hard abs.

"I – nothing," I stopped having plans after I found out that

Mack was released and could be heading her way. "I've reserved all my evenings for you."

That was as much as I could say to her right now without worrying her about her own safety.

"Oh my god, I'm so sorry." Lucy stood in front of the door, having opened the door without knocking.

"I, uh, I should, I should. Um, Jenny wants to go shopping. Just letting you know that we're leaving." Lucy blurted out the words.

With Lucy still standing there, I adjusted myself, trying to hide the boner in my pants and stood up as straight as possible.

"Good to know." I meant that, it was a good sign that Jenny wanted to go shopping.

"Have Clare take you." I added.

"Will I see you tonight?" Lucy's words flowed out of her mouth smoothly, now fully recovered from the shock earlier.

"I have other plans." My eyes went to June's.

"Oh? A hot date?" Lucy asked, though she sounded like she was snooping for information.

She had started to get on my nerves. I wanted her to be gone like five seconds ago. She shouldn't be in here, in the first place. "Do you have a problem with that?"

"No, of course not. You do whatever makes you happy." Lucy turned around and left without another word.

17

June

Although I hadn't known Lucy for very long, I felt like we could be good friends. There was this Zen air about her. It made people feel calm, relaxed and at ease. At the same time, she wasn't too Zen – so intimidating – that you felt like you were with a sophisticated Buddhist monk.

She was what my mother considered the perfect daughter. On the outside, she had a great fashion sense, hairstyle and make up that my mother would consider on point for a wealthy and well-bred Asian woman. Inside, well, that was not something I could judge. But from what I've seen and heard so far, she was the perfect woman.

Sad maybe, that my mother still worshiped that outdated thinking. While the world had moved on from centuries of stereotyping, dictating how anyone should behave, I remained stuck. Always striving for my mother's approval.

But then, who wasn't?

I had tried for years to change her ways, but I knew better than to to hope she'd change. Sometimes, being happy with myself – finding happiness within was much more important than looking for the joy that was attached to the approval that I would never receive.

I felt sorry for Lucy finding Kai and me in that situation. It was awkward. The shock must have caused the poor woman to lose her ability to converse properly. It just wasn't like her to say something so forward.

But that didn't mean last night with Kai wasn't fun. It was like having the chocolate bar that I had denied myself for centuries. My crush on him had lasted too long. And now that I finally had a taste of what it was like to be in bed with him. I wanted more.

But I knew it had to end somehow.

Ten dates should do it.

Ten minus one.

If we did what we did last night, having the same fantastic sex on each date, then it would definitely be enough. Maybe.

I forced myself to push all the dirty thoughts away – mainly what I wanted to do with Kai – and focus on work.

For the rest of the day, Kai waited outside patiently for me. Needless to say, he had again moved his whole office over. Camping at the corner of the waiting room, working on a coffee table. I had pointed out that he could work at the cafe downstairs, but he refused. I even suggested letting him use one of the empty private suites that was reserved for VIP patients, and again, he rejected the idea.

He said he just wanted to be near me.

Sweet.

And too cute, even for Kai.

I didn't need him to do that. Though it did make my heart sing.

The other part of me couldn't help but wonder what game he was playing. Chloe had warned me that men like Kai always have something up their sleeves – waiting to trick innocent women like me.

Was I innocent, though? People like to think that I was. Perhaps I was, there was no way for me to tell.

Word traveled really fast where I worked. The nurses loved nothing more than good gossip. Linda, the middle-aged nurse who had known me since I was a teenager, told me all about it over a short coffee break.

At first, they thought that Kai was some contractor that my father had hired for the hospital. And I, as usual, had to manage the contractor while they were at work. Things got a bit ridiculous when he donated his sperm. They then said that I had started some kind of program where I promoted the sperm, by having the donor pose as a billionaire within my clinic. Then it quickly escalated after someone confirmed that Kai had placed a bid at the charity event last night. According to the office gossip, the sperm donor had fallen in love hopelessly with the fertility doctor.

There was more, Linda said, but she wouldn't tell me to save me from rolling my eyes too much. All in all, the nurses were happy and enjoyed seeing a handsome guy around. Even if it was around my office.

I had no idea all this gossip was going on, and I didn't like it. People never talked about me. Apart from how nice I was, or rather how big a doormat I was. Anyway, that meant I had to kick Kai out of my clinic.

Well, perhaps after I see this couple from Cheng Du, China.

"Hi, I'm Dr. June Bennet, nice to meet you."

"You speak *pu tong hua*?" The woman answered with a strong accent.

"No, I'm sorry. *Dui bu qi, ni xu yao fan yi ma?*" It meant, 'sorry, do you need a translator'?

Normally, for our overseas clients, we would ask if they

needed a translator before the appointment. The language barrier somehow slipped through the cracks, but we'd soon fix that.

"Yes. Yes." The couple both nodded at my question.

Immediately, I called our translator, but he didn't pick up.

The couple exchanged a few words to each other, then the husband got up and left. I couldn't tell if he was angry that we weren't prepared. And he was partly correct, if he was, we should have done a better job at going over their file. I made a note to discuss it with Siti before I called the translator again but it went straight to voicemail. Then I asked Siti to find him.

The wife stared at me with nothing but an awkward smile. And in return, I gave her an even more awkward smile, with an apology.

A few minutes later, the husband came back to the room with someone. I could hear as he approached the door that he was laughing at something funny.

Kai.

He shouldn't be here.

"Oh no, no, no he's not our translator." I shook my head, feeling a little embarrassed that my patients had misunderstood me completely. "Siti, can you..."

"It's okay, Dr. Bennet." Kai put on a straight face and a tone that indicated there was nothing non-professional between us. Then he poked his head out of the room to let Siti know to ignore my last demand.

I watched Kai and the couple, talking and laughing among themselves. They talked like they had known each other for years, like they were just a bunch of good friends catching up at a coffee shop. I felt like a massive third wheel or fourth in this case, like I should take the hint and leave my own office and let them get on with their conversation.

Two very long minutes later, the woman said to me teasingly, "you lucky girl."

Now I couldn't wait to drill Kai on what they were saying to each other in Chinese.

"Dr. Bennet, are you aware that you have an award-winning actress and director sitting in your office?" Kai raised one of his eyebrows. No, of course, I didn't know. And I appreciated his knowledge on this matter. I should have guessed, the couple were exceptionally attractive. Especially the wife, she had one of those flawless, dewy Korean skin tones that was nearly impossible to obtain unless you lived indoors twenty-four seven all while never being exposed to the sun.

"Do I? I'm so sorry. It was very ignorant of me." I said apologetically.

"No, it's okay. This guy is more famous." Mr. Song pointed his finger at Kai.

"He makes the news more than us." Then he let out a hearty laugh. His English had a very strong accent, but it was perfectly understandable. It seemed like he had no problem understanding me either. We would have no problem having our session without a translator. Without Kai.

I made a mental note for Siti to do a little research on the internet for our patients from now on, just to make sure that we knew who walked through the doors. Not in a weird spying, privacy-invading way – just the normal stuff that was widely available on the web. We could have the president of some country sitting in front of me and I wouldn't know, due to my lack of interest in following news or global political affairs.

"Have I seen anything that you made?" I asked, attempting to make conversation. And to test my patient's English, to collect enough proof that we didn't need Kai there.

"In Chinese mainly." The man added.

More proof that he understood me, but did the woman?

They switched back to Chinese again like they were discussing something they didn't want me to know.

"Oh, that's a shame." And I really meant it. I have never pointed at a TV or billboard at someone and said, oh I treated him or her. It was something that I never planned to do due to patient-doctor confidentiality. But it would be nice to have the fantasy though.

"Mr. Song said he will send you some links later."

"Thanks." I wondered if it would be weird to see my clients on the screen, knowing that I had seen their most private parts.

"And he said you should consider opening a clinic in China. He said he had many friends that came to you, and they all loved you. And many more of his friends were yet to pay you a visit."

Well. That was exactly what the group had planned. They wanted to send me to China years ago, but it fell through. The project was shut down quickly after the pandemic. I sometimes saw that as a blessing. If I had gone to China any time earlier than planned, I would have been stuck there for years, not knowing anyone there but Kai.

I wondered how many of Mr. Song's friends that came to me before were famous and that I had no idea about. Would any of them appear in the movies that Mr. Song was going to send me?

"Thank you. It's good to know."

I had to get control of the appointment back. The first part of the consultation had very little to do with the couple's problem. But I didn't want to stop them talking either. These sessions could be so daunting and stressful for the patients. If a little conversation with Kai helped the couple to relax, then so be it.

I knew that it was really my subconscious trying to keep Kai here a little longer.

I managed to move the session along and discussed what the patients wanted. A lot of people that I came across were very private about their fertility problems, especially the females. They couldn't help but feel like a failure for not being able to get pregnant. However, not this couple. They didn't seem to have any problems sharing their fertility problem with Kai.

I found out that Mrs. Song had been a very successful actress all her life and had decided not to pursue motherhood until later in life. Now, at age 45, and happily married, she wanted to have at least two kids of her own. And they also wanted to consider a surrogate after two years of trying without luck.

I left the men in my office section while I led Mrs. Song to the examination room. Through a translator on her phone, Mrs. Song told me that she had suffered three miscarriages in her life. That they had even taken two years break on their careers to try to conceive. Going on holiday after holiday, trying to conceive at a beautiful location while they were most relaxed. Month after month, nothing happened.

That was when they had decided to get medical help. Like a lot of their friends, to avoid paparazzi, they had chosen to come to America for their fertility treatments, where no one knew who they were.

Part of me felt privileged and the other part of me felt like I was holding their fate in my own hand.

"He's very famous in China. Li Zong." Mrs. Song said, surprising me when she used English.

"Li Zong?" I asked, not sure who she meant. Her husband was Mr. Song.

"Yes, Director Li. The most handsomest. The most successful. Every lady wants to marry him." I got it. Mrs. Song was calling Kai *Director Li*, and I guess that was something they do in China.

"I have no idea." That was partly true. I had known that he was a big deal but on what scale though, I truly had no idea.

"Like Donald Trump, but better... he's handsome."

I chuckled at that. "Well, if you ask around, I'm sure some people consider President Trump handsome too."

He wasn't my type, not by a mile, but you never know what people were into.

"Maybe you can have him to lead your country." I said, referring to Kai.

"Oh, no, no, no. Then he has everything. Money. Beautiful. Sexy. Power."

Mrs. Song's English wasn't as good as her husband's, but I understood her. In the end, we managed her first examination successfully, without any further assistance from *the translator.*

I gestured for Mrs. Song to remove her skirt and lay on the table as I drew up the curtain and stood on the other side for her modesty.

"I think his mother is a tyrant." Her tone turned serious. "Be really careful. I think they think you want his money."

That was new to me.

I was known to as a lot of things in my life, but gold digger was definitely a first.

"I'm not after his money."

She was already on the table. Our eyes locked.

"No matter. They are the top richest. The worst." She added, "I made more money. My mother thinks I want my husband's money."

I should feel offended, but I wasn't. It was the way she said those words, her sincerity that made me understand that she was genuinely being kind to me. What she said was advice, and concern, from one non-gold digger to another.

"Does she?"

"Yeah. Every time I buy clothes, bag, she scolds me. Wasted her son's money. And the media too."

"That must be annoying."

She chuckled. "Yes, they say I too princess to give birth. Too afraid I get fat after baby."

I smiled awkwardly at the woman in front of me with her legs spread wide, while I poke at her privates, looking for anything abnormal.

Suddenly, her words hit me. Was I to be judged by Kai's mother, Kai's family and the media of his world? I felt like the roles had reversed, and I was the one lying on the bed, exposed, with strong lights shining into my privates for the whole world to judge me.

As soon as Mr. and Mrs. Song walked out of my office, Kai walked in with a big silly grin. Kai waltzed in like he was a performer on stage, moving his arms with exaggerated movements, his face animated with happiness.

"Lunch time, princess." He announced. I knew that. But he didn't know that I would normally work through lunch, catching up on the paperwork that I never seemed to finish on time.

"I don't do lunch." I announced matter of factly.

He frowned with disapproval. "No, that's not healthy. You must eat."

That was a misconception. Eating wasn't necessarily healthy though, especially with the kind of food most people eat. While eating could make you sick, not eating on the other hand, could make you healthy. Depriving your body from food makes it recycle old cells and grow new ones. That was why intermittent fasting had become such a big thing. Not all doctors received the memo on this though. A lot of them still worshiped the textbooks that got them their medical degree centuries ago. And that was why the opinion on the subject was so divided. People are entitled to believe what they want to believe, and I never really bothered trying to change anyone's mind about it.

"It is. Trust me. I'm a doctor." Ha! That was right. I used that to my advantage whenever I needed to. And right now seemed fitting.

"If you come to lunch with me, I'll let you have dessert." His cheeky smile indicated that he didn't mean sweet fluffy things covered in whipped cream and sugar. Though the thought of him covering me in whipped cream and sugar sent a shiver down my spine...I pushed the thought away and looked up at him.

His dark brown eyes were so mesmerizing as he pleaded with me. "Please?"

Right away I regretted looking into those eyes of his. I couldn't say no to those eyes.

"I only have an hour."

"An hour is exactly what we'll need." To see his big silly grin again made my heart sing. "Come with me. Your lunch is already waiting for you."

Right.

He was one of those guys who ordered for their women. Personally, I thought that was so disrespectful. Was asking such a hard chore, was it really that hard of an effort? What if I was a vegetarian? Or allergic to garlic or something like that? I normally judge a date very quickly based on that. If they ordered for me, assuming that they knew my taste, I would mentally check out of that date and the evening would be ruined.

The thing was, when it came to Kai, all my principles seemed to become non-existent. I was kind of excited to see what he had in mind for me. How much he thought he knew me, as if knowing my food taste was the greatest test of winning my heart.

I followed him out of my office like he knew this hospital better than me. Like he was the one who had been working here for years. He greeted every staff member that walked past us, using their first name. Some of them, I shamefully only knew by their last name, and I'd never bothered to learn their first name.

When he led me out of the hospital, I started to think that I had made a mistake.

"Kai…" I pleaded with him. "We can't go anywhere. I really only have an hour, well fifty-five minutes…"

He hushed me gently. "I know, we're here."

We stood in the middle of the parking lot, but his car was nowhere to be seen. Even if I had agreed to eat out at a restaurant, it would have to be fast food. And a very fast one, at that. As in, grab a hotdog from a food stall fast.

"Kai! I have three procedures scheduled this afternoon and I cannot be late for them." My neck felt warm, and I was afraid of what was coming next. A rash that surprised me when I least expected it – and I noticed that stress often seemed to be a factor when it came to visit.

Being professional was what I shot for in my career. I couldn't risk being too sloppy with my work. People often wondered if I pulled any strings to get where I was. My father being the director of a medical group obviously made people wonder. My brother, also a successful doctor, could obviously put in a good word for me if I had asked him to. Not to mention the uncles and aunties of mine who were very influential in their careers – also in the medical and drug industries – and could easily send me to high places without me even trying.

I could have accepted their help and had an easy life. I could have sat back and called it a day.

But that wasn't me.

I *always* picked the hard route.

So no, in short, I have to be good at what I do. I couldn't bear people talking behind my back – saying that I was a shitty, incompetent doctor, and that I was the head of Bennet Fertility Group because I was a nepo-baby, and not because of my own hard work.

The door to the RV parked in front of us opened up and interrupted the insecurity demon chipping away at me. A tall, bald man in a white shirt, with black pants, and a red apron wrapped around his waist appeared. "Welcome Mr. Li and Dr. Bennet. Your lunch is ready."

I stared at the guy and then back at Kai. I couldn't mutter a word to say in this situation.

"What on Earth are you doing now?"

"Come inside and have a look." Kai said with a happiness that invited me to come play with him. Truth to be told, I was excited to see what trick he was about to pull out of his sleeve.

Inside the RV was decorated with soft lighting. At the front was the usual section where the driver and passenger would sit while the vehicle was on the road. The rest of the space was bare apart from one long table on one side of the wall, and a medium size table that could be removed for seating on the other side.

On the long table I saw a display of food. It was a buffet with multiple plates of ready to eat delicacies. When I say delicacy, I'm not joking. Though they were just simple food – salads, pastas, pizzas, sandwiches, and a variety of rice. But the chef must be some kind of magician. He had successfully transformed the most boring everyday cooking into exotic mouthwatering meals with clever and beautiful plating.

I felt my stomach knot with hunger when I saw a variety of proteins – grilled chicken, steaks, smoked salmon, boiled eggs and pan-fried tofu. All of them were presented in ridiculously gorgeous arrangements as well.

"What is this?" I gasped for air. I didn't know what to think of all this.

"I don't really know what you prefer to eat, so I got the cook to whip up a bit of everything. I hope there's something that takes your fancy."

"You did all this for me?" I couldn't believe how much the display touched me.

"No, my cook did."

I scanned the room but couldn't see any sign of cooking nor was there a proper kitchen. "How?"

"Yeah, I borrowed a food truck and had my chef prepare everything there." Kai gave a wave of his hand, as if borrowing a food truck and having a chef were no big deal.

"I recognize the guy." I said, after a closer look at the chef.

"Yeah, he's some TV chef who works part time at one of my kitchens."

One of his kitchens?

"You mean your chef from one, one of your restaurants?" I asked. Kai nodded gently. "Wouldn't that affect your business?"

He laughed as if I had said something hilarious. "No, our kitchen is well-staffed so they can do without their head chef for a couple of hours."

"So, he isn't really part time then?"

"Oh no, of course not. He's the head chef and the main consultant for my restaurants, the European ones at least. But it gives him the freedom to do other stuff like being on TV. You know, that also helps with the visibility of my restaurants, so why not?"

"As well as the freedom to cook up a feast for you on demand," I teased as I waved my finger around the room like a magic wand.

"This is nothing for Marcus."

Yes, that was his name. Marcus the TV chef. What was his surname again? He's British, that was the only thing I could remember about him. I felt a little embarrassed that I couldn't recall his full name.

"Please don't tell me you host some of your parties in this thing?" I looked over at Kai, hoping to not give away my thoughts.

Dirty thoughts had been crossing my mind far too frequently lately and I could totally see this as one of his private sex parties on the move.

"This?" He seemed a little baffled by my words and I didn't feel like I had asked anything too difficult to answer. "I just bought it this morning. You like it?"

I shook my head. "You just went out and bought an RV, just like that?"

The sound that came out of me wasn't one that I recognized. When you live in New York, nothing surprises you because freaky things happen all the time and nothing ever shocks you. Kai had done just that.

But Kai was well ahead of me in this little game of his.

"No, silly. I didn't go out and buy it. I was at the hospital all morning."

"Obviously." I glared at him, wishing he'd just come out with whatever little nugget of information he was about to drop on me.

"My PA did all this."

Duh. Silly me.

"Still, you organized all this just for," I paused for two seconds, couldn't bring myself to say the word *me*, "lunch?"

"Again. No, not really. My PA did most of it."

It sounded like we were both in denial. "That's just semantics, Kai. You paid for it. You asked for it. You did this."

I couldn't believe that he would do something so nice for me.

He denied that he had anything to do with it, and perhaps, in his mind, he really thought that he had no part in this. But he did.

Still, it was the thought that counts. It didn't matter if his PA organized most of it. This had to be the most romantic thing that anyone had ever organized just to have lunch with me.

"Why did you do that though? You could just get me a box of salad, a sandwich and a coffee."

"Well, Siti said you never had lunch. I've seen how busy you are. And I can't bear the thought of you being disturbed by your colleagues, or patients at the hospital's cafe or in the cafeteria during the very little time that you called lunch time."

He took a bite of a chicken wrap before he continued. "Don't get me started with eating in front of your desk. Oh, don't get me wrong, you have a nice office. Still, it's a little depressing to see you eat at the desk where you discuss your patients' pussies and dicks."

"Shut up! That's rude." Though I never thought of it that way, I now felt a little grossed out about my own desk.

"I think you deserve a little quiet time all to yourself. Well, kind of with me as well. Have I answered your question?"

Yes, he definitely did. A little too well.

"That was really sweet of you."

"Not really. It was a little self-serving. I wanted to spend some quiet time with you too."

I settled on a bowl of salad and some boiled eggs. Too many carbs would make me sleepy, and I couldn't afford to have a foggy head for the procedures later. Besides his chicken wrap, Kai ate a pizza with some smoked salmon. We sat beside each other and in the middle of the RV, at the table. Marcus, the British TV chef – I really couldn't recall his surname and was too embarrassed to ask – served me sparkling water that I requested.

I felt a little put out having a famous chef waiting on me. I only hoped that he didn't feel the same way.

We sat quietly during our lunch. I couldn't think of anything to say to Kai apart from thank you. If it wasn't for the awkward celebrity chef waiting at the corner of the room, I would have ripped Kai's clothes off to show him how much I appreciated his gesture.

18

———

June

My heart rate wouldn't settle after my lunch with Kai. I sat at my desk studying my patients' case one last time before the procedures. None of the information seemed to register in my mind.

It was like my brain had a mind of its own. No matter how I tried to concentrate, my thoughts kept going back to Kai.

I knew for a fact that Kai Li wouldn't do what he did over lunch to impress just any woman. And the high bid just to date me? He didn't have to, his charm alone would win anyone over. I was flattered that he did all that for me.

Ten dates would have been enough.

Ten ordinary dates. I would even be okay with it if we didn't end up in bed again. Those dates were a dream come true for me...sort of. I couldn't bring myself to admit that I had such a shallow dream – that I simply wanted to date my secret crush.

I wanted more out of life, of course. Being a doctor was a career choice – not my dream – and I knew that from the very beginning. Having a perfect family – husband, children, dogs –

was something I also wanted. Living in the twenty-first century America had made that dream almost unattainable, though. Most of the people I know came from broken families. Perhaps seeing my parents marrying and dating different people had made me want this perfect family more not less.

Happily ever after was too much to ask from a guy like Kai.

He wouldn't marry someone like me. I could never be his someone special. I didn't mind being just another one of the women who ended up in his bed. But...with everything that he'd done for me over the last few days, he'd given me hope that I could be the one, his forever.

I shook off the thoughts and tried to think about my procedures.

Nope.

Being his forever meant something else. Something crazy. With Kai's parents' unhappy marriage as an example, he wouldn't marry until he was certain his chosen bride was his forever. Jenny told me one evening that all women wanted their fairy tale ending, and it seemed like Kai was ready to offer one – to one lucky winner.

The winner would have it all. She'd share everything he'd built from his empire to his bed. as well as the biggest prize of all...his heart. How many women ended up with broken hearts because of him, though? We all played a game where only one could win, like that famous TV show, Squid Game, where only one person could come out alive and unharmed.

It scared me to death thinking about it. Over the last few days, I have heard a thing or two about his complicated family. Would his hard to please mother even allow a part Asian American woman to enter their kingdom?

Besides that, Kai had an appetite that no one could ever fill. And I didn't mean his appetite for food. He had a hunger for achievements. It was a massive void that nothing could ever fill.

It was that hunger that drove his success in business, the urge to own businesses and properties across the world. He loved hosting and attending the craziest and silliest parties one after another. Then there was his love of trying dangerous sports that gave him thrills. He liked dating different women, and only beautiful women who were top of their class – and doing God knows what with them. He lived such a loud and noisy lifestyle completely opposite of mine. And I knew that there was no way I could ever fill that need of his, that excitement that he chased after in life.

It seemed to me that he had this new obsession with me. It couldn't be fake – I could see it in his eyes. As complicated as Kai could be, his eyes never lied, not to me anyway.

After lunch, he was the gentleman he'd been for the last few days, and escorted me back to my clinic. My clients this afternoon were all high profile. One was a politician whose name I wasn't allowed to disclose to anyone. They were traveling from Taiwan especially to see me. She'd wanted to have a child all her life but hadn't met the right person yet. Now that she was ready, her womb wasn't. I was chosen to *fix* the problem so she could get pregnant with the help of sperm she'd hand selected. I couldn't afford to fuck this up and it made me nervous.

I took out my favorite Zen kit. This one was just a notebook with a black ink brush pen. I removed the lid of the brush pen and flipped to a blank page, the one after my last entry three days ago, and started drawing circles. Or Zen circles, some people might call it. None of them were pretty or to my satisfaction. My hand was somewhat shaky and shuddered as if I was terribly cold. With great effort, I inhaled a large breath, and then breathed out as the brush pen touched on the white paper.

These weren't the kind of Zen circles that you saw in art galleries, or fancy cafes. Mine were tiny and often flawed by my shaky hand. I did it as a way for me to study how sturdy my hands were and how calm my mind was. And after a few pages of deep breathing and tiny circles, my mind would calm down and my hand would behave again.

But today, it took much longer to calm my nerves.

Twelve pages later – my longest record to calm my nerves – things started to switch. My breath was long and deep, the tremors gone.

Although the surgery later wasn't a life threatening one, every surgery carries certain risks. It was something doctors should always remind their patients of. But – touch wood – if the surgery went well, the woman could regain her opportunity at motherhood.

Unwanted distracting thoughts kept popping up left and right throughout the day. The tremors that I thought that I had under control decided to challenge me again. The fight with distractions was never an easy one. It was much like fighting food cravings and always losing.

From time to time, Kai's face would pop up in my mind. My thoughts of him were as persistent as the actual person. I could never kick him out of my office, no matter how much I wanted to. I took another deep breath and tried not to overthink what was going on between us.

I had never struggled so hard in the operating room. It was so bad that I sweated continuously and demanded to have the air conditioned blasting at top speed and lowest temperature. My freezing assistant nurse was starting to worry that we were going to run out of tissues to wipe my brow with.

Kai was up to something. Another uninvited thought invaded my mind.

His phone was constantly buzzing while we were having lunch. For whatever reasons, he'd chosen to ignore it – didn't even take a look at his phone. As soon as he dropped me off, instead of parking out in front of my office like he did for the last few days, he left.

Has he gone cold on me now that I've slept with him?

The procedure took longer than I had originally planned. It was entirely my fault. I should have been more professional and focused solely on my patient, and the *very* important task right in front of me. But where did Kai go? What was he hiding?

I really should pray and thank the god that protected my client. The operation was performed badly but was still successful. And my medical license was still intact, which meant so was my reputation. Soon, my high-profile client would be able to bear children after proper care and rest.

A small part of me thought that I was special. I thought that Kai wasn't going to sleep with me and then do the disappearing act. A universal act that I was warned of by my best friend, and all those Netflix shows that I had watched throughout my life. I felt foolish for believing that he would treat me differently. I admit that the lunch clouded my judgment. Who did something for a woman that he wanted to sleep with and then disappeared? Many men do that, of course. Kai included.

I was secretly hoping that his friendship with my brother meant that I deserved a little more. Perhaps the extra sweet and considerate lunch that he kindly threw my way was it. Would he have done that if my brother wasn't his best friend? Shit, was it pity or kindness that he threw my way?

It hurt.

My head was messed up.

I felt pathetic.

Kai had officially ruined me.

I DON'T MIND BEING wrong.

But that was a lie that I told myself and the world.

That lie had earned me popularity among my peers. Who didn't like a nice fluffy doormat to walk all over? Someone they could easily bully?

I wasn't someone who had a strong belief in anything. Changes were necessary. They were part of life. When they came, I welcomed them with open arms. But I never said that changes weren't hard. My parents' divorce. Chloe's fake death. My brother lying about her being alive. None of those were easy to deal with.

Right now, I don't want more changes. I don't want to be wrong.

Kai was not there to greet me when I finished my operation. His little team was gone. The reception area seemed weird without him there. There was no trace of him, like he and his team had never existed. Siti seemed to love the silence that had returned. If she hadn't mentioned how quiet it was now that they were gone, I would have thought that I fantasized the whole thing, that Kai and his people were never ever here, and it was all a dream.

It would have been much simpler if it was just a dream.

As soon as I finished a routine checkup on my VIP patients, I darted out of my office.

I patrolled the hospital floor to floor, from top to bottom, just in case Kai was hiding somewhere, ready to jump out and surprise me. Next, I walked around the parking lot, looking for expensive looking cars, or any cars with dark tinted windows – no one jumped out from any cars to surprise me. Then reluctantly, like a drunken ex-girlfriend on Valentine's Day, I drove around different places looking for him. I even went to all the restaurants and establishments that I knew he owned.

I could have picked up the phone and called him. But I wasn't sure I could face what he was going to tell me. I was a grown up and this wasn't my first rodeo with being dumped. Yet, I've never felt like I needed to know the reason why I got dumped or ghosted until now.

Kai came on to me so hot for the last few days that a small moment of cold felt odd and unacceptable. I parked my car across the street from Kai's building and waited, entering a stalker mode that I didn't know I had in me. This must have been how stalkers started obsessing over their subject. Shaking off the thoughts – a loud laugh escaped me.

"What the fuck is wrong with me?" I asked myself.

A knock on my window startled me. I recognized the face next to mine, only inches away separated by a piece of glass.

"Hi Dr. Bennet, are you here to see Mr. Li?" The doorman asked politely. Their security camera must have seen me. Kai would want a building with good security. It still surprised me how fast someone came checking on me. I'd barely been stopped there for five minutes.

A career as a spy or private investigator was definitely out of the question for me. So was obsessive stalker girlfriend.

"Yes, I was supposed to check on Jenny," I lied smoothly, "Mr. Li's guest. I am a little early, so I thought I would wait in the car."

I felt guilty for being caught red-handed. I wondered if he saw right through me.

"Oh, of course." Then it occurred to me that I had completely forgotten that Kai had deliberately tried to hide Jenny's whereabouts. And I had accidentally mentioned her name. He mumbled into his tiny mic on his collar before looking back at me. "Ah I see, no one is at the property I'm afraid. They haven't returned since this morning."

No one? What did he mean?

I thought about asking him to call me when someone returned, but that would just raise some red flags. Besides, he probably wouldn't anyway. "Thanks, Mr...."

"Jeff. Just call me Jeff."

"Thanks Jeff."

Driving off was the only thing a sensible person should do. What made me drive here and camp out in front of Kai's building in the first place was probably hurt. That was the only explanation that I could think of.

Or I could wait here until he gets back.

Shit! He had done it again.

Three years ago, I thought that we were going somewhere, and then he left without saying goodbye. The only difference was that we didn't sleep together back then.

The hurt was worse this time. Tremendously worse. I thought sleeping with him would fix my obsession. I was wrong.

I drove away, to my place, looking around as though my apartment was unfamiliar to me. Home didn't feel like home. His ghost remained there, even though he'd only spent a very short time here. The mug he used for coffee sat there next to the sink mocking me about his disappearance.

The quicker I accepted this change, the better. Life must go on.

I flattened out, face up, on my bed. My eyes fixed on a spot on my ceiling. My face felt heavy from the mixture of oil and make up on it, and my body felt a tad sticky for whatever reason, yet I had no will to drag myself to the shower.

The room wasn't really quiet. It never was here in my apartment. However faint it was, I could hear the street, sirens, cars honking, and occasionally people shouting. Then my tummy decided to join in, like it had a mind of its own.

If I hadn't had lunch today, I wouldn't feel hungry at this point in the evening. This has been my experience with fasting. The more often I eat, the more I feel the urge to eat.

I dragged my unwilling limbs to the kitchen. I knew I wasn't going to find anything in the fridge apart from some sparkling water. I hadn't bought any food for a while since I started trying out intermittent fasting. I opened the door anyway.

Food.

I rubbed my eyes, just to make sure I wasn't dreaming. Pre-packaged food stacked neatly on the shelves. Fruits and what looked like salad filled the vegetable drawer. A tray of eggs. A loaf of bread. Who put all this food in my fridge? There was more than one person with access to my apartment. Mom, Dad, Lincoln, Chloe, Liam and my assistant. It could be any of them. But why?

I wanted to know who did it, but my need to know wasn't as strong as my need to avoid social contact. It was one of those people who cared about me, that much I knew. For now, it was enough. There were still people in the world who loved me. Even though Kai Li didn't. Not that I ever asked him to. But our one date together was so bad that he gave up after that.

I took out the first box I could grab and opened it. Lasagna. Perfect.

I stuck the whole box inside of my microwave. The plastic that came with it was safe to be microwaved, even though I could totally hear my mother nagging me for doing so. I couldn't care less about eating microplastics or having *negative* energy in my blood. Any kind of energy will do.

Not caring how the lasagna looked, I tipped the whole thing upside down onto a plate and stabbed a fork in it. I could have eaten it straight out of the plastic tub. It would save me from washing one less thing.

Damn. That was what being civil did to me.

Whatever. I could just throw away the plate when I was done with it.

The lasagna tasted fine. It was definitely not my mother's cooking. Not that she was a bad cook, but her version of lasagna was comforting, greasy and *ugly*. Even when it was upside down,

I could tell that the person who made it definitely put a lot of care into it. It was so good that it could rival some upper-class restaurants.

Wait. Who actually bought this?

Mom was the only person who would cook lasagna. No one else in my family would choose to buy a lasagna like this. Not even Chloe. Sure, they might buy something from a supermarket, but not in a good quality reusable Tupperware container like this with 'cooked with love' written all over it. There was no way you could get something like this in New York City.

I rushed to the fridge and opened the tubs one by one. Pork chops. Steaks. Steamed vegetables. Egg fried rice. Chicken fried noodles. Vegetarian looking sausages. None of these things were from the same restaurant. Unless it was made to order. Still no clue of who brought the food.

Turning around, I headed right for the bin underneath the sink. There I found it. A large paper bag with the word Calling on it. One of Kai's restaurants.

Kai did all this? It was probably his assistant. Still...why?

I refused to believe that it was just something he did for everybody. Nobody would do that. Mr. Doorman confirmed that he hadn't returned.

I'd had enough of these mixed hot and cold messages.

I picked up my phone and dialed the only number I knew who could explain all this.

"Where is he?" I demanded without a hello from the other end.

"June?"

"Where. Is. He?" I repeated. My impatience was going to pierce through my phone.

"Kai?" My brother's thick skull finally registered. "I haven't heard from him." *Shit.* My hand lost its grip, and my phone dropped on my floor.

"Hello." I heard my brother shouting from the phone. "Are you okay?"

A chill traveled up my spine. Something had happened to Kai. Or Jenny. Or Lucy.

I didn't want to imagine the worst. But this was the kind of shit that happened to him.

The mean, billionaire dude with a reputation like his.

I knew in my gut that they wouldn't all disappear at once. It must have something to do with the missed calls that he got during lunch.

Picking the phone back up and putting it on speaker, I left it on the kitchen island. "He's gone."

It hurt when I heard myself saying that.

"Where is he?" Lincoln sounded shocked. It had to be the first time he'd heard this information.

"I asked you that question first."

"Right, I don't know. But it doesn't make sense."

"What doesn't make sense?" I needed to know if he had any clue that could point me to Kai.

"He, um..." I could hear Lincoln's hesitation.

"Now is not the time for bro code."

"I wasn't supposed to tell you this."

"He's gone missing for fuck's sake, whatever it is, you can tell me." I stopped caring about the way I talked to my big brother. And it apparently didn't seem to bother him either.

"Right. He might be mad at me for telling you, but I'll deal with it." Lincoln said. And I wanted to kick him for wasting another second with that stupid intro.

"Get the fuck on with it." Said the erratic woman that was me.

"He asked for my blessing to be with you."

"What did he do that for?"

"Bro code. Of course."

"Right. Continue."

"He said he wanted to stay in New York, for good, to be with you. So, it doesn't make sense for him to *be gone.*"

"Are you sure he wasn't kidding?"

"No, I know him. He was dead serious about you."

"Then how do you explain this? Another disappearing act!"

"What do you mean by another?"

I felt embarrassed about telling Link that it was the second time he ditched me. But I knew he would keep asking if I didn't.

"Three years ago, he asked me on a date. Then he just up and left."

"Oh that."

"Oh what? I know that *oh*. You know something. You better tell me about it." I said, though my big brother wasn't normally one for revealing secrets.

"His father was dying then. Kai went back to say goodbye to his father."

"He didn't say." He should have told me. Did he think I wouldn't understand? "*You* didn't say."

"It wasn't my place to say anything."

"His dad…"

"Still alive. Hung on and got stronger after they made peace with each other."

"Link, I'm scared." I took a deep breath in and breathed out the words. "I have a bad feeling."

"Are you sure he wasn't planning some kind of surprise?"

"I don't think so. He's gone. Everyone's gone."

19

———

June

I woke up the next day with an idea.

If what my brother said was true – that Kai really cared about me – he would have planted someone to watch over me. He was the kind of person who over prepared, who went overboard on most things, especially when it comes to safety. Him seeing Mack attack me that day, would trigger his protective side – amp up the security around me – if he truly cared.

After my brother was taken a few years ago, Kai had his security team extend their care, which covered my family as well. We had bodyguards following us everywhere we went that drove us crazy. It only took about a month for my parents to voice their opinions. Very angry opinions. They loudly demanded Lincoln call it off. The funny thing was, Lincoln didn't even know anything about it.

It struck me that I hadn't been approached by Mack since that or heard anything about him. Did Kai have something to do with that? It was odd that the police hadn't contacted me. Was

Mack still in jail? Did someone bail him out? The day the police took him away, they mentioned something about keeping in touch, collecting statements and pressing charges. So far, I've heard nothing.

Curiosity urged me to find out what was going on with Mack, but something more important was on my mind. If Mack managed to get out of jail, then there wasn't anything I could do about it.

Right now, I couldn't really tell if I was being watched.

I hadn't been paying any attention to my surroundings lately. I wouldn't know if I was being watched by one person, or a whole team of them.

I scanned the footage from my Ring doorbell, the only surveillance I had in the house. There was nothing really suspicious going on outside my house. I did notice that I had new neighbors move in across from my apartment. But that was a week ago. They couldn't be Kai's team. Could they? Kai would have to be really organized to have someone move in before he arrived. I don't think that he planned for this to happen. For *us* to happen. Besides, if my neighbors had something to do with Kai, why didn't Clare greet or say something to them when they saw each other two days ago on one of the videos? Of course, it was possible that Clare was pretending not to know them.

Despite the fact that I hadn't had any news about Kai, learning how he felt about me made me feel slightly better. At least I knew that he wasn't toying with my heart.

An erratic laugh escaped me. Then another one. I felt ridiculous for thinking that I could approach sex like a man. That all I needed to get Kai out of my system was ten dates he'd bargained for at the auction. That I could just fuck him out of my mind.

Then sense prevailed. Calling Kai shouldn't make me feel pathetic, like a sore loser who chased up a follow up after a one-night stand. Yet, there was this unknown force that stopped me from doing it.

Truth or denial?

There was so much I wanted to know. Was he safe? Why did he leave? Where did he go? Why didn't he leave me any messages?

But I wasn't sure how I would respond if the truth wasn't what I wanted to hear. What if he was in danger? What if the sex wasn't up to his standard and he decided that he wanted someone else? Perhaps he was in trouble with the Mafia.

No, I shouldn't speculate any more, I would only drive myself crazy.

Finally, I picked up the phone to call. It went straight to voicemail.

Typical. I was worried about what he might say to me, and he wasn't even available to talk.

I tried multiple times after that, leaving five to ten minutes in between calls. All went straight to voicemail.

I thought about trying Lucy or Jenny, who could possibly be traveling with him. But I didn't really get a chance to ask for Lucy or Jenny's numbers. Though it was rather unprofessional, I found Jenny's number through the hospital database which I had access to at home.

It got my hopes up when someone picked up at the other end, but it wasn't Jenny. She had made up a fake number and I should have guessed that. At least I tried.

That meant I was left with one option: testing out my idea.

I called in sick and had Siti arrange for one of the doctors on my team to cover for me. She panicked when I told her I wasn't going to come in at all. And panicked more when I told her that I wasn't actually sick and wanted her to lie about it. The thing was, I had never had an unplanned day off my whole career as a doctor. My team had gotten so used to me always being there, but I think it's time they learn to deal with the situation when I wasn't there – suddenly.

The controlling and workaholic part of me wanted to know how Siti and my team were going to handle my absence, but I shook off worry. It was exactly that bad habit of mine that had led me to my current stress and unexplained high blood pressure. The *enlightenment* hit me like the cold air on a winter morning as you leave the bed. For years now, I denied my lifestyle had anything to do with my high BP, and a high resting heart rate. And suddenly, I was no longer in denial and staring right at the fact face to face.

Still in yesterday's clothes and with messy bed hair, I headed to the parking lot. I was too tired and upset to change out of my clothes when I returned from my failed stalking mission. After my call with Lincoln, who'd promised to try to find Kai, I'd spent the night binging multiple Netflix documentaries, munching on a large double cheese pizza and wallowing for the rest of the evening before passing out in bed.

The elevator trip down to the parking lot had given me a vague impression of how awful I must have looked. My neighbors were either staring or too afraid to look at me.

As soon as I got inside my Tesla, I checked myself in the rearview mirror and saw the hot mess that was me. Really, I couldn't blame my obviously very concerned neighbors for staring.

The gray smear of makeup that decorated my face suggested that I had been crying. Had I been crying? Probably. I honestly couldn't remember. I'd been very upset, that was all I knew for sure.

From now on, I was never going to trust any beauty influencers or sales assistants when they told me their makeup was waterproof. Not that I was planning to cry all the time. People don't buy waterproof makeup because they cry all the time, but just in case. For that one unexpected day when there was something really – or not – worth crying about.

I gathered enough saliva in my mouth and wet a piece of tissue. *Gross.* I couldn't help feeling disgusted as I cleaned myself with the self-made wet tissue. Perhaps I was wrong earlier about my senses, they hadn't returned. Not one hundred percent.

With my face cleaned, I drove out of the parking lot. I didn't know where I was heading. The street was busy with rush hour traffic. I drove around for a little while. Finally, I found a street quiet enough and slammed my foot on the gas until I hit a streetlamp with as much impact as I could muster.

Fuck. The airbag hit my face hard. So hard that I was struggling to stay conscious. The streetlamp bent with its light now closer to my car, like it was bowing down to say hello. For a moment, I thought it was laughing at me and my Tesla, for failing to take it down.

This was a bad sign. The streetlamp shouldn't be communicating with me. I needed to stay awake and conscious.

Focus.

The crash had attracted some people walking by. There were different voices talking to me, asking me simple questions that I struggled to answer right now.

"Lady, are you okay?"

"Do you want me to call anyone for you?"

"Should I call 911?"

"Are you hurt?"

"Can you move?"

Suddenly, I was being dragged out of the car.

"Hey dickhead, you're not supposed to move her!" Someone shouted. My eyes remained half opened – as much as I could manage right now but my vision was not quite in focus.

"You aren't supposed to move me." I whimpered.

"Put her down."

"The ambulance is on the way." Another voice intervened.

"Do we have a doctor here?"

"I'm a doctor." Weakly, I answered.

"Doctors don't do stupid shit." A familiar voice snapped. I recognized the voice, and the strongly accented English.

It wasn't Kai.

But wait, it was Dave. Kai's favorite bodyguard. If Dave was here, that meant Kai was near.

"Where is Kai?" My vision came back into focus.

Dave's head shook ever so slightly.

I knew Dave was large, but he appeared even larger when he picked me up. A black van approached us, and someone opened the back door from the inside. It drove away as soon as we got in like it was a getaway car.

"My car?"

"Someone will take care of it." Someone in the van answered. An American by the sound of it, though I did not recognize who that person was.

The back of the van was exactly how I imagined a spy vehicle would look but a lot less humble. It was equipped with a laptop on a small camping table and chair. I sat up and gathered as much air as I could to clear my headache.

"Where is Kai?" I asked again.

Dave answered with another head shake.

"You don't know?" I needed to hear it from him.

"No."

"Why are you here? Why aren't you with Kai?"

"Mr. Li wanted me to take care something." I knew that I was the *something* he meant.

"What about Clare?"

"Mr. Li."

My theory was correct. Kai indeed had someone watching over me. Not just anyone, but his most trusted bodyguard who hadn't left his side since he was a boy after escaping from his kidnappers.

"Is Kai in danger?" I asked. Dave stared at me, face blank.

"Say something." I demanded.

"I don't know."

"Have you called him?" Dave didn't need to play the game of chicken with his boss.

"Yes."

"And?" I knew his English wasn't good, but it had started to get annoying having to fish words out of him.

"No one answered."

"Try something else." I barked, "call your other team, the team in China, or his mother's team, what about Jenny's team, and Lucy's team? Who else has a team of people watching them? People like them can't simply be gone right? They are being watched all the time. It's practically impossible."

Dave let me finish without interrupting me. As much as I liked that about him, I hated him for losing Kai. "Dr. Bennet."

"June." I corrected him.

"Ju–, Dr. Bennet," I let it go as he clearly couldn't bring himself to call me by my first name. "I called my sources. They all said, don't know."

"So," I paused. That only meant one thing. "Kai's in danger."

Dave wanted to have me checked out by a doctor, but I refused. So stupid coming from a doctor. I could have suffered a concussion or worse. But I didn't care.

I felt perfectly fine.

After further questioning, I found out the reason Kai left. Jenny and Lucy went missing. They were last seen at a Japanese hair salon up town. Their CCTV showed the two women were escorted into an SUV by four suited Asian men. Dave recognized one of them, an ex-vet who served in the same unit as him. These men worked for Jenny's husband, that much was clear.

There were no bodyguards by their side at the time. Clare was told to wait in the car. The girls told her that the salon had their own security. It was an upper-class salon frequented by the rich and famous and they wouldn't let anything happen to their clients. Clare wasn't convinced at first, but she turned giddy when she saw a few of her favorite A list movie stars inside.

Their words were true though. To a certain extent.

They were taken outside the hair salon, as soon as they stepped out of the door. Everything happened so fast. The ladies were supposed to call Clare when they were done, so she could go and pick them up. But they didn't, they must have forgotten.

Clare and her team chased the car for quite a few blocks, but the kidnappers eventually escaped.

I couldn't imagine all that happened during my lovely lunch with Kai. I couldn't help but wonder, if Kai had picked up his phone during lunch, would it have made any difference?

Kai, Clare and a few of his team left for China – the only possible place Jenny's husband would have wanted her.

"Wait, are you saying after all that happened, there are only you and two other people left in this country?"

He hesitated. "Yes."

It didn't make sense, Kai would up security after an event like that. It didn't quite make sense that it was only Dave plus a van with two other team members.

"What are you hiding from me?" My tone was serious, and that seemed to take Dave by surprise.

"Nothing." There was half a second delay in his response. He had to be lying.

"Why are you still here?"

"I already said." Dave said, his face still expressionless.

"Did you plan the kidnapping?" I knew he wouldn't, but I needed to make him confess.

"No, no, no." No pause this time.

"Did you plan all this to make Kai disappear? Is he in danger?"

"No, no, no, no, no."

"Tell me what you are doing here?" Volume control had already left the building, and I was shouting. But I could tell that he was about to break.

"Okay. Okay. Calm down." He put out both of his hands in front of me. As if they had the power to block off my rage.

"Talk! Now!"

"We had Ander."

"Ander who?" I shouted the unfamiliar name.

"Mack Ander."

"Mack…" I covered my mouth.

"Yes, we take care of Ander." Fuck! They *kidnapped* Mack.

"What are you doing to him?" I pressed. Though Mack probably deserved whatever they wanted to do to him, kidnapping was illegal. After everything Kai had been through, why would he abduct someone and keep them captive?

"Nothing. We watch him."

"You guys kept him captive." I couldn't bring myself to say the word kidnap.

Dave nodded.

"Thank you for being honest." My voice went back to its usual volume. "You can tell me the truth. I can handle it."

Now that made sense, some of Kai's team must have been

sent to make sure that Mack was being supervised. With Mack out of the picture, Dave didn't need a team of hundreds to watch over me.

The only problem was, they had no idea what they were dealing with.

"Do you know about Mack's connections?" I felt like it was time I shared.

"No. We got nothing."

"Of course not. That was a fake name. His other name is Mack Sun, his Chinese name is Ting Yen, which could also be a fake name. He used to work for one of the triads in Hong Kong."

Dave stared at my face as he heard the word *triad*. His gaze was intense. And I felt like he was trying to see right through me or burn a hole in my skull.

No one spoke for a few seconds. Dave was clearly thinking as lines showed up between his eyebrows on his expressionless face.

"How you know?"

I chuckled awkwardly. "Well, let's just say I'm not as innocent as you all think I am. I've crossed paths with him." I had a past that I wasn't proud of. A past that I had never really shared with anyone. Not even my family.

"You knew the boss?" Dave kept surprising me with his ability to ask straight to the point questions. Language was no barrier to him.

"Yes," I thought about not saying his name, but what was the harm. "Dannie Wu."

We stared at each other without saying another word for what felt like a very long minute.

"Dannie. Wu. Dan. Tin." He spat out each word slowly.

"You know him?"

It was subtle but I knew that both his breathing and heart

rate were racing. That was the perk of being a doctor. I could tell these things.

"Mack Ander was Dannie's guy?" He answered my question with another question.

"I don't know if Mack still works for Dannie. But based on the fact that he asked me for money a few days ago, I am going to say no. At this very moment, he probably isn't working for Dannie."

"Dr. Bennet," Dave cleared his throat. "I make big mistake."

"How so?"

"Mack. Dannie. Dangerous."

"You didn't know. You did all that to protect me." I cut in. I knew why Kai took Mack. That was no excuse for kidnapping someone. However, I wanted to reserve the shouting and lecturing for Kai. For when I see Kai face to face. "Listen. At this moment, we don't know if Kai is missing. Maybe his phone is on an airplane mode."

"His plane land last night." Dave interrupted me for the first time. His face was growing more impatient by the second.

"Please, let me finish. Kai might not be able to contact us for whatever reason. Like you said to me, Jenny and Lucy were taken. So, for all we know, he was on his way to help them. If we find one of them, we'll find them all."

"I think we take Mack. Dannie take Mr. Li."

"I don't think Dannie would do that."

"Dannie does take people." Dave protested.

"I didn't say he wouldn't do such a thing as kidnapping." Dave's face changed, "calm down Dave. I don't think Dannie was stupid enough to take someone like Kai. One, I don't think Dannie cares about Mack enough to kidnap someone like Kai just for fun and revenge. Two, Dannie hates hassle. And kidnapping a high-profile crich asshole like Kai would definitely give him a huge headache. So, I can say that Dannie had nothing to do with that."

To be honest, I was only speculating. I had no idea what Dannie would or wouldn't do. Saying all that made me feel better. I only hoped that Dave bought into it.

"This is good news."

"Well, I suppose." I gave an awkward, small laugh. "But I cannot guarantee that Dannie won't hurt Kai in the future. He sees that as a fun way to pass time. And Kai kidnapping Mack has probably put a target on his back."

That I knew for sure. Let's just say that Dannie was an eye for an eye kind of person. If you ever wronged him, he would make sure that you paid for it. That thought sent a shiver down my spine. I hadn't thought about Dannie in a long time. Not properly. When Mack showed up, I tried with all my might not to go there.

"Dr. Bennet." Dave's already very serious face changed. I didn't know that his face had another dimension worse than what it already was. This was a someone died face. I stared at him blankly. I couldn't find any words to say to him.

"Yes, Dave."

"Forgive me."

"What's wrong?"

"I must leave you and go find my boss."

"Can you take me with you?"

"No. I cannot." His voice was stern. It had an authoritative tone to it.

"Why not?"

"Dangerous."

"You can protect me." If I started talking like him, would he understand me better, or would he think that I was mocking him?

"Dr. Bennet."

How was I going to convince him to take me? If I ever want to find Kai, he was probably my key to it. "I'm going to go to China to find Kai whether you like it or not. Traveling alone is no strange task to me."

"You stay here." His brows curved up ever so slightly – a bit too much emotion to deal with for the poor guy today.

"Look. You want to find Kai, right?"

He nodded.

"And you were told to protect me, right?"

"Yes."

"If I come with you to China, you could do both. This way, you haven't broken your promise or assignment about protecting me." I said with my sale-sy voice, like when I tried to get some new toy funded for my project with the hospital board.

He didn't answer me.

But the corner of his lip rose ever so slightly.

Thank you for reading. This is it for June and Kai for now. Find out what happens next in Billionaire's Cruelty.

Thank you for reading my book. If you liked this story, I think you'll enjoy my FREE book **Dark Desire**. Here's an exclusive sneak peek for your eyes only.

Emily

"EMILY, we'll be back around nine. Don't let the kids stay up too late." Jessi, my sister-in-law, said from the doorway to the living room.

As if her twin girls would ever listen to a thing I said. The door closed, and I turned to my twin nieces. "Who wants ice cream?"

The two little girls, identical blonde, sweet tyrants, screamed with joy as they looked back at me with gray eyes so similar to mine. They could be mine, if I wasn't so busy all the time. I pushed the thought away and stood up from the pillow fort they'd built around me to head into the kitchen.

Harry, the baby brother of the twins, slept in a playpen near the dark gray leather sofa, so I left him there. He was a growing boy, and he needed his sleep. Soon enough he'd join his older sisters in the kitchen with me.

I found the girls on bar stools around the marble island in the kitchen. It was the kind of kitchen any baker would love. It was Jessi's kitchen, after all, and she needed three industrial sized ovens. I turned to the fridge, the same stainless steel as the oven, stove, and microwave, and asked which ice cream the girls wanted.

"I want strawberry, please, Aunty." Breanna, always the polite one, informed me sweetly.

"Yuck! I don't like strawberry! I would like rocky road, please." Rhiannon, the bossier of the two and always the most opinionated, cried out from her perch by her sister.

They were two peas in a pod, but they were also quite different when it came to their personalities. Even if they were identical.

"You two don't know how lucky you are to have a mother who's a baker," I muttered, more to myself than to them. I pulled out two cartons of ice cream from the freezer and a plate of brownies from the drawer above it. I microwaved the brownies for a minute and added the ice cream to each bowl, before I added a spoon and gave the bowls to the girls.

I'd only put in small amounts, the girls were still little after all, and sat with them, a small bowl of my own in front of me. "What movie are we going to watch, girls?"

The girls began to argue about which family-friendly movie they wanted to watch first, and my thoughts drifted. Jessi and Trent were off for a charity ball, and I'd been enlisted to watch the girls and baby Harry. I knew the routine. I'd helped with babysitting since the girls were first born and had also helped with my other nieces and nephews.

Over the last five years, what was a small family of three brothers and a sister, had turned into one huge family. I often spent time flying back and forth to watch the children who resulted from my brothers' unexpected, but totally welcome, romances. The hard men I'd barely known in my younger days had now become men with a softness around their hard edges, and I was a spinster.

I looked at the bowl in front of me, totally untouched, and imagined a candle on the top of it. The birthday song played in my head, and I had to swipe a tear away. How had all of them forgotten it was my birthday? I hadn't received a call from any of my brothers or my sisters-in-law. Even Trent and Jessi had forgotten about the event.

I'd kind of hoped that one of them would remember, that there'd been a surprise element to tonight's babysitting gig, but no. Just a charity event somewhere in downtown Myrtle Beach that they'd planned to attend. Jessi had looked glorious in a black velvet gown, and Trent was always impressive in a tux.

I swiped at the blonde ponytail that had fallen over my shoulder and gave the girls a wan smile.

"What's wrong, Aunty?" little Rhiannon asked softly. She put her spoon down and put her tiny little hand on my cheek. "Do you have a sad?"

"I do, honey, but you two make it all better. And Harry, of course."

"Do you want to watch a grown-up movie instead of one of our movies?" Breanna added from her stool.

"No, honey, it's fine. Let's wash up the bowls and settle in. A nice long cuddle with you two will make it all better." I loved my siblings and their children, but sometimes, I wanted what they had for myself.

I didn't resent that I was the family's version of Mary Poppins. I just wanted them to recognize that three flights a week was too much, and that I needed time to myself. And to have my special dates noticed. I only really had one, after all; why had it been so hard to remember this year?

Jessi and Trent had a new baby to deal with, as did Mason and Laura. They'd adopted a lovely little girl a month ago to add to the two children they'd had previously. Ember and Kevin only had one child, a beautiful little version of Ember that they'd called Bridget after her mother. That still amused me, that Ember's real name was Bridget Jones.

I'd loved Ember from the moment I met her, and that voice? She was a wonder, but then all of my sisters-in-law were wondrous. Then there was me. The family caretaker and a spinster. What a life.

The girls surprised me and fell asleep twenty minutes into the movie. We'd piled up on the broad, black velvet couch in front of the large screen television, one on each side of me, and I was now stuck between them. I didn't want to wake them up, but my phone began to buzz. I struggled for a moment and wanted to scream when the phone almost fell off the edge of the end table, but I caught it.

I opened the screen to see a text from my friend, Roxie Simpson, on the screen.

<Hey, girl, happy birthday. Want to celebrate with me after my set?>

I grinned, the pain in my chest eased just a fraction. I thought about what to say, about what she offered, and decided that, yes, I did want to celebrate.

<Are you sure you want to party with an old woman like me? I'm twenty-seven now!>

The response was almost instantaneous, and I grinned wider.

<Shut up, you aren't old. You're only a few months older than me. Meet me at my apartment around ten?>

<I'll be there. I have to wait for Trent and Jessi to get back, then I'll be there.>

I felt a little better about life after that, and I couldn't wait to see what Roxie had in store. She wasn't the kind of person you'd associate with a woman of my class. My father owned hotel chains across the world, but she was one of the best friends I had. Now that Jessi was a wife and mother, I spent a lot of time with my best friend too busy to talk to me.

I'd met Roxie at a fundraiser I'd been part of. She'd helped to organize the event, and we'd hit it off. She'd been in a wonderful lavender suit that fit her form, but she'd looked classy and well put together with her makeup in place and her manners impeccable. I hadn't known she was a stripper until she told me. Exotic dancer, that's what she called it.

Only she wasn't just an exotic dancer, the woman had skills

and had won competitions all over the country with her performances. She continued to perform, but in her spare time, she volunteered with the charity I'd become a part of. She worked at some kind of exclusive gentlemen's club, code for strip joint, but she'd alluded to the fact that it was far more than that.

I'd often wondered about those allusions, and exactly what Roxie did to earn her money. She lived in a nice apartment on the outskirts of Myrtle Beach and drove a nice car. She always looked impeccably dressed, unless she was at home, and then she'd put on jeans and a tank top, or shorts and sweaters. Basically, she was just like me, except I lived in a mansion, didn't really have a specific job, was rich, and the world was my oyster. She had to work for her money.

I wasn't judging her; that wasn't the problem at all. On the contrary, I was quite intrigued about Roxie's life. She said she found her routines to be an escape, and the other tasks she did; well, sexual gratification was always a good thing. I wouldn't know. But I wanted to.

I took the girls up to their bedroom, put them each in their little pink fairy princess beds, and left a nightlight on for them. Jessi and Trent would be back soon, and I'd be on my way. I went downstairs to check on Harry, found him awake, and gave him a bottle while we waited.

"Your mommy and daddy will be home soon, my little love," I said to him as he stared up at me with eyes so like Trent's. Like mine.

I never had time to date or find a husband, but at night, when I was alone in my rooms at whatever hotel I called home for the moment, I'd think about my future. Right now, it looked empty and bleak. I wanted a family, and the look of happiness that my brothers now wore. I wanted a baby of my own and a family.

Or so I considered. I knew I wanted children, but maybe not

right away? I grinned a little as I burped Harry over my shoulder and felt his little snuffles fall back to snores. Such a tiny little being, and so sweet.

The problem was, I wanted that same sweetness for myself, but I also wanted some of the wildness that Roxie had told me about. Parties where everybody ended up naked, and the private rooms some of the patrons of the club rented for their own escapades. I wanted to know more about that world.

I wanted to explore it and find out what it was all about. I was more than ready to find out what happened in the world of the grownups. I might have been rich, but I was also very sheltered, and I wanted to tear that shelter down.

I'd formed a plan by the time Trent and Jessi came back to the house at nine. I headed back to the hotel, changed into an outfit I'd hidden away in my suitcase of secret wonders, and looked at myself in the mirror. I'd applied a little makeup, just enough to make the gray in my eyes lighter, and had curled my hair into long waves. The lace top, with a shelf bra to protect my modesty, and short white skirt spoke of my innocence, but left little to the imagination.

I added a pair of white heels, then left the room with a bag in hand. I went down to the parking garage, found the family car that was left there for any of us to use, and drove to Roxie's place. She let me in with a scream of excitement and a hug.

"Girl, it's been a month since I've seen you! How are you?" She offered me a drink, and we'd both sat by the time I got around to answering her.

"I've been rushed off my feet. I keep flying from place to place, and I tell you, I'm tired." I sipped at the wine she'd given me and set the glass on the table.

Her living room was done in white, glass, and gold trimmings. Tasteful but not gaudy. I didn't want to ruin her carpets with red wine if I got clumsy, so I'd asked for white wine.

"Why don't you tell them to hire a nanny, honey? You can't keep living like this."

I looked at her with a little guilt on my face before I smiled. "I told Trent tonight that I needed more time to myself, and I wouldn't be watching the kids so much. I need to be here to work on that project we've started, and I'll be around, but I won't be flying back and forth between Laura and Mason in Charlotte, and Kevin and Ember in Tennessee. I know they all want someone they trust around their kids, but you're right, Roxie. It's time for me to spread my wings." I left out the part where I wanted her to help me do just that. For now.

"Okay! Good for you! I'm glad you finally did that. It will be nice to have you around." She was two feet away on the other end of the white damask couch. I couldn't help but compare myself to her.

She wore a black leather bustier type top and black leather pants, yet she still looked sophisticated. Maybe it was the black patent leather Prada kitten heels, the way her blonde hair was never out of place, or maybe it was the fact that Roxie never sweated, even in the heat, but she always looked so cool and collected, in control. I admired her. Those blue eyes helped too. They were so... bright.

I felt underdressed, and maybe a little trashy in my attempts at sexy but sophisticated. I looked down at my lace top, something I would never wear to any place my brothers or parents might see me, and wondered if it wasn't a childish choice. Something someone pretending to be sophisticated would pick.

If it was frumpy but stylish, then I could pick it out. A suit that leaned a little to the too tight was about as risqué as I usually went. This outfit was my first attempt to fit into Roxie's world, which was much different from my own. Even if her world was full of power, controlling that power, and money. Not so different from mine, but the power struggles flowed different ways.

"Right, girl," Roxie said as she nudged me with her manicured fingers. "What do you want to do for your birthday? Where do you want to go?"

I looked at her, my breath caught in my chest. I had a plan, a cunning one, if she'd play along with it. "I, uh, I want a favor from you. Please."

"Alright?" she said, a darkened eyebrow arched at me questioningly.

"I want you to take me to that club. The gentlemen's club. I want to see what it's like in there. What the men are like, what happens with the women. I really, really want to find out for myself."

Her ruby red lips twisted into an amused smirk, and her eyes looked at me with pride. "Oh, girl. You want the birthday of a lifetime, then?"

"I do. Badly. Please, will you take me?" I waited, my hands clenched together as she looked me over. She just had to say yes. It was my birthday, and she was the only one who remembered!

Dylan

"You're a descendent of Jesse James, aren't you?" a woman at the end of the conference table asked.

My gaze flicked to the woman, and I noted round, out of date glasses, fuzzy hair, and a little too much fluff around the hips. She had a twisted little mouth that looked cruel, and I wondered who she was and how she'd come to be here.

"I am, yes, in a way. I'm adopted, but the man who became my father is descended from his son, as a matter of fact." It wasn't a point of pride, just something I'd had to learn to deal with over the years. Every now and then someone would crop up to ask me if I had special knowledge about the gunslinging outlaw from long ago.

I was born in 1986, so how could I know anything about a man who died over 100 years before I was born? It was a familiar question, though, and one I'd grown bored with long ago.

"He was such a handsome man," she crooned from the other end of the table, and I tried not to roll my eyes. The man had been a murderer and a thief; his spawn had tried to live good lives, despite their ignoble birth, and to get on with life. We didn't see him as a romantic hero, even if he had been handsome.

"I suppose if you consider murderous bank robbers handsome, well, I guess he was," I muttered and looked away. The woman I'd been waiting on, Liz Kearny, came in to the meeting room at last.

"Dylan James, as I live and breathe, how are you?" Her wide, red painted smile greeted me and hid the lust in her eyes. At forty-two, Liz was still a fine specimen of a woman, but she was married. I wasn't interested.

"I'm good, Liz, I'm good. I needed to speak to you about some property." I sat and indicated the seat across from me. I kept my voice low so the woman at the other end of the table wouldn't hear us.

"I know, your PA told us all about it. Excuse me." She paused, turned her head to the woman who had asked me about my ancestry, and called out to her, "Imogen, what did you find out about that land for Mr. James?"

"The land has been bought out by the Thompson family. I'm afraid, we're too late." She didn't even look down at the papers to verify what she'd said; she just knew her job and did it well.

"I thought that might happen. Liz, can't you find me something to work with here? Some way of getting them off my back? Or lawn, so to speak?" I gave her my most charming smile and added a gentle tease to my voice.

Her eyes went soft, and her face relaxed as I allowed my head to lean a little closer to her. It was a stupid ploy, but when you want something as much as I wanted to expand my resorts, Sky B-n-B, out here to Myrtle Beach, well, you did what was necessary. I'd wasted a lot of time already because I'd had to deal with things at Pebbles, the resort chain my adopted father had left me in charge of when he retired.

"I'll find you something. Something you can't turn down." Her voice was husky, and her eyes were like a laser focused on mine.

"I would appreciate that," I murmured seductively and let my tongue flick out to wet my lips.

My family had started a chain of hotels when great-great-whatever grand-daddy Jesse, Jr, had fathered a daughter. She had turned a boarding house into a string of hotels out in Kansas, and the coming generations expanded it west. By the time I came along, the family had a hotel in almost every single state in the west. Now, I wanted to move the family east, and Myrtle Beach was a hidden jewel I wanted to wrap in a platinum setting. I hadn't counted on the Thompson Hotel chain's resistance.

"I guess that's all we need to talk about for now. Thank you for the work you've done so far, Liz. I'll expect a call if you find something suitable." I stood, buttoned the panels of my suit coat, and made to leave.

"Oh, now, as your real estate agent, Dylan, I can't just let you leave empty-handed. I have a wonderful house going if you're looking for a private home on the waterfront." She started her spiel, and I shut her down.

"Not interested in that, just resort property. Take care now." I inhaled deeply as I left the room of one of the top estate agencies in the area, and made my way to the parking garage. I needed to relax. I'd been dealing with this family for two long months now, and I had deserved a break.

I decided to take the night off and head out to the gentlemen's club I'd been introduced to upon my arrival. I'd met up with an old friend, Freddy Sinclair, and he'd shown me the best parts of this wonderful little beach town. He'd also shown me the spots the tourists would never find out about.

Like Elmo's. The strip club/sex club I kept my nose out of kind of place. It was exclusive, kept quiet, and entry was by invite only, if you were a man or woman looking to partake in the custom Elmo's had to offer.

I liked the finer things in life, and the girls at Elmo's were of the highest caliber; I'd give them that. I hadn't found exactly what I wanted there yet, but I knew patience would pay off. It always did.

I made it to the club and walked in the secluded entrance in the back. From the front, the place looked like an abandoned store with three levels. Red paint covered every square inch, and the place looked like a gaudy dump. It didn't look much better in the back; all of the windows and every surface had been painted black. There was a shiny new gold knob on the door, however, and I put my hand on it but didn't turn.

Beneath the round knob was a palm scanner. If it accepted your palm print, the door would open on its own, as it did now. "Welcome, Mr. James."

The door person was a rather breathy and busty brunette, but she was off-limits. "Thank you, Miss Maples. Lovely to see you again."

"A pleasure as always. What will it be today?" The owner of the club didn't often sit and guard the door, but sometimes she could be found here.

"I just need a quiet place to watch some beautiful ladies dance their hearts out." It wasn't a past-time I'd take part in back home in Kansas, but here, I'd learned to live a little on the wilder side.

I could be me here, with all of my proclivities and vices.

"Enjoy the show; Roxie's on in ten." Miss Maples turned away even as she spoke, my presence already forgotten as someone else buzzed in.

I ordered a drink at the bar and sat. The shoddy exterior, designed to keep out curious onlookers, did not match the interior. The first floor housed a bar, a stage, and a small club on the other side of that. The club was a separate part of the first floor, one I rarely went into because I wasn't into rave-style hedonism. I was much too old for that crowd.

I preferred the darkness of the stage area and to watch the pole dancing magic. Roxie would be on soon, and I wanted to speak to her anyway. I'd noticed her quite a few times, but I hadn't spoken to her yet. I wanted to know if we could, perhaps, take part in one of the peculiar arrangements available at Elmo's.

I watched her go through her routine, effortless beauty, stunning grace, and skills beyond measure on display. Roxie never disappointed her viewers, and the tips she brought in proved that. She started a new routine, and I waited, my interest growing. If she could move like that on a pole, how well could she move on a man?

Sexist, perhaps disgusting, but people didn't come to Elmo's to find love; they came to relax, get turned on, and maybe fuck, if they were lucky. I saw Freddy, the man who had introduced me to the place, and wondered... Was he Roxie's protector now?

Freddy was a very handsome man, I'd give him that, and he'd never had problems with women. Those brown puppy dog eyes and blond hair kept the ladies on a leash, begging to take care of him. I, on the other hand, had black hair, dark gray eyes and was so tall and broad women often found me intimidating. If the broadness had been fat, it might have softened my appearance a bit, but every inch of me was covered in muscle. I worked hard to maintain my health, and I didn't allow an ounce of fat to form on me.

I didn't often have a problem finding a bed partner, though; there were plenty of women brave enough to take the challenge I offered them. Women with eyes that gave off sparks of defiance, that eventually ended up begging for me to make them mine. I never did, though. The minute their will broke, I was done and moved on to the next. A handsome face made that much easier.

I wanted Roxie, but if she was under Freddy's protection, then I'd have to look elsewhere. A dainty blonde, small and delicate, caught my eye. She had on a silky emerald robe that flowed out behind her as she walked around the room, in search of a man to entertain. There were about eleven other customers in the room, but she didn't spend much time with any of them.

She flitted around, nervous, with a fear in her eyes. I would guess it was that fear that drove the men to send her away. Nobody wanted an unwilling partner. That was the cost of protection after all. The arrangement was about sex, and nothing more. We would pay to protect the ladies, in a sense, and in exchange, we were free to enjoy each other. We were all adults, however, and knew that arrangement meant sex.

If the woman wasn't into a guy, then she could turn him down, no problem. Most arrangements were made through Miss Maples or Roxie. It was all done in a way to protect all involved, from all manners of problems, and could be ended without notice to either party. Maybe this woman would do that for me? If we could get rid of that fear.

"Hello there, gorgeous," she said softly as she made her way up to me. I looked her over, noted the sweet swell of large breasts beneath the panels of the robe and a slim waist too. The perfect little doll for me to play with, maybe.

"What's your name, angel?" We all knew the women used fake names, but we played along. They needed their privacy and dignity, after all.

She wore a white mask, a wide ribbon of silk with the eyes cut out so they could see. The white looked almost silver it was so shimmery, and on this young woman, it made her appearance more tantalizing while enabling her to remain anonymous. All the girls in training wore them as a way to let customers know they were new, and as a way for them to maintain their dignity until they were sure this was the life they wanted. That strip of silk would allow her to return to her life without anyone knowing what she looked like without it.

"Why, I think you just gave it to me." She spoke with a deep Southern accent, the kind that made my balls go tight. Sweet, submissive, and so sultry.

"Indeed? Would you like to sit?" Her eyes had darted around nervously, her hands clasped together until she sat. She relaxed the moment she did, and I wondered if the heels had pained her. Six-inch heels were hard for any woman to stand in.

"How long have you been here, angel?" I asked and flicked a hand toward the bartender. A waitress brought over a glass of the beer I'd been drinking and a glass of wine for the lady.

"It's my second day, but I've been a pole dancer for three years now. I came up from Georgia just to check out the scene." She didn't look much older than twenty-three, I noted as I looked her over. She had pretty brown eyes, straight but large white teeth, and a lovely smile. It was just a shame her chin was a little too long and her nervousness hadn't completely receded.

I could look past those problems, if she'd calm down a little more. Let me see who she really was and what she really wanted from life. Some of the girls who came to Elmo's came to seek fame. They wouldn't find it here. They might find a protector who would help them find it, but fame didn't come from Elmo's.

It was an exclusive, prestigious place, but the ultimate goal wasn't to propel a dancer to stardom; it was to provide men, and some women, with sexual partners. This little angel wasn't going to last long here, I was afraid.

"I guess you'll learn to fit in then. It's still early. You might settle in just fine." It wasn't proper to ask a woman how she ended up at Elmo's, but one thing was certain, they were there under their own free will. Some had even found protectors who moved them out into their own newly-purchased houses and put them on an annual income.

That was the ultimate goal here, to never have to work again. Not a "real" job, anyway. Mistresses for hire, that was what the place boiled down to.

"I guess I will." She sipped at her wine prettily and looked at my chin, not my eyes. Hers flicked up to mine for an instant and then shied away. It wasn't an act, I decided; she was afraid.

"You know you don't have to do anything you don't want to right? You're perfectly free to dance if that's all you want to do." I'd been versed on the rules well and warned about repercussions if I didn't follow those rules. No meant no, and anything other than acceptance would get a patron banned.

"I know, but I thought I'd try. At least once, you know? I've never done that before, just slept with a man for money."

"It's awkward, I assume, for you ladies?" I hadn't really thought about it. Most of the women I'd met here had been eager, curious to find out what hid behind the cool façade.

I was sure more than one would be amused to find me with the kitten who had found herself lost in the big, bad world. I didn't want to turn her away, because she might prove to be exactly what I wanted.

"It is, but most of the women here want to sleep with the men they choose. It's not like we have to do it. They want to. I just haven't found a man I want to do it with yet."

"Then, I suggest you wait for the right one, angel. There's no rush." I smiled and sat back as Roxie began another set.

It was almost nine, and she'd be done soon. I'd talk to her and then go home, I decided. It had been a long day, and I'd only found disappointment so far. Maybe a night's sleep would cure that.

Get your FREE copy of Dark Desire now!

ALSO BY

Also by Summer Cooper

DARK DESIRES
A billionaire dark romance series
Dark Desire (FREE now!)
Dark Rules
Dark Secret
Dark Time
Dark Truth

BARRE TO BAR
A billionaire second chance series
Dancing With Lies (FREE!)
Dancing With Temptation
Dancing With Doubt
Dancing With Guilt
Dancing With Redemption

TWISTED INTENTION
A billionaire revenge romance series

Twisted Beauty (FREE now!)
Twisted Love
Twisted Fate

Mafia's Obsession
A hot mafia romance series
Mafia's Dirty Secret (FREE now!)
Mafia's Fake Bride
Mafia's Final Play

Screaming Demons
An MC romance series full of suspense
Rough Start (FREE now!)
Rough Ride
Rough Choice
Rough Return
Rough Patch
Rough Road
Rough Trip
Rough Night
Rough Love
Check out Summer's entire collection at
www.summercooper.com/books

Also by Susu Chin

This is Susu's debut novel. Stay tuned for more captivating love stories and heart-pounding romance to come.

ABOUT THE AUTHORS

About Summer Cooper

Besides (obviously!) reading and writing, she also loves cuddling her dogs, shouting at Alexa, being upside down (aka Yoga) and driving her family cray-cray!

Follow Summer on Facebook | Instagram| Goodreads | Bookbub

Get in touch at
hello@summercooper.com

www.summercooper.com

About Susu Chin

Susu Chin is a passionate romance writer making her debut Billionaire's Promise co-writing with Summer. She's already at work on her next project, promising even more heart-racing and swoon-worthy moments for her readers.